HER LOVING HUSBAND'S CURSE

Meredith Allard

Copperfield Press

Copperfield Press
www.copperfieldpress.com

Publisher's Note: This is a work of fiction. Names, characters, places, and incidents are a product of the author's imagination or used in a fictitious way. Any resemblance to real persons, living or dead, or to businesses, companies, events, institutions, locales, entertainment personalities or programs is entirely coincidental.

Book layout ©2013 BookDesignTemplates.com
Cover design by LFD Designs for Authors

"To My Dear and Loving Husband" by Anne Bradstreet and *The Merchant of Venice* by William Shakespeare are in the pubic domain.

{1. Trail of Tears—Fiction. 2. Salem Witch Trials—Fiction.
3. Vampires—Fiction. 4. Salem, Massachusetts—Fiction.
5. Literary—Fiction. 6. Historical—Fiction. 7. Paranormal—Fiction.}
I. Title

ISBN-10: 0-615-61368-3
ISBN-13: 978-0-615-61368-0
LCCN: 2012904295

Printed in the United States of America

When you were born, you cried and the world rejoiced. Live your life so that when you die, the world cries and you rejoice.

~Cherokee Proverb

PROLOGUE

I am among the masses as they limp and drag toward some foreign place they are afraid to imagine. Even in the dimness of the nearly moonless night the exhaustion, the sickness, the fear is everywhere in their swollen faces. The weaker among them, the very old and the very sick, the very young and the very frail, are driven in wagons steered by ill-tempered soldiers. The riders are not better off than the walkers, their sore, screaming bodies bumped and jostled by the wobbly wheels over the unsteady forest terrain. No one notices as a few drop like discarded rags from the wagon to the ground.

"Here!" I cry. "Let me help you. I will find water for you to drink."

But they pass me without looking. They see nothing, hear nothing. They walk. That is all they are. Walk. That is their name. Walk. Or "Move!" That is what the soldiers scream in their faces. They struggle under the weight of the few bags they carry and stumble under the musket butts slapped into their backs. And still they do not see me.

I wave my hands in the air and yell to make myself heard over the thumping of thousands of feet.

"Here!" I cry. "Who needs something to eat?"

I push myself into the center of the mass. Men in turbans and tunics, women with their long black hair pulled from their faces as they clutch their toddlers—all focus their eyes on a horizon too far away. One old man, unsteady under the weight of the pack he carries, stumbles over some rocks and he falls. The soldiers beat him with their muskets—their futile attempt to make him stand. The man tries to push himself up but cannot, so the soldiers try the whip instead. The old man prostrates himself on the ground, arms out, face away. He has accepted that this is how he will die.

"Step around him!" the soldiers bark. And they do step around him, their eyes straight ahead. They do not see the old man any more than they see me. To acknowledge the fallen elder would force them to admit that his fate is their fate and they will all die here among un-

1

known land and foreign trees. The old man does not stir. He does not lift his head or seem to breathe. And the people pass him by. When they stop to make their encampment for the night, the old man does not arrive.

I throw my hands into the air again, my frustration boiling the blood in my brain. "Let me help you! Why will you not listen to me?"

"Because they cannot see you."

I have seen the man before—his blue tunic, his white turban, his solemn bearing—and he has seen me. He is an elder, his hair silver, his face a ridged map of everything he has seen, every thought he has had, every prayer he has said. There is wisdom behind his wary glance and oh so tired eyes.

"That's ridiculous," I say. "I am standing here among them."

"You are the Kalona Ayeliski. They cannot see you."

"The what?"

"The Kalona Ayeliski. They cannot see the Raven Mocker."

I watch the walkers, hundreds of them, their heads bowed under the weight of losing their possessions, their land, their ancestors, everything they had in this world and beyond, and I realize the man is right. They do not see me. They have never seen me.

"What is a Raven Mocker?" I ask.

"An evil spirit. All the Raven Mocker cares for is prolonging its own life force, and it feeds from others to do it. It tortures the dying and hastens their deaths so it can consume their hearts. The Raven Mocker receives one year of life for every year its victim would have lived."

"I am no Raven Mocker. I mean harm to no one."

"Ever?"

I turn away, watching the families reuniting after the long day's walk, children crying for their mothers, husbands searching for their wives. They are setting up their campsites, eating the meager gruel and drinking the few drops of water given them. I cannot meet the man's eyes.

"Not for a long time," I say. When the man's stare bores through me, pricking me somewhere I cannot name, I shrug. "I do not hasten death in anyone," I say. "Not anymore."

"We shall see," he says.

CHAPTER ONE

Sarah Wentworth didn't know how her life would change the first year of her marriage. She sat on a bench near the Massachusetts shore, protected from the high August sun by the shelter of overhanging trees. She watched the families on the narrow stretch of beach of Forest River Park, the children digging holes in the rocky sand, the mothers gossiping under the shade of striped umbrellas, two grandmas in their old-timey bathing suits and floppy straw hats, knee-deep in the water, walking back and forth in the laps of the waves, talking intently between them. Beyond them small white boats bumped and bobbed in the water, unattached to any dock, floating at will.

She was attuned to the laughter of children, and she watched the families eating at the picnic tables on the grassy expanse beneath the trees, lounging in portable chairs, playing games, enjoying the late summer day. She watched the tourists park their rental cars on the dirt lot and walk to Pioneer Village where costumed docents showed visitors around the historical replicas of wooden homes, medicinal gardens, carpenter's sheds, and stocks for the naughty, explaining life in Salem, then Naumkeag, in the 1630s.

Before my time, Sarah thought.

She stood with a wistful look at the mothers tending their children, enjoying her time alone with her thoughts after her shift at the library, Forest River Park a short block across Lafayette Street from Salem State University where she worked as a librarian. Though it was a year since she moved to Salem, there was still a magic about the place for her, a quietness, a calm she couldn't associate with anywhere else. It might be a Massachusetts thing, a Salem thing, or a seaside thing, she wasn't sure, but people were different there. They smiled at you. Said hello. There wasn't the mad-rush pace you see in larger cities where she had lived, like Boston or Los Angeles, except, she now knew, in their driving. Since she was a girl, she had always found something serene in the ocean, the peace of going home, she thought, and in Salem she had the tranquility of the bay every day.

She walked to the end of the park and waved to the shirtless teenage boy sitting in a lawn chair outside the gate. She headed down Lafayette Street, right on Derby, finding her way home. Thinking of her husband in their bed, still sleeping as the brightest daylight hours dwindled away, she smiled. She stopped in front of her wooden house, the one with the two peaked gables on the roof, and she realized she had such a fondness for the old thing. She and that old house shared a secret between them, after all. It was almost exactly a year to the day when she first stood on that lawn, fascinated by the museum-like home, needing to know it better. And then James had appeared, handsome and pensive in the shadows, reaching out to touch her cheek. Even then he knew her. Before she knew who he was, he knew her.

She walked past the crooked oak tree and touched the brown slats of the exterior walls, then looked through the diamond-paned casement window into the great room, the shelves of books, the flat-screen television mismatched against the old-fashioned furniture, her black cat asleep on the long reading chair. She looked at the sky, the light hazy, fading behind the breeze-blown trees. The air was cooler now, less heavy, the heat of summer fading into the beginning of a memory, and it was growing darker earlier, which Sarah liked.

She opened the green front door, walked inside, and pet her cat between the ears. She watched the sun drop away, first a pink light on the horizon, then blue, then dark. She glanced at her bedroom door, still closed, then at the wooden ladder leading up to the loft-style attic. I need to get up there soon, she thought.

"Hello."

She felt her cheeks blush hot at the sound of his voice. There he was, James, handsome as always, tall, gold hair, stormy night-black eyes, the smile that lit her up from the inside out. She stood on her toes and pointed up her face so he could kiss her, which he did.

"Hello yourself," she said.

They kissed again, and again, until the heat settled within her and she had to pull back or risk being distracted. She dropped her arms from his neck, nuzzled close to his cool skin, then stepped away.

"Not tonight, Doctor Wentworth. The exhibition starts in an hour."

James's eyes narrowed. "Jennifer should have supervised it," he said.

"But I'm the only one with personal experience from that time." She looked at James, his ghost-white complexion, the hardness behind his flat-black eyes. "I suppose you were here then too." She smiled, trying to lighten the mood. "I'm all right," she said.

They left their wooden gabled house hand in hand. On Derby Street they passed the House of the Seven Gables, the Salem Maritime National Historic Site, and the U.S. Custom House. It was fully dark, the water steady in the bay, the boats bobbing with the flat-line rhythm of the low tide. The tourists cleared away when the museums closed at five p.m., and the locals were enjoying a last summer hurrah, dining under the stars at the restaurants along Pickering Wharf. It was a quiet night in Salem. Peaceful. The remaining humidity lingered like a soothing blanket, Sarah thought, protecting us. Protecting us from what, she wondered? She didn't know, but suddenly her palms went wet and her breath stilted. She looked around, searching for anything that looked menacing or frightful, but she saw no one but James. She looked at him as he pressed his wire-rimmed eyeglasses against his nose, and she knew his strength, all of his strength, would keep them safe. She dismissed her shudders with the thought that she had been spending too much time in the seventeenth century lately. After that night, when the exhibition was over, she could immerse herself fully in the twenty-first century again.

When they turned down Lafayette Street and walked onto the campus of Salem State University, James's lips tightened and his shoulders closed together. Jennifer and Olivia waited for them inside the library. Jennifer, an auburn-haired beauty, and her mother, Olivia, ever the gypsy with her peasant skirts and coin earrings, were Sarah's dearest friends, her Wiccan friends, and she was happy to see them.

"Bickering witches," James said, but he smiled when he said it.

Olivia patted Sarah's hand lightly, as if she were afraid of breaking her. "Are you all right, dear?" she asked.

"You need to stop tip-toeing around me," Sarah said. "I put the exhibition together. I've been working on this for weeks. I'm fine."

"James doesn't look fine," Jennifer said.

"I know," said Sarah. She looked around expecting to see one more face, and she was surprised when it wasn't there. "Where's that new guy you've been gushing about, Jennifer? I thought he was coming."

Jennifer shook her head. "Soon," she said.

They walked in silence to the Winfisky Gallery at the Ellison Campus Center in the North Campus, passing students with their backpacks slung over one shoulder, most walking in pairs chatting, others riding their bikes or listening to music blasting through their earbuds. Sarah felt her heart cough in her chest when she saw the sign outside the museum: The Salem Witch Trials, 319 Years Later. James's hand tightened over hers, and though it hurt, his grip was strong, she squeezed back, trying to comfort him. After watching the doom on Olivia's face, and the gloom on Jennifer's, Sarah had enough.

"Stop looking at me like I'm going to explode!" she said.

Olivia exhaled. Jennifer smiled. James looked away.

"I knew you'd be all right," Jennifer said. She nudged James's arm. "I told you she'd be all right."

When they turned the corner near Winfisky Gallery Sarah saw the people waiting. Most were tourists with their walking shoes and cameras, ready for one more witch museum to visit, as though the Salem Witch Museum, the Witch Dungeon Museum, Witch House, and the tours weren't enough. But there were others there too, locals as well as friends and families of the art and design students who created the exhibits.

Inside the gallery Sarah found the students making last minute adjustments, turning the statue of Rebecca Nurse to the right, straightening the painting of Gallows Hill, lighting the portrait of John Hathorne sitting center at a witch trial. James wandered from wall to wall, staring into the art as though he could reach through the paintings and the pencil drawings to the seventeenth century on the other side and wring a neck or two. Maybe I shouldn't have brought him after all, Sarah thought.

"Should I open the doors, Mrs. Wentworth?" a student asked.

"Yes, Natalie. Go ahead."

The people came in, oohing and aahing at the artistic interpretations of the Salem Witch Trials. Families and friends hugged each other, proud of their students. A few wiped away tears. Sarah nodded, pleased with the response.

Olivia stepped beside her, slid her arm around Sarah's waist, and squeezed. "This took such strength for you, Sarah. Look how far you've come in just a year."

"Thank you," Sarah said.

Olivia leaned close and whispered. "Jennifer said there's a recreation of the...the..." She shook her head, unable to continue.

"The dungeon? It's in the next room."

"Show me."

Sarah led the way. It was dark inside, and she could barely make out Olivia's short-cropped red hair and steel-gray eyes in the flickering light of the flameless candles. The recreation of the dungeon was 70 by 280 feet, made of oak timbers and siding, and inside were dirty, suffering-looking women mannequins in seventeenth century rags, chained by irons to the wall. Most of the women had no bedding, though one had a sad excuse of a straw mattress. One mannequin woman was on her knees praying. Another lay prostrate, her eyes open, staring at a God in heaven who could not or would not help her. She was dying, or already dead, it was hard to tell. Sarah watched the women, some with their witch-accused children clinging to their knees, and she was surprised to feel nothing. Maybe she had relived the scene so often in her dreams that seeing it played out with life-sized dolls didn't affect her. She felt Olivia watching her, that detective seeking clues look only Olivia could do.

"You're all right," Olivia said.

"I told you I was fine."

"I didn't believe you."

"I know."

Olivia stepped closer to the exhibit. "Where are the bars?"

"They didn't need bars. We were chained. If anyone tried to escape they were immediately executed whether they were tried or not, whether they confessed or not."

Olivia's hand went to her heart. "Why do only a few have bedding?"

"We had to pay for everything. We had to pay for the bedding, a flat straw mat, useless though it was, and we had to pay for food. The prisoners who couldn't afford to pay went without. We had to pay the salaries of the sheriff, the magistrates, even the hangman who would take our lives away. The bit of light here is brighter than it was then. When it's dark, that's when your mind plays tricks on you. Everywhere was a shadow where monsters could hide."

Suddenly, in the space of a thought, the numbness went away and Sarah was there again, in 1692. She saw herself in the dungeon alongside the mannequin women, only they were living now, all of them suffering. The pain of it all, the horror and the sadness, were real and she had to shake herself back into the present. Olivia placed a comforting hand on Sarah's shoulder, and Sarah exhaled.

"We had to pay for the privilege of having our bodies searched for witch marks. We paid to have our heads shaved. Sometimes I could hear James arguing so loudly, begging them to treat me well. 'Name your price,' he'd say, the grief cracking his voice. 'Name your price for some kindness for my wife and I will pay you that and tenfold more.' But I suffered with everyone else. They barely gave us enough water to drink because they thought they could coerce a confession from us if we were thirsting to death. When it rained it flooded inside and we'd be up to our waist in rainwater, urine, and feces, and often that was the only water we had to drink. The rats would bite our legs and arms. Some prisoners went mad. The only thought that kept me sane was knowing that James was trying to set me free. After a while I was shipped to Boston with other prisoners because the jail here was full. But I was already too sick when I arrived."

Sarah closed her eyes. Her hands reached for her stomach, then full with the baby that should have been born. Suddenly, the pain, so strong just moments before, dissipated into a dull tugging. When she opened her eyes she realized a few of the visitors had gathered around, listening as though she were a museum tour guide. When they moved onto the next scene, Olivia put her arm around Sarah's shoulders.

"I am so very sorry, Sarah."

Sarah leaned into the warmth of Olivia's embrace. Olivia reached into her bag and pulled out a tissue, dabbing at her eyes, and she dabbed at Sarah's too. Sarah kissed her friend's cheek, grateful for this second mother in her life, wondering where she would be without her wise Olivia. Olivia gestured toward the end of the exhibit.

"I think there's someone who needs more comfort than I do," Olivia said.

Sarah saw him across the darkened room, James, his beautiful face twisted into a torment so powerful she thought he'd be permanently scarred. She saw the blood spots at the corner of his eyes, visible under his wire-rimmed eyeglasses. She took his hand and kissed it, but he was so caught up in the nightmare-like panic he didn't feel her caress.

"James? Jamie? It's all right."

He stared at the exhibit, his black eyes wide, almost child-like, as though he couldn't believe what he was seeing. As if the monsters of his imagination had come to life and he was mesmerized by them. As if he were afraid the exhibit would disappear before his eyes and he would never understand. Sarah looked at the scene that held him in stop-motion terror. He was staring at a woman mannequin, dirty, ragged, kneeling between two walls with barely the width of her body as space between them. She couldn't sit. She couldn't stand or lay down, caught in pain-filled limbo.

"Why is she trapped between the walls?" he asked.

"She hasn't had her trial yet," Sarah said. "Sometimes they kept the accused witches in these tiny spaces hoping they would be in such agony they'd confess. Everything in the dungeons was about forcing confessions."

"But she's trapped," James said, hysteria creeping into his voice, the sound a nails-on-chalkboard contrast to his usual mellow tone. He dropped his head into his hands, his eyeglasses hanging down his nose. "No. No," he said. "You hadn't had your trial. You never had your trial." He looked at Sarah, a trail of blood slipping down his cheek. "You weren't here were you?"

It wasn't a question. It was a statement. You were not here. Sarah stroked his face, wiped the red away, his pale-blue cheek streaked pink.

"Were you here?" A question now.

"It was a very long time ago."

"Were you trapped between the walls?"

Sarah nodded. James walked closer to the mannequin stuck in a perpetual half-up, half-down stance, the never-ending torture everywhere on her face.

"Oh my God," James said. "You were trapped between two walls? And couldn't lie down? Couldn't sit? Couldn't stand?" No matter how tight he shut his eyes he couldn't stop the sobs. "Oh my God," he said again. "Elizabeth…"

She took his face between her hands. "My name is Sarah."

But James turned back to the mannequin, drawn to the horror the way lookie-loos gape at accidents on the road, not wanting to see the carnage yet unable to look away. Sarah stood between James and the mannequin so he had to see her.

"The reason they removed me from the walls was because of the money you paid them. You did help me, James. You did."

"It was too little too late and you died. Oh Lizzie..."

Sarah took his hands in hers. She felt a shard of glass poking her heart from the inside out at the sight of her miserable husband. "I thought the exhibit would help us face the sadness from this time so we could be done with it. I hate feeling like there's this whole part of our lives we have to tip-toe around."

"Do you really feel that way?"

"We need to remember these times, James, the good and the bad. They're a part of who we are, the good and the bad."

"There is no bad of you, Mrs. Wentworth."

"Or you."

James shook his head. "I'm not so sure."

She wiped his cheeks with the back of her hand, then stood on her toes, leaning up, kissing his lips.

"Let's just say these times, as horrible as they were, are a part of us. And now that we've faced them head-on we're ready to leave them behind and focus on the wonderful, perfect years ahead. The madness can't touch us anymore."

"There is always madness, Sarah."

"But it's our turn to be free of it. We've earned it."

James smiled with a pensiveness that said he wasn't so sure. Sarah took his hand.

"Come with me, Doctor Wentworth. A few of your students have spotted you and we need to wash your face before anyone wonders why you're bleeding from your eyes."

James went into the men's room and washed his face. He was quiet as they left campus. On Lafayette Street, Sarah took his hand again, but she didn't lead him toward home. She led him into Marblehead, where the fancy people lived. She walked, faster and faster in the nook of a neighborhood, past the trees, the colonial-style homes where doctors and lawyers had their offices inside, through the parks. It was, Sarah thought, a perfect place to raise a family.

James stopped. "Where are you taking me?" he asked.

Sarah smirked, caught like a naughty child. "I thought we could visit Jocelyn and Steve. Their new house is down the block."

"Are we going to see Jocelyn and Steve or Billy?"

"We're going to see the whole family."

"Sarah..."

Sarah turned away. She looked at the red brick houses, the yellow houses, the colonial-style churches with the steeples on top. As they neared the green-covered coastline and the bay in the distance she strained to see Jocelyn's house, certain that if she could get James there he would understand.

"Sarah..." He touched her cheek with his fingertips, his face still pulled from the wretched dungeon. "I know you want a child, but we can't have one."

"Jocelyn and Steve have Billy."

"Billy's adopted."

"We could adopt too."

James turned away. "Do you know what problems Billy will have with a mother like Jocelyn? How are they going to explain her differences away?"

"As long as children have a loving home who cares if their family is different? He'll think his mom works at night and sleeps during the day. What's wrong with that?"

"How are they going to explain to that little boy that his mother drinks blood?"

Sarah wanted to scream. She felt goosebumps in her gut and her head ached. Again, she remembered the baby from so long ago. Her hands nearly went to her stomach, but she stopped herself. Why was James so set against a child?

Because he was dead.

But he seemed so normal, Sarah thought. Did the fact he didn't breathe matter in any meaningful way? She didn't think so, but she didn't know how to convince him.

"I'm going to Jocelyn's," she said. "You can come with me or you can go home, but I'm going."

Her pace quickened in time with her racing heartbeat. Was she angry? Worried? She thought she might be dying inside. It hurt too much to know James didn't want everything exactly as she did.

She kept walking, faster and faster, hoping he'd go home, but he caught up to her in two quick strides. They walked the tree-lined streets in silence, lost in their thoughts. They were near the harbor now, near Marblehead Neck, and Sarah saw Castle Rock Park, a lookout for fishing fleets and pirate ships in colonial days. She felt the soothing sweep of the Atlantic Ocean in the air. In the distance was the mouth of the harbor, jagged and green, the sailboats rocking, the lights inside the houses beaming like curious eyes at the strangers on the road. It was a dark night, the stars resting, and everyone else had cleared away. The benches and picnic tables were empty, the swimmers gone. They were only a few miles from Salem, but to Sarah this was another world entirely.

She gazed longingly at the homes, some modest and narrow, others mansions with harbor-front views and personal docks. She was most attentive to the homes with swings and basketball courts behind the garages, lawns decorated with slides and kickballs. She looked at the gardens, the roses, the sweet Williams, the wild flowers, the American beeches, one fine tulip tree, and the requisite oaks. She admired the shrubs and the herbs, and she remembered suddenly that she used to like to grow things. In her previous life, in Los Angeles, she had a few rose bushes she cared for, along with two lavender bushes and assorted petunias and daisies. In her previous life, in the Massachusetts Bay Colony, she grew herbs and vegetables. When they were married the first time, when she was Elizabeth, James made a point of admiring her front yard garden. She grew tomatoes, carrots, cabbages, and onions in the raised beds within the brown-wood fence. She would walk the gravel pathway to tend the beans and pumpkins in the copious land behind the house. There was no aesthetic value to gardens in the seventeenth century—they were for food and medicinal purposes—but sometimes she gathered native woodland flowers and set them out inside the house. They were wealthy enough to hire all the help they needed, and in truth she didn't need to lift a finger, but she was a farmer's daughter and she liked getting her hands dirty, digging in the dirt, feeling the roots in her hands, delicate yet vibrant, strong yet fresh. When Sarah saw Jocelyn's house down the block she thought she might like to start gardening again. She would like to create something new.

Jocelyn's new home was pale-yellow, a single-level, ranch-style house with a green lawn and manicured bushes. James stared at the swing set behind the house.

"What happened to all the land?" Sarah asked.

"What?"

"Our house was surrounded by land. What happened to it?"

"I didn't need more than what the house stood on so I sold it all, piece by piece."

Sarah looked at Jocelyn's house. "We're here," she said.

"I see."

"Will you come inside?" She wanted him to go inside. She wanted him to see what she saw whenever she was near the happy little Endecott family, and she wanted him to relent and see that they could have that too.

James sighed. "For a while," he said.

But he didn't step forward. He had that little-boy-lost look, a 'why' between his brows. He spoke to the blades of grass beneath his feet.

"You knew when you married me your life would be different. A baby is the one thing I can't give you, and I know that's what you want more than anything right now. Don't you know how that hurts me? But I'm not like ordinary men, Sarah. I'm cursed."

"You're not cursed, James."

"Only a curse could turn me into a three hundred and forty-nine year old man who doesn't look a day over thirty. Only a curse could turn me into something that's seen the Salem Witch Trials, the American

Revolution, the Trail of Tears, the American Civil War, World War II..."

"But a curse is a bad thing. You're not a bad thing."

James looked like a child left to find his way out of a haystack maze, where everywhere you look there's one more row of taupe-colored straw the same as everywhere else. She rested her head against his chest and listened to the hollowness. There were nights when it was still a shock to remember he was silent inside.

"But the baby..." Sarah said.

"What baby, Sarah?"

"I can feel her. She's calling me."

"Sarah..."

She had to restrain herself from reaching out toward the phantom child. Her voice dropped to a whisper. "Grace."

"Grace has been gone a long time." James took Sarah into his arms. "I'm so sorry, honey. I'm so sorry my curse makes it impossible for us."

Sarah went numb. She felt the way Olivia looked when she went into a psychic trance—detached from her body, her mind, the earth beneath her feet.

They were shrouded in the shadows when the lights in Jocelyn's living room went out. The lamp upstairs went out too. But the den stayed bright. Jocelyn. She wouldn't sleep for hours yet. James glanced at the illuminated window, then looked at Sarah with a maudlin grin, as if to say, "This is why we can't adopt a child. The baby will have a father whose light stays on when the others have gone dark."

Sarah turned toward home. She thought of running away and leaving James behind, but something stopped her, unseen but tangible. She remembered the fluttery thread-like line she felt binding her to James, and the silken thread brushed her knotted shoulders, lassoing her frustration and releasing it to skid across the ocean, to the moon, and beyond. As suddenly as her frustration came on, she felt a wave of contentment wash over her as though she were standing in the bay at high tide, and instead of aching for the child she had seen so clearly in her mind's eye a moment before, now she ached for her husband. When she looked at him she saw the man who loved her every night for over three hundred years. And I love him just as much, she thought. That was all. It was a simple sentence. No fancy similes. No poetic metaphors or alliteration or assonance. But it was so true. I love him just as much.

James brushed a dark curl from her cheek and pressed her head to his chest. "I don't want you to be unhappy," he said.

"I can never be unhappy with you. You're my dear and loving husband."

"And you are my Sarah. *My* Sarah."

He brushed another stray curl from her face, the bay breeze was whipping her hair from its clips, and he kissed her, softly at first, then passionately. Sarah parted her lips, receptive to him. She wasn't through wanting a child, she knew, and they would continue the discussion another time. They didn't need to settle anything that night. They had time.

When they arrived home, James swept Sarah into his arms and carried her into their bedroom. He undressed her slowly, though she was always impatient when she undressed him. She could never wait as he could. When she connected with him that way she was transported, first somewhere far away where there was only wholeness and peace, then back to herself and she knew who she was in the world. Where she was supposed to be, in that house, at that time, in that place. When the moment was over, her panting done, when James was on his back pressing her head to his chest, when he stroked her hair from her forehead past her shoulders, twirling her curls through his fingers, he was silent for the longest time. Sarah pressed her cheek into him, trying to feel even closer. Sometimes, no matter how hard she tried, she couldn't get close enough.

And then, as if he could read her mind, he said, "We'll be all right, Sarah. Just the two of us. I'll never leave you ever."

"And I promise you the same," she said.

She felt cold suddenly and trembled, the hard bumps rippling her skin. She didn't understand the rawness she suddenly felt, as though she were left exposed in a winter storm, and she closed her eyes and calmed her breathing the way she used to whenever she woke up from a nightmare. There was an echo to James's voice when he said, "I'll never leave you ever," and Sarah realized she was afraid that one day he wouldn't be there. But that will never happen, she thought. He promised me he would never leave me, and I believe him.

And she did.

CHAPTER TWO

Late the next afternoon Sarah watched the top layer of night descend like a blanket over Salem. She was antsy waiting for James, so she straightened up the bookcases, cleared off the counter in the newly re-modeled kitchen, and sighed again at the ladder leading up to the attic. She startled at the woodpecker-like knock at the door and looked through the window, shuddering when she saw the man outside. While it wasn't the pock-faced monster come to drag her away, this visitor wasn't any more welcome and she wondered if she could pretend she wasn't home.

"What's he doing here?" she said.

"Who is it?"

James came out of their bedroom and looked over her shoulder to see an unshaven black-haired man in dark glasses though the sun was gone.

"It's my ex-husband."

"What's he doing here?"

"I have no idea."

Sarah was hesitant as she opened the door to the man she had been married to for a decade. He looked small, Nick, wearing a black sports coat over a white button-down shirt untucked over blue jeans, rubbing the stubble of perfectly trimmed three-day-old beard.

"Nick," Sarah said. "This is unexpected."

"Sarah..." Nick held his arms out like they were high school buddies connecting at a reunion. "It's been too long, babe. I was in town to scout a location so I thought I'd stop by. How've you been?" He looked Sarah up, down, around, and back again, smiling the whole time. "You're look-ing hot, Sarah, I have to say. I see you lost that weight you gained."

Sarah sighed. "Nick, I'd like you to meet my husband, James. James, this is Nick Corelli."

"Good to meet you, Jim."

Nick stepped around James, who was standing his full height, his eyes glaring, his mouth set, a preternatural barrier between the intruder and his wife. Nick glanced around the newly remodeled kitchen, tapping the stainless steel appliances and the cabinets like he was testing melons for ripeness. James leaned against the bookcase, his arms crossed in front of him like a battle shield, his lips a flat line. Sarah thought he looked ready to pounce.

"Nice house," Nick said.

"It was built in the seventeenth century," Sarah said. "So was most of the furniture."

"I like old things. That's why I married Sarah." Nick winked at her. "Sorry, buddy, but I guess you get sloppy seconds." He laughed as he ran his hand across the wood wall. Sarah hoped he'd get a splinter somewhere painful. "So what do you do again, Jim?"

Knots twisted James's jaw. "I'm a professor at Salem State University," he grumbled.

"That explains the old stuff. What do you teach?"

"James is an English professor," Sarah said.

"You married an English teacher?" Nick laughed, that loud guffaw that always grated her nerves to Parmesan cheese. "You never could keep your nose out of your books, Sarah. Here I'd be telling her about all the celebrities I met, the exotic locations of the movies I was producing, everything she needed to know about my day, and she didn't even hear me."

Sarah smiled at James, and when he saw her, the devilish amusement in her upturned lips, he nodded. Her years with Nick became a joke suddenly, a romantic comedy with a happy ending, with another man, a beautiful man, the only man she ever loved.

Nick continued, oblivious to the silent conversation between them. "I don't have time for books," he said. "I'm too busy with my movies. Did

Sarah tell you I was a producer? Two films up for Academy Awards in the last three years. My latest film will break every box office record ever known. It's a vampire movie. Vampires are popular now, right? Why not tap into it? My buddy Sam's finishing up the screenplay as we speak. We should be ready to begin production in January."

"What's the name of your movie?" Sarah asked, casting a wary glance at her husband.

"'The Vampire Killers.' It's about a ring of vampires who roam the streets searching for vengeance for the wrongs they've suffered. They're a motorcycle gang but they're also vampires. Since they're immortal they've lived through all these important historical periods like the Trail of Tears, World War II, the fall of the Berlin Wall, you know, olden times."

James glared at Nick. "The Trail of Tears?" he said. "What do you know about the Trail of Tears?"

"Indians are like vampires, Jim—they're always popular. You know, Cowboys and Indians, feathers and peace pipes, *Dances With Wolves.* You Lone Ranger, me Tonto. That shit sells."

James glowered over Nick, his fists clenched into white balls behind his back, and Sarah worried he might try to drink the smaller man for dinner. Not that she entirely minded the idea.

"How dare you," James said, pointing an accusing finger in Nick's direction, the thunder rumbling his voice. "How dare you make a mockery of the Trail of Tears. You don't know how they suffered. You can't fathom how they were ripped from their homes. You didn't see their faces, hear their cries in the night. You didn't watch them die."

"Are you Indian?" Nick asked.

"No."

"Then what do you care? It's just a movie, Jim."

Sarah stood up, her hands out, a barrier between the men. "I just remembered," she said. "We need to meet Jennifer and Olivia in an hour. Don't you remember, James? We need to meet Jennifer and Olivia in an hour."

Nick laughed. "All right, I get it. Enough time with the first husband. We don't want the second husband getting jealous." Nick opened the door and stopped. "You seem happy, Sarah," he said. "You were a mess before. Never sleeping. Never happy."

"I was having nightmares."

"Those nightmares." Nick threw his hands into the air. "She'd wake up screaming in the middle of the night and scare the living hell out of me. Does she still have those ridiculous dreams? God help you if she does. You were always so weak, Sarah."

James's eyes became squints of black light. He gripped the seventeenth century chair in front of him, and with one squeeze the wood crumpled to the ground. With the chair disintegrated under his grip, he dropped it and took one long step toward the intruder.

"James!"

He froze at his wife's command. He bit his lip, clenched his fists, and disappeared into the bedroom muttering expletives, slamming the door behind him. Nick stared after him, then looked at Sarah with surprised eyes.

"He has trouble hearing sometimes," Sarah said.

"What did he do to that chair?"

"Like you said—everything in the house is old."

She walked Nick out to the rented black Mercedes by the curb. Nick nodded toward James, who was watching them from the bedroom window.

"He seems kind of angry," Nick said.

Sarah smiled. All the love she ever had for James, then and now, filled her and radiated brighter than the white-milk moon shining above. "I'm very happy," she said. She looked at James, who heard every word, and she spoke for him and him alone. "There's nothing angry about James. He's a kind, brilliant, thoughtful, sensitive, affectionate, caring husband. I'm lucky I found him." For James she whispered, "Again."

"You should get his hearing checked."

"I will."

As Sarah said good night to her ex-husband, she hoped she would never see him again. Back inside, she put her hands on James's shoulders, trying to rub away the tension Nick's presence caused. James leaned into her hands, closing his eyes, and Sarah felt his muscles loosen and his skin cool. He sighed, and he turned her face toward him with his hand.

"What were you thinking, Sarah? How could you marry him?"

"I'm not sure myself. Maybe I had to experience a bad marriage so I could find my way to you."

"I never looked for anyone else. In over three hundred years, I never wanted anyone else."

"That's not fair. I didn't know about you. If I had known you were waiting for me I would have come running. But I'm here now." She sat on his lap and pressed her head against his shoulder. As she nestled against her husband, his coolness soothed her agitation.

"You became so angry when Nick mentioned the Trail of Tears," she said. "I thought you were going to take a bite out of him."

"The thought did occur to me."

"I wanted to bite him myself." Sarah nuzzled her face into James's neck and gently nibbled his skin with her teeth. "I'm going to bite you instead," she said. Then she looked into his dark-night eyes. "Did you see the Trail of Tears?"

"I did."

"Will you tell me what happened?"

"Another time."

"You always say another time. When will it be another time? We're here now. Tell me now."

"I'll tell you, Sarah, but I can see you're tired. Go take a bubble bath. I promise. Another time."

It wasn't very late, just around nine o'clock, but James was right. She was exhausted. She kissed his lips, his cheeks, his forehead. When she could finally let go of him she went into the bedroom to grab her robe.

When she passed the open door she saw James at his desk, staring into the nighttime void. She watched him, loving him. Suddenly, she understood why Nick had shown up unannounced—so she could compare and contrast, then and now, sad and happy, hot and cold. See how far you've come, Sarah, she thought. Look at that beautiful man sitting there. He loves you. He has always loved you. Only you. Ever.

She went back to James and kissed his cool cheek. "I love you," she said.

"I love you more."

He pressed a stray curl from her cheek, and she brushed some gold strands from his eyes. She kissed his cheek again, then went into the bathroom and turned the dial in the tub, wanting the water as hot as it would go, as though she had to soak away the memories of her ex-husband having ever been in the house. She poured half a bottle of lavender-scented foam under the running water, got undressed, and lowered herself into the tub. She leaned back, closed her eyes, and let the stress of the night disappear with the popping bubbles. When she felt cleansed, she grabbed a towel, dried herself off, wrapped the towel around her, and watched her anxieties whirl down the drain. She pressed her ear against the closed door, and when she heard his shuffle she smiled. She knew James was waiting for her. She thought of his beautiful face, the smile that could brighten any night of the year, his broad shoulders, his muscular arms, his hands that knew everything and everywhere about her, and she left her towel on the floor.

I am home. I had been drifting, mainly through England, mainly London, though often I went to the Cotswolds, finding comfort in the storybook lime-stone villages with the potted flowers in the windowsills and the marketplaces and the river valleys and the water meadows. In the 1820s life was not so different in the English countryside than it was in the seventeenth century, and I found continuity there. Occasionally, I left England for France, and sometimes I left France for Italy or Italy for Switzerland, but it was always back to England, mainly London, though sometimes Bath or Kent or Stratford. I spent time in Cambridge at university. Then I needed to go home. I needed to step into our house, sleep in our bed, feel you near me again. I had been numb for oh so very long. But now I am here and you are still gone. I cannot live without you, and yet I cannot die. What do I do? Oh my God, Elizabeth. What do I do?

The loneliness overwhelms me. My empty arms ache. Everywhere I look in our wooden house, every chair I sit on, every window I look out, all see is you. I must leave this place. I came back to find you and all I have found is a despair I can never recover from. There are too many haunted nights in this place. Even as I am, I fear the phantoms. Only when I sleep, in the shroud of my daily death, the ghosts say good-bye sometimes. I cannot stay.

Dear Elizabeth...where should I go?

I wandered. I journeyed out west into the barren frontier where brave men, women, and children ride their covered wagons to who-knows-where under harsh circumstances for new chances. I remember being like them once, when Father and I left London for the Massachusetts Bay Colony. Now I am back to my old haunts in the Smoky Mountains, the hardwood forests, the streaming valleys, the green-covered slopes, the spruce firs at the peaks. My neighbors, the Cherokee, who have lived in this land for over one thousand years, call it "Sha-conage" or "Place of blue smoke."

A few times I have tried to make conversation with the Cherokee man who is my closest neighbor. He is a strong-looking, broad-chested man, youngish, perhaps the age I was when I was turned. I often see him reading books and newspapers and writing his thoughts into a bound journal. I am drawn to him, I think, because he reminds me of myself, the way he dotes on his pretty wife and two young daughters, the way he is drawn to read and think. They are who we could have been, Lizzie, and I like him for it. I have tried to talk to him, offered to share books, but he does not acknowledge me. I wonder if it is because I am not Cherokee, but he has white friends who come to trade with him so I do not think that is the cause. Do you think he knows what I am?

Since no one will know me I am left to spend my time as I will. Last night I hammered the last pegs into this one-room, one-window log cabin under the hardwood trees. I can hear the soothing river flowing just yards away, trickling over rocks and edges. I am certain that here, nestled high in this nook in the mountains, that I can kiss the close-looking stars, kiss you, if I stretch hard enough. There is nothing in this cabin but heavy quilts to sleep on, a heavier quilt to block the light, a few books, paper, quills, tips, and ink. So I'm writing, trying to make sense of everything—your life, my life, our lives together. Your death. My death. My life after my death. I am writing to you because you are still all I have to live for.

CHAPTER THREE

James locked the drawer to the desk in the great room, turning the antique-looking key, snapping the latch. He looked for Sarah, but she was in the kitchen on the phone with Jennifer, paying little attention to him. He would share the contents of that drawer with her soon. But not now. They had only been married three months. There would be plenty of hours over many years when he could share more of everything he had seen. He stopped, listened to Sarah laugh at something Jennifer said, and he smiled. It was still his favorite sound in the world.

He sat on the sofa, put his feet on the glass coffee table, and turned the television channel to the Boston Celtics game. Sarah thought it was funny that he enjoyed watching sports, turned as he was, but it made perfect sense to him. The battle between the teams. The victor, the vanquished. The struggles, the conquers. The doing, the dying. The winner, the loser. It was like a hunt, he said, and he loved it. Sarah said good-bye to Jennifer and left her cell phone on the table near the hearth. She kissed James's cheek, then stretched out on the sofa resting her feet on his knees. She picked up her book from the end table, *The Scarlet Letter* by Nathaniel Hawthorne, and started reading while the high-energy cheers from the home crowd in TD Garden filled the room.

"Why are you reading that?" James asked. "You saw the idiocy of the Puritans first hand. You experienced it yourself. You don't need a fictional account of it."

"Hawthorne was born in Salem and I thought I should brush up on his work. I haven't read him since college."

James nodded. "I should probably read him again too. I was thinking of teaching a Hawthorne seminar next autumn. I wanted to run the idea by Goodwin at the department meeting tomorrow night." He looked at Sarah's cell phone on the table. "So what was Jennifer cackling about?"

"Her new boyfriend."

"She's not talking about getting married again, is she?"

"No. Not really."

"Who is he?"

"You should know. You're the one who invited him to our wedding."

"Who?"

"Chandresh Mankiller."

James started at the name. "I didn't realize they were dating," he said.

"They are." Sarah paused, her chocolate-brown eyes fixed on him. "He's like you, isn't he?"

"Like me?"

"The nocturnal type?"

James laughed. "Yes, he's the nocturnal type. Along with koalas, aye-ayes, and the red-eyed tree frog."

"And vampire bats."

"Yes."

Suddenly, like a slap against the sound of the cheering basketball crowd, was an unmistakable howl, the kind you hear in horror films when the Wolfman is on his way. Sarah dropped her book to the floor and looked at the window.

"What's that?" she asked.

"Not what. Who. It's Howard."

"Howard?"

James nodded toward the full-moon sky, and Sarah sucked in her breath. He opened the door and Howard walked in, horizontal, one leg on each corner, yellow eyes, gray fur. Strong, husky, powerful. When Howard saw Sarah he pulled one front leg behind the other, bowing. Sarah backed away, pressing into the wall between the window and the door, sneaking a furtive glance at the moon as though she wanted to turn it crescent at the snap of her fingers, or send it tumbling into the ocean.

"Sit down, Howard," James said, gesturing at the sofa. "Sarah? Come sit with us." She nodded, but instead disappeared into the kitchen. "Excuse me," James said as he followed Sarah.

He leaned close to her and waited. Finally, she asked, "Is it safe having him here now?"

"It's Howard."

"What if he attacks us?"

"Are you afraid of me?" James asked.

"Of course not."

"If you can trust me, then can't you trust Howard too? Do you think I'd let him into this house if there were any chance he could hurt you? Don't forget—Howard is Timothy's guardian."

"A werewolf who crossed party lines to adopt a vampire son."

"Exactly. Now come back. He can hear every word we're saying."

Sarah followed James into the great room. She paused by the wall, unsure a moment longer, but she did finally sit next to Howard on the sofa.

"I'm sorry, Howard," she said. "I've learned a lot about the supernatural world this past year, but sometimes the paranormal part still comes as surprise."

"I apologize for coming in my current condition, Sarah," Howard said. "I didn't mean to scare you. You should have seen your face when I walked in the door!"

James laughed, Howard laughed, but Sarah stared, marveling at the wolf-man sitting on her sofa as though he had stopped by for a spot of tea.

"Humans can't hear me like this," Howard said. "It sounds like howls and barks to them."

"Howard said he's sorry he scared you," James said.

"It's all right, Howard."

"It's probably better she can't hear me," Howard said. "She's not going to like what I have to say about Kenneth Hempel."

James kept his eyes light, his features easy. He didn't want Sarah to worry about that annoying little reporter again. He laughed as if Howard told a joke.

"I heard through a journalism professor at the college that Hempel started a blog where he's going to share everything he knows. He's already reposted the article he published in the *News*."

Sarah was staring at Howard, her head tilted to the side as though if she strained hard enough she might understand. James didn't want her to understand.

"Hempel's also self-publishing a book about his vampire hunt. Seems anyone can publish any crap they want these days." Howard turned to Sarah and spoke to her as if she could understand. "Luckily, no one pays much attention to the indie books," he said.

James felt the worry crawl up his spine, rung by rung, until it rested in the smile he wouldn't drop so Sarah wouldn't guess something was wrong. He smiled the way a madman in the mental ward smiles, amused by something only he can see.

"The blog is up, James. I've seen it myself."

"That's not good," James said.

"What's not good?" Sarah asked.

James shook his head, unsure what to say.

"Tell her this," Howard said. "Timothy is having a hard time. I need you to talk to him, James. I think he's depressed."

James turned to Sarah. "Howard thinks Timothy is depressed." He said the words quickly, hoping they flowed to the right cadence, no strange offbeat in his tone.

"Depressed about what?"

James relayed Howard's words: "About looking like he's fourteen when he's eighteen now. He had a crush on a girl in one of his classes and she wouldn't give him the time of day because she thought he was a little boy."

"Will you talk to him, James?" Howard asked.

"Of course," James said.

James opened the door, and Howard scampered away free and wild as any wolf roaming the plains. As he shut the door, James felt weighed down by a black-hole worry about the damage Hempel could cause if he went through with his plans to share his knowledge about vampires with the world. Should he tell Sarah? Did she need to know that Hempel was on the hunt again? James thought back to that day, just five months before, when he had gone into the sunlight and survived, proving to Hempel that he wasn't a vampire, though he was. Hempel had been convinced, and James was no longer a suspect. He had taken himself out of the running for Hempel's Vampire of the Year award. So why did he feel nervous knowing about Hempel's latest plans?

Sarah walked to him, pressed her head against his shoulder, held his hand in hers. She looked wistfully out the window the way Howard left. "How did Howard come to adopt Timothy?" she asked.

James shook his head, pressing away his fears about Hempel so he could concentrate on his wife. "I think Geoffrey turned Timothy," he said. "I don't know that for a fact, but Timothy was left to fend for himself the way I was—completely abandoned. He was all alone like I was, afraid of what he had become. He needed someone to help him."

Sarah sat on the sofa, patting the cushion beside her.

"Tell me," she said.

James sat next to her. He slid his arm around her waist, pulled her close, breathing in deeply, savoring the scent of strawberries and cream. He could live forever wafting in that delicious fruity haze. He pressed Sarah's cheek to his chest, and he stared over her head out the window as he remembered.

"It was about four years ago now. I was living in Washington State at the time, teaching at the University of Washington Seattle, when I got a call from Howard saying he found a vampling, a young one, living alone and frightened in the woods.

"'He's just a boy,' Howard said. 'I tried to help him, but he was too afraid to come to me.'

"'Afraid?' I said.

"'It was a full moon,' Howard explained. 'I heard the boy crying and I saw the blood on his cheeks so I tried to talk to him, but he was frozen with fear when he realized he understood a talking wolf. He ran away as quick as a flash, and as fast as I am I couldn't catch him. Now I can't find him and I don't know where he went to stay out of the sun during the day. You have to help me find him, James. He's just a boy and he's scared.'"

"What a kind man Howard is," Sarah said. "I didn't know."

James nodded. "The sight of the frightened vampire boy touched him and he had to do something."

"So you came back to Salem?"

"Yes. When I arrived I saw a very human-looking Howard, his shirt rumpled, his beard untrimmed, his hair messy, his eyes red-rimmed. He couldn't rest until he found the boy, so that night we went into the woods to search for him. At first there was nothing, no sounds, not even the scamper of animals or the rustling wind. Then I caught his scent and the sound of feet crunching fallen leaves. I moved as soundlessly as I could since I didn't want to frighten him away. Finally, I saw him huddled against a tree, his knees pulled to his chest, his face and blue shirt stained with large pools of blood, some from his tears, and some from some previous feeding or injuries, I couldn't tell. The sight tore at Howard's heart, and it touched mine too. At least it touched where my heart used to be."

Sarah shook her head. "You're like the Tin Man from *The Wizard of Oz*, James, wishing for a heart you already have."

"Perhaps," James said. "The sight of Timothy touched my memories of how frightened and alone I felt when I was new to this life, and I understood what Howard felt because I had to help the boy too. I walked to him, and when he saw me he jumped as if he would run away.

"'It's all right,' I said. I moved toward him as if I were approaching a strange dog with my hands out to let it smell me. I knelt next to him and spoke softly. 'Don't be afraid,' I told him. 'I'm just like you.'

"Timothy pulled into himself, his knees closer to his chest, his arms so tight around his legs they nearly wrapped around his back, an immortal ball of fear.

"'It's all right,' I said again. 'My name is James. What's your name?'

"Timothy's black-night eyes looked like pinholes against his dead-pale skin, watching me as I inched closer to him. He must have sensed I meant him no harm because he released his grip some and he found his voice.

"'Timothy,' he said. He looked at himself, his bloody clothes, the fresh blood from his tears on his hands. He looked confused, as though he hardly remembered his name himself. 'I'm Timothy Bryston.'

"'How old are you, Timothy?'

"'I'm fourteen.'

"'Where's your family?'

"He heaved with such sadness he couldn't speak, and he shuddered so hard I was afraid he'd damage himself even with his preternatural bones. I rubbed his back until he settled. He looked even younger than fourteen then. 'They're dead,' he said through waves of sobs. 'All of them. My mom and dad. My sister.' He held his blood-streaked hands out to me, pleading. 'What's wrong with me?'

"'You're all right, Timothy,' I said. 'Tell me what happened to your family.'

He paced the rocky forest ground, tripping over heavy tree roots he didn't see through his blurred, swollen eyes, then stopped suddenly, his head in his hands. "'We were driving home and another car zoomed around us. My dad lost control swerving away and our car smashed into a tree.' Timothy dropped to his knees under the weight of his anguish. 'They're all dead! And I should be too! I was dying, everything was slowing down, everything was growing darker, but this man pulled me from the car and said he could help me. I asked him if he could help my mom and dad, and he said I'd thank him later. I woke up here in the woods.'"

"That does sound like Geoffrey," Sarah said.

James grimaced. "Yes."

"Did Timothy recognize him at our wedding?"

"I don't think so. He hasn't said anything."

Sarah shook her head. "That poor baby, all alone in the world without his parents and terrified at what he had become."

"I understood how he felt. I told him I was very sorry about his family, and I told him he didn't need to be afraid anymore since Howard and I were there to help him. I looked back at Howard, the father's concern already settled in his eyes. He stepped out from behind a tree, tentatively at first, fully human, heart wide open, like the arms he held out ready to embrace this boy he already knew would be his son. He kneeled near Timothy and smiled.

"'I'm Howard Wolfe,' he said. 'I'd like to help you, Timothy, if you'd let me.'

"'There's something wrong with me,' Timothy said, holding out his bloodied hands as proof.

"Howard laughed. 'It's all right,' he said. 'There's something wrong with me as well. You'll see in about a month. If you'd like to stay with me, I think that would be fine. James here is just like you, and he's going to help you too. Your life will be different now, but it's nothing we can't figure out together. Would you like to stay with me, Timothy?' I thought Timothy would burst into a fresh flood of red tears, he looked so relieved."

"I thought vampires and werewolves are enemies," Sarah said.

"It's never been true. At least not as long as I've been around."

"How come Geoffrey doesn't go to see Timothy the way he comes to see you?"

"I don't think he even realizes he turned Timothy. He's never said anything about it."

Sarah shook her head. "Sometimes people don't say everything they know," she said.

James nodded. He took his wife into his arms, holding her close. He guessed she knew he was keeping something from her, but that was his job, to protect her, to keep everything bad away from her. He was her safety cushion, her soft place to fall, shielding her from everything wrong in the world. He decided not to tell Sarah about Hempel. Not now. She didn't need to know.

But he needed to know. Later that night, while Sarah slept, he sat at his desk and turned on his laptop. One Internet search later he was staring at the blog with the finger-pointing words he remembered:

Do vampires lurk in Salem? The demon tales from long ago may not be as fictional as many have come to believe. Do you know any demons? Or, perhaps a better question is, do you know any vampires? Before you laugh you may want to consider the facts. Vampires may be prowling as close as your hospitals, your favorite clothing stores, your dentists's offices, even lurking in Salem State College.

How well do you know those whom you encounter every night? Where are they going? What business do they tend to? While it's difficult to believe that the undead are real, it would be to everyone's benefit to consider such possibilities. These blood-devouring night creatures aren't merely figments of imagination from books and movies, but they're out there, among us, feigning human lives to be all the closer to our blood. We are their natural food source after all.

James saw the addendum under the original article, and he read that too:

I am in the process of gathering the final pieces of evidence I need to prove the reality of vampires. I will have names, facts, and details soon. I hope everyone will follow me on this journey as I disclose once and for all the undead who have cloaked themselves in darkness these many years.

James shut down the computer and stared out the window, wallowing in the silence of a sleeping Salem. It was just as Howard said. But James had hope. Since writing the original article Hempel had dismissed James from his list of suspects. They would be fine.

Dear God, James thought. Let us be fine.

They say the Indians are uncivilized with their barbaric customs. Forget their depraved heathen gods. The Indians should conform to the gods of commerce. Besides, they have no title to the land. They do not believe in land ownership. And the discoverer has rights too. What is the point of discovering land if you cannot have it when you find it?

But the Cherokee assimilated. They converted. Their children go to proper schools. They have a written language, a syllabary, invented by Sequoyah over twenty years ago, and they have laws and a Constitution. They abolished clan revenge and other acts considered too savage for gentle American sensibilities. The women spin and weave while the men raise livestock and plant crops. They own their own plots of land, no longer shared as one whole. Most have become God-fearing, Bible-reading, prayer-speaking Christians. Many have become wealthy. Some further south are slave owners, a sad concession to their wish to conform. The people here are farmers, but others are doctors, lawyers, writers, teachers, professors, and journalists. But no matter how well they follow the leader they will always be Other.

It's the land, Lizzie. The Americans are greedy for the land. And now they will force the people to go away when they will not leave it all behind. When they will not pretend they were never here. It's beginning already.

As I look through the window all is dust. Even into the night the chalky air rises and swirls, settling on cornstalks, clothing, faces, leaving a pallid mask on everyone. There is the grit-covered white man I see here often who comes to trade with the natives. Now he is speaking to my neighbor.

"Ridge and Boudinot signed the treaty in Georgia," the white man says.

"No," says my neighbor. "Chief John Ross won't allow it. He thinks we can keep our land."

"It's done, Friend. They're taking your land and sending you away."

"No," my neighbor says again. "Chief John Ross has gone to Washington to talk to the government. They will listen. They will see why it's wrong to take our land."

"Ridge and Boudinot thought there was no way the government would let you keep the land—that's why they signed. Removal will start soon. I thought you should know."

The trot-trot-trot of horse's hooves comes faster and closer. I heard it long before the men talking outside. Suddenly, the horse stops a few feet away. I see the stern-faced, blue-suited officer dismounting, his bayonet at his side. My neighbor's family have come outside, his mother-in-law, wife, and daughters, huddled close to one another, watching.

The wind picks up, and everyone disappears in the dust. Through the haze I see the officer nod at the white man. He doesn't look at the native man or his family as he walks through their open doorway. He scans their possessions, their basic furniture, the spinning wheel, the beads and stones and pestles. He eyes my neighbor's pretty black-haired wife with a suggestive gleam that boils rage from the soles of my feet to the tips of my hair. For a moment I am back in Salem in 1692, and I feel the constable at our door, cruel as he drags you away. I can hardly restrain myself from ripping the officer man to shreds. How dare he impose himself on this family. What have they done?

The native man must also sense danger and he stands protectively in front of his women.

"What do you want here?" the white man asks.

"I have orders to take inventory of the belongings inside," says the officer.

"So you can confiscate it for yourself or sell it?"

"I have orders."

"Seems awful late into the night for that. Can't you come back tomorrow?"

"I'm here now."

The officer brushes further into my neighbor's house, his back stretched tall, shoulders back, a sad apology for his height—the Napoleon complex, I believe it's called. He needs to make a show, the man in the uniform, the man with the orders. This is all a show of Power. You will do what we make you do. When we want what you have you must give it to us. When we want you to leave you must leave. There is no other way.

The white trader notices me and nods. I can see in his face he is kind, but I have come away from the window. I do not want to be noticed. I hear the officer mount his horse, and the horse trots away, faster than he came. My neighbor and his family are left alone for one more night.

CHAPTER FOUR

James arrived at his office in the library, turned on the computer, and logged in to check his e-mail. There were the usual messages, white noise from the English department, notes from students asking about assignments, requesting extensions, making excuses, or all of the above. He remembered the red-filled bags, and he took them from his black backpack and slid them into the brown-paneled icebox beneath his desk. He hit the button to print his notes for his Shakespeare seminar that night, impatient because he was late to meet Sarah in the library. They would be home together soon, but he wouldn't lose one moment with her. He wanted to spend every hour of every night with her, holding her, kissing her. He missed her when she wasn't there. And if he could steal a kiss before he had to teach, he would.

He stopped when he heard the footsteps come down the hall. For a moment he thought he heard Hempel's heavy, plodding steps, but he shook that paranoia away and heard short, shuffling paces instead. He smelled musk, so it wasn't a student since twenty-something boys don't douse themselves in Old Spice. After the knock, he opened his door to see Goodwin Enwright, head of the English department, fiftyish, balding, wearing a white button-down shirt and brown tie over blue jeans and running shoes.

"James," said Goodwin, "I was hoping to catch you before you left for class."

"Here I am." James gestured to the chair where his students sat during office visits. Goodwin shook his head.

"I can only stay a minute. I have an idea for a new class I want to run by you."

"What is it?"

"Vampire Literature."

39

James struggled not to gag, jump, or scream. "Goodwin, I don't know..."

"Hear me out, James. We've been stagnant as a department for a while and we need to be innovative. We're a university now."

"I know. I saw the sign outside."

"We want to shake things up, so we took a poll of English students and asked for ideas for new classes. Turns out they're crazy about vampires. So what if we offer a vampire literature class? And what if you teach it?"

James didn't know whether to laugh or cry, but since he would bleed from his eyes if he cried, suspicious during a conversation about vampires, he chose to laugh, or at least force a hearty smile. "I don't know anything about vampire books, Goodwin."

"Sure you do. Everyone does, unless they're dead." Goodwin slapped James's shoulder like they were buddies out for a beer. "You're not dead, are you?"

"Not very."

"I bet you know more than you think. There's that book that's so popular with the girls these days. What is it?"

"I don't know."

"Sure you do. The one about the sparkly kid?"

"*Twilight.*"

"That's it. I was thinking the class could cover the development of vampire literature. People think Bram Stoker's *Dracula* was the first vampire novel, but it wasn't. Sheridan Le Fanu's novel *Carmilla* and *Varney the Vampire* by James Malcolm Rymer came first."

"*Carmilla* is about a lesbian vampire who preys on a lonely young woman."

"See, so you do know some of the books."

James sighed. "Maybe you should ask Angela to teach the class. She's younger. She might like the idea."

"Younger than who? We just went to her fortieth birthday party last month at the Lyceum Bar and Grill. I distinctly recall seeing you and Sarah there. So Angela's forty, and what are you? All of thirty now?"

"Something like that."

Goodwin pulled over the empty chair and sat down. "You're one of the best we have in the English department, James. The students rave about you on your evaluations every term. We want someone young, someone the students like to teach the class. We'll try it out once and see how it goes. What have you got to lose?"

James rubbed his eyes beneath his glasses. "It'll have to be a night class," he said.

"What could be more fitting?"

James shrugged. He wasn't concerned that Goodwin suspected anything, but he was unnerved that he was the one asked to teach the class. Teaching about vampires? It was too ridiculous. But he couldn't think of an excuse, a good excuse, in the moment he had to come up with one, so he nodded.

"Excellent," said Goodwin. "I knew you could be reasonable when you wanted to be." He walked through the open door, then turned back, his hand on the doorknob. "It'll be fine. Just start with the early stuff like *Carmilla*, *Varney the Vampire*, and *Dracula*, pull in some Anne Rice, throw in that sparkly kid and another one or two of the newer books and you've got a class. You can send me the course syllabus next week."

While James waited for Goodwin's shuffling footsteps to disappear, he stared out the window, trying to find the humor in the situation, Professor Wentworth teaching a vampire literature class. He looked at the time on his computer screen, grabbed his book bag, and locked his door. As he headed to the elevator, he decided he was right to agree to teach the class. He didn't want to make himself conspicuous by being too difficult. He thought of the line from *Hamlet*, Act 3 Scene 2, the play his seminar was discussing that night. "The lady doth protest too much, methinks," James said aloud. Gertrude was complaining about the queen in the play within the play meant to represent her own mean deeds.

James was complaining about the vampire books when he was afraid others would see...

"I think the vampire class is a great idea."

"Timothy..." James looked around to be sure no one else was close enough to hear, then shook his head at the dark-haired boy. "First of all," he whispered, "you should know better than sneaking up on me, and second of all, it's rude to listen in on conversations behind closed doors."

"I didn't sneak up on you since I was here first, and I can't turn my hearing off, and neither can you."

"That's true enough," James said. "I'm surprised you think the class is a good idea. Last year you were ready to tear Levon's throat when he said how he didn't like vampires."

"That's why this class is a good thing. It'll show people how everything they know about vampires is based on myths and legends."

"The class isn't about outing vampires. Those myths and legends are the basis for most vampire literature."

"I know." The elevator opened and they stepped inside. Timothy looked thoughtfully at the doors as they closed, and James could see some idea forming within the boy.

"That's it!" Timothy shouted. His black eyes widened, the smile brightening his young-looking features, and he grabbed James's arm, nearly pressing James into the steel wall in his enthusiasm. "People should know the truth about vampires!"

James shook his head. "We've had this conversation before. People won't understand..."

"Listen! I'll write a book about what it's really like to be a vampire! I'll write about my life, about the car accident where my parents died, how the vampire man bit me, how I was turned, how you and Howard found me and helped me. What a great part of the story, how this werewolf adopted a vampire boy! I'll write about how it's hard because I'm eighteen but still look like a kid."

"Timothy..."

"No, wait—here's the thing: I'll say it's a *novel*. I'll pretend it's *fiction*. I'll make up names and everything. This way I can be honest about my life but not have to worry about being discovered. But at least there'll be a true vampire story out there, something based on reality instead of that *Dracula* garbage."

The elevator door opened and Timothy skipped away, through the library to the campus outside. James shook his head, thinking it might not be such a bad idea. At least Timothy didn't look depressed anymore.

Sarah stood on the corner of Lafayette, staring at the skeleton-like scaffold of the new library building. The night lights were on, and workers with their hardhats in their hands wandered past. The cranes stopped. The only movement came from the students moving to and from their classes.

"Hey, Mrs. Doctor Wentworth."

Sarah saw Jennifer standing a few feet away in the parking lot. She walked around the orange construction cones to hug her friend.

"How are you feeling?" Sarah asked. "The library isn't the same without you."

"I'm better. I'm back at work tonight."

"I thought you were playing hooky. I thought maybe you ran off with Chandresh."

Jennifer smiled coyly. "I really was sick, but," she giggled like a teenage girl, "I did see Chandresh."

"Did you?"

"He came over to take care of me. He made me a potion his father used to make to cure people when they had influenza."

"Did it work?"

"It's not the same formula I use for healing, but I'm better. See?"

Jennifer spun around like a fashion model on a runway to show how healthy she felt. She looked at the skeleton frame and nodded. "Isn't it beautiful? We're going to have a library to beat even Harvard."

"It'll be a lot of work moving in," Sarah said.

Jennifer smiled. "We can have your strong husband and my strong boyfriend help."

Sarah looked toward Meier Hall, wondering if James had arrived. They walked to the U-shaped building and looked through the first-floor window of his Monday night classroom, but it was dark inside. "He must be in his office," she said.

"Let's go."

They walked past the construction zone, down College Drive, past Rainbow Terrace and the Marsh Conference Center to the Central Campus. The trees were peeping well, the leaves displaying all of autumn's beauty like impressionist brushstrokes of cadmium orange, crimson red, and yellow ochre.

"It's October already," Sarah said. "It seems like just yesterday when I saw James at the Witches Lair last Halloween. Time goes too fast."

Jennifer sighed. "I think last year was the first good Halloween James ever had. He's usually pretty grumpy about it."

"He told me he ran into Kenneth Hempel at your mom's shop that night."

Jennifer stopped. "What made you think of Hempel?" she asked.

"I was remembering last year. Why?"

"Just wondering."

Jennifer looked at Sarah as though she were deciding something. She shook her head, so whatever she was thinking, her answer was no. They arrived at the library, but there was still no sign of James. It's well dark now, Sarah thought. He should be here.

"Maybe he's running late," Jennifer said.

"James doesn't run late."

"Maybe he's in his office."

Sarah shrugged. "I'm not worried. It's not like there's a vampire hunter after him."

She meant it as a joke. It still made her smile to remember how James had outwitted Kenneth Hempel. He liked to remind her it was her idea to keep him out of the sunlight as much as possible, but that didn't matter, she said. He was the one who had to go in the sunlight when it was too painful for his eyes, and he was the one who had to convince Hempel he wasn't what he was.

Sarah put her bag into her desk drawer and hung her sweater over her chair. She looked out the window, reminded that it was dark, and she wondered where her husband was. On the nights when she worked, Sarah arrived earlier than James, but he would come to the library as soon as the sun dropped, kiss her, go up to his office, to his classes, and back to the library to kiss her again before they went home. She kept busy, filled out book orders, answered questions, researched information. She looked into the returns bin and saw it overflowing. She scanned bar codes and found a wheelie cart.

"You can get a student aide to do that, you know," said Jennifer.

"I don't mind."

Sarah wheeled the cart into the stacks and reshelved the books. She remembered her first nights in that library, how odd she found Jennifer's intuition, and how beautiful yet strange she found James. She remembered how she came to recognize her attachment to him, and how she began to search for him, wait for him, light up fluorescent whenever he appeared. And then, on cue, as if he knew her thoughts, there he was, James, coming out of the elevator, and she felt the same joy at the sight of him. He kissed her lips.

"Sorry I'm late," he said. "I was detained."

"By a vampire hunter?"

James was always pale, a dead-blue undertone to his ghost-white complexion, but Sarah watched him go slate-gray.

"I was just joking, James."

He smiled and kissed her forehead.

"No hunters here tonight," he said. "I'll talk to you after class. Wait until you hear what Timothy's up to."

He kissed her lips again, then left as quickly as he could without drawing attention to himself. Sarah watched the way he went, out the door, across the campus, toward Meier Hall. She turned to Jennifer, who was still intent on her work.

"Are you sure you want to date a vampire?" Sarah asked. "They can be difficult."

"I've known James my whole life. I know all too well how difficult they can be." Jennifer looked at Sarah. "Is he still saying no about the baby?"

"We haven't talked about it since the exhibition. I don't know..." She waved her hands around her, her fingers out, grasping for the words she needed to make herself understood. "Maybe James is right. Maybe there would be too many problems with James being..."

"Nocturnal?"

Sarah smiled. "Yes. Nocturnal."

"Jocelyn and Steve are doing great with Billy."

"I know."

Jennifer directed a student aide to replace some books abandoned on a study table. She walked close to Sarah and said, "I think you should do another reading with my mother."

"I don't know, Jennifer."

"Sarah, my mother is one of the most powerful witches alive today. Witches from all over the world visit her seeking her advice. Martha moved here from Alabama for the sole purpose of working with her. If you have questions, about the baby, about anything else, my mother can help you. She can find whatever you need to know."

Sarah laughed. "Olivia is one of the most powerful witches in the world?"

"Yes, Olivia. She's very modest about her abilities."

"She must be. I had no idea."

"I don't think even James knows the extent of her powers, and he's known my family since 1693. She should be the high priestess of our coven, but she passed the title onto me last year because she had been high priestess for over twenty years and she thought it was time for me to take over. Trust me, Sarah, you wouldn't believe the strength of her magical gifts. She helped you before, and she'll help you again."

Sarah remembered her psychic reading at the Witches Lair when she first arrived in Salem. At the time, she dismissed Olivia's prophecy as ridiculous—if frightening—nonsense, though every word of it turned out to be true. If Sarah decided to get a new reading, at least this time she'd know what to expect: Olivia speaks in riddles when she goes into a trance. But maybe Olivia could help her make sense of this on and off need for a child that came light—dark—light again like electricity from a switch. Sarah felt her heart telling her something, but what? If she was supposed to adopt a child, if there was a baby out there meant to be hers, then she would welcome it with open arms. If it was meant that she should have a child, then it was meant that James should too. They were a pair. A pair of what? James liked to joke. Just a pair, she'd say. Like matching socks? Yes, she'd answer. We're a pair of matching socks. We go everywhere and do everything together, then spend our nights knotted up.

"You're softening," Jennifer said. "Say yes already so I can tell Mom. She's been dying to get her hands on you since the exhibition."

"I'll think about it," Sarah said.

Jennifer turned back to the computer, logging into the database. "So when will James and Chandresh tell us about their time on the Trail of Tears together?"

"They were on the Trail of Tears together?"

"I don't know much about it. James certainly never told me. When I asked Chandresh how he and James met he mentioned the Trail of Tears. James lived near Chandresh and Bhumi, his wife, and their two daughters in the Smoky Mountains, and James went with them when they walked to Oklahoma."

"Chandresh is married?"

"Was married. His wife died on the trail."

"Jennifer..."

Jennifer shook her head. "I know what you're thinking so stop thinking it. I'm not worried that Bhumi's ghost will suddenly appear and win him back. You're a unique case, Sarah. It doesn't happen that often."

"You never know, Jennifer. Reincarnations can just show up unexpectedly."

"Chandresh isn't expecting Bhumi to come back, so I'm not either. He said when he said good-bye to her he meant it, and his life is now in Salem with me. He's an amazing man, Sarah. After everything he's been through, he's still so strong. He's not bitter about anything. He's made peace with it."

"I understand the attraction to a strong, amazing man," Sarah said. "So are you going to be Mrs. Mankiller soon? Going to try marriage a third time? Your mother's been married four times, so you have to try at least two more times." Jennifer blushed, and Sarah nudged her arm. "I see you've been thinking about it."

"We're not engaged," Jennifer said. "We've been talking, that's all."

"You're not worried about having a vampire husband with the last name Mankiller?"

"His name was Mankiller before he became a vampire, Sarah. Mankiller was the name given to those who protected the village from invaders."

"He sounds like a great guy, Jen. I'm so happy for you."

"Thank you. Honestly, my mother wasn't so thrilled when Chandresh and I started dating, but she's come around."

"What could she have against Chandresh? She doesn't mind vampires."

"She thought the reason I was dating Chandresh was because of his connection to James and..." Jennifer stopped suddenly. She shook her head, closed her eyes, her lips pulled into a tight line to prevent any further words from escaping just then. When she opened her eyes she smiled. "Chandresh has the greatest respect for James," she said. "He's always talking about what James taught him, what a strong role model James has been, how James helped his family after they arrived in Oklahoma. I know there's more to the story, and I was hoping maybe we could get James and Chandresh to tell us."

"I haven't been able to get any stories out of James," Sarah said. "Whenever I ask him about his past he says another time."

"Be patient with him, Sarah. He spent a long time living in his memories."

When James came back, his class over, he stopped by the door, watching her, always intense when he looked at her. Suddenly, Sarah felt complete compassion for him. He wanted to live in the now and leave the past behind, and so did she. Whatever will be will be, she decided. As long as they were together, everything would be fine.

CHAPTER FIVE

James sat at his desk in the great room, muttering expletives at the book in his hands. He slammed the cover shut, opened it, flipped the pages, then shut it again.

"I cannot believe this crap," he said to the tailless black cat, who stretched on the reading chair and yawned. He held the book out. "Have you ever read trash like this?" he asked. But the cat only fell asleep again.

He heard Sarah stirring in the bedroom and looked at the time—two in the morning. She padded into the great room, and he felt her warm hands on his shoulders. He felt human whenever she touched him.

"It's past your bedtime," he said.

"I could hear you muttering from the bedroom." She looked over his shoulder at the book in his hand. "What are you reading?"

"*Dracula.*"

"Why? You know that book makes you mad." He told her what happened with Goodwin, and she laughed. "So you're teaching the vampire literature class?"

"I thought it was best to go along."

"Some vampires books are all right. It might be fun."

James shrugged. "Perhaps."

Sarah flipped open the cover, skimming the pages, reading the synopsis on the back. "It's fascinating the way Stoker fits the pieces together with the newspaper articles and journals from the other characters as they hunt Count Dracula. You get everyone's point of view of the story."

"Everyone's point of view but the vampire."

"What do you mean?"

"In vampire stories you get everyone else's opinion about the vampire—what they think, what they feel, what they know. Why don't we hear from the vampire? Why doesn't the vampire ever have a say?"

"Probably because no human has ever been a vampire so they don't know how to speak like one. Besides, Anne Rice writes from the vampire's point of view."

"There's one."

"You still haven't told me why you don't like *Dracula*."

"Because it's ridiculous. What vampire do you know can turn into a bat or scale walls like Spiderman?"

"None?"

"Of course none. Have you ever seen me turn into a bat or scale a wall?"

"Never." She held his face between her hands, her warmth calming him. "If people don't know you exist then how can they know the truth? They have to use the myths and legends to guess what vampires might be like, and let's face it—vampires don't have the best reputation."

James nodded. She brushed his gold hair from his eyes and kissed his forehead.

"You've always said people can't know your kind exists. Isn't it better if they don't have it right, that they make up stories? If they knew the truth then you'd be exposed, and that can't happen. Isn't that what you told me?"

James smiled. He looked at his wife, her dark curls loose around her shoulders, her lips full, open, and smiling, the spaghetti straps of her pink nightie with the lace lines falling down her shoulders. He pulled her onto his lap and kissed her peach-like shoulders.

She wasn't as distracted as he was. "So am I right, Doctor Wentworth?"

"You're always right, Mrs. Wentworth."

"They're just stories."

James leaned back, twisting Sarah's curls between his fingers. "But the legends originated from people's fear when they encountered the magical," he said. "Anything related to the supernatural people assume is evil."

"You're not evil, James. I've never known anyone more loving than you."

He kissed her shoulder again. "At least I was able to write up a syllabus. The class will look at the earliest vampire folklore and legends and how those legends evolved over time. Then we'll compare and contrast the legends with the progression of the vampire novel. The theme will be 'The Curse of the Vampire.'"

"You're not cursed. You're special."

"I'm very special."

"I'm serious, James."

"So am I. The earliest folktales from Eastern Europe say vampires were cursed by Satan to outwit death. Perhaps they're right."

"You have nothing to do with Satan." Sarah slapped her hand in the air, dismissing the Devil himself. "I don't believe in Satan. And I don't believe hell is a pit in the center of the earth. I don't believe in Dante's Inferno or that Bosch triptych with Adam and Eve and the Garden of Eden on one side and the torturous punishments of Hell on the other. We're our own Satans. We create our own hell."

"That's what my father used to say."

"Your father was the wisest man I've ever known. Except for you."

He didn't argue with her. He would give her whatever she needed, do whatever she wanted done, say whatever she wanted to hear. As long as she smiled, that sweet, beautiful smile, he would be content. He would protect her whenever she needed protecting. He had superhuman strength, extraordinary sight, supersonic hearing. Immortal life. As long as his secret stayed safe, there was nothing to fear. A scratching thought, like sandpaper on his spine, gnawed at him, and he heard the name Hempel somewhere in his middle ear, but he shook his head and sent it away.

Sarah kissed his cheek, and he leaned into her, savoring her warmth.

"There's no such thing as the vampire's curse," she said.

James held her head to his chest, loving her. He looked out the diamond-paned window and saw the blackout night stretching from one horizon to the next. He heard Sarah's breath slow, felt her body grow limp, saw her eyes close. He slipped his arms around her to carry her to the bedroom, but she started suddenly and stopped him.

"I'm not going to bed yet," she said.

"It's nearly three in the morning. You need to sleep."

"Not yet. I'm changing my schedule. I'm asleep most of the time when you're awake, so if I went to bed later and woke up later, we'd have more time together."

"You've never been a night owl. Even three hundred years ago you were ready for bed as soon as the sun went down."

"No, James, I mean it. I'm going to change my schedule."

"All right, honey. Whatever you want."

He rubbed her back, down her spine, up to her shoulders, down again. He wasn't surprised to hear her breathing slow to sleeping. He carried her to bed, laid her down, covered her with the blanket, and kissed her forehead. She opened one eye as he walked to the door.

"I love you," she said.

"I love you more."

She was already sleeping. He turned back, kneeled by the bed, stroking her hair, kissing her forehead. He thought about the night in front of Jocelyn's house. Sarah's need for a child was so tangible then he felt it reaching out to him. That child she was so certain was there—he felt the child touching him, clutching its tiny fingers around his, and it scared him. How could he be a father? How could he explain?

"Daddy is cursed," he could say, or "Daddy is a leech. But don't worry. Daddy won't ever suck your blood. Sure, Daddy used to bite people and suck them dry until they died, but things were different then. We didn't have technology like we do now."

He would have to explain why he could never visit their schools, meet their friends, attend Fourth of July barbeques. He could be there for the fireworks, he supposed. He would have to explain why he was so pale, why he didn't eat dinner with them, why he always looked the same. It couldn't possibly work.

Besides, Sarah hadn't mentioned the child since that night. Not with her words anyway. Sometimes, when things were quiet, when they were at home together, he saw her stare off at something far away, and he guessed she was imagining the child. Sometimes, whenever they were out, walking the Salem streets, when he was taking her to a restaurant for her dinner, or to Jennifer's, or to Olivia's or Martha's, they would pass a family and he saw her eyes cloud as she watched the mothers with their children. Then, when they visited the Endecotts, she would light up joy whenever little Billy appeared, running to him, laughing, clasping him to her heart. And, when she thought he wasn't looking, her hands went to her stomach, reaching for the baby that was no longer there. She thought he didn't see her, but he did. The sight of it sliced at his chest where his heart used to be, and he knew what it felt like to be staked by wood. That's what it felt like to him every time he saw his wife long for that child. But he stayed stubborn. It was for the best, he thought. They were enough for each other.

He watched Sarah sleep, heard her soothing heartbeat, and he felt a new wave of calmness. Suddenly, someone unseen but all-knowing whispered in his ear. "She'll be a wonderful mother," he heard. "And you'll be a wonderful father too."

James shook his head at the formless voice. "No," he said.

"Yes," he heard.

He looked around, expecting to see someone standing beside him. It was a rich voice, a deep voice, formal yet comfortable, strong yet familiar, and it left him warm inside when normally he was oh so very cold. He was certain he knew it, but it sounded detached somehow, like it was distorted through a scratchy intercom. He shook his head again, trying to separate the fantasy of the voice from the reality of the room around him. He saw no one but Sarah asleep in their bed. He must have imagined it, he decided, though he continued to feel warm inside. Suddenly, he felt a starburst of truth illuminate every concern he ever had about bringing a child into their home. The light was so bright he shielded his eyes with his hand.

Was it possible? He knew Sarah would be a wonderful mother. She had the kindness, the patience, the affection, and, most importantly, the love any child would need. And he would love the child too. He never doubted his ability to love a child, only the child's ability to love him. But Sarah loved him, turned as he was. And their child could too.

Their child.

James smiled. He leaned over Sarah, kissing her cheek. He thought of that sad time all those years before when he had mourned not only Elizabeth's passing but their child's too. He blinked away the bloody film blurring his sight. He laid down in bed next to her, spooning her, and closed his eyes.

The voice spoke again. "Yes," it said.

James smiled as he relaxed into the radiating warmth.

"Yes," he said.

CHAPTER SIX

J ames awoke to the clunk-clunk-clunk of nails hammered into seventeenth century wood. He pulled aside the blackout curtains and raised the blinds, seeing the sunrise-colored autumn leaves drop one-by-one to the wilting lawn while storm clouds gathered over the bay, adding more gray than black to the night. He was waking earlier since it was getting darker earlier, a good thing with Sarah waiting for him.

Orange and black. That's all he saw when he walked into the great room—orange and black. And pumpkins. Witches, ghosts, skeletons, Frankensteins, even, he sighed, vampires decorated the walls and the bookshelves while strings of glowing plastic pumpkin lights lined the diamond-paned windows. A display of autumn harvest squash sat in a Happy Halloween basket on the granite island in the kitchen, and he saw the witch-themed potholders hanging from hooks.

Sarah skipped toward him like a dancing preschooler. "What do you think?" she asked.

"Is this a joke?"

"You live in Salem and you think Halloween is a joke?" She stood on her toes and reached her arms around his neck. "Besides, who better to celebrate Halloween than a vampire husband and his ghost wife?"

James was too distracted by the decorations to answer. He hated Halloween for all the same reasons he hated *Dracula*. If humans thought ghouls and goblins were their greatest threats, how little they understood. When he looked at Sarah he half-expected her to be orange and black and wearing a pointed witch's hat. She must have seen his agitation because she dropped her arms and stepped away.

"Jennifer told me you're a grouch around Halloween. You're looking a little puckered, Doctor Wentworth." She walked toward the decorations as though she were siding with them against him. "They're decorations. They're meant to be fun, allow grown-ups to feel like kids again for a little while every year, but if you hate them that much I'll take them down. I don't want to look at that annoyed face for the next two weeks."

James looked at the caricatures of green-faced, sharp-fanged, cape-wearing vampires, cackling witches on broomsticks, shapeless, booing ghosts, howling werewolves, glaring square-faced Frankensteins, and he shook his head. But he saw Sarah admiring the pumpkin-painted porcelain plates, the haunted house flags, the Witches Brew cauldron by the door, her face flushed like a costumed girl ready for candy Halloween night. He reached for her hand when she smiled that smile he lived for. He would do anything to keep that smile happy.

Again, the thought that she would be a wonderful mother.

Again, the voice. "Yes," it said.

"Yes," he said.

"Fine. I'll have everything down by tomorrow night."

"No, Sarah…" He put his arms around her though she tried to push him away. "Keep the decorations. Keep whatever will make you happy. All I want is for you to be happy." She stopped resisting and relaxed into him. "What do you want, Sarah. Tell me what you want to be happy."

"You make me happy," she said. "You're all I need. And…"

"And what? A child?"

Sarah pushed the air from her lungs. She pulled away from him, her dark eyes unsure. "I thought there was no way…"

"If you want to adopt we should."

"What about all the reasons you had about why it could never work?"

"We'll figure it out."

"Are you sure?" She held herself still, as though she were afraid he would change his mind and this joyous moment would fall away from her like water through cupped hands.

"There's only one thing I have ever been more sure about, and that's you."

Sarah smiled. James could see the peace settle over her, an iridescent halo. She crossed her arms, pulling him, closer, closer, as though
she wanted to merge with him. They were already one, James thought,
each a part of the other.

Sarah looked at the orange and black. "You'll have to get used to the
decorations. Kids like Halloween."

James laughed. "I know, honey. I know."

While James was at work that night, Sarah felt the restless leg syn-
drome shaking her bones. A child. James agreed to adopt a child. Where
she had managed to subdue the longing when she thought he would
never agree, now that he was open, he was willing, the manic I-have-to-
have-it-now need she felt outside of Jocelyn's house returned, its full
force rattling her, trapping her under an avalanche of want.

"It's going to take time," James said before he left. "There's a lot of
paperwork to fill out, and there's interviews, and background checks..."
Sarah laughed at the look on his face when he said 'background checks.'
Then he winked at her. "How far back do you think they check?" he
asked.

In search of something to keep her body busy and her mind occupied, she went for a walk. She walked far and fast, away from the bay
down Derby Street to Essex, around Washington Square and the green
expanse of Salem Common. The night was crisp and cool, not yet cold,
the richness of autumn with the barest hint of winter fade. The houses,
the shops, everywhere she looked was Halloween. Round, orange
pumpkins sat bundled on porches, some left whole, others carved jack-
o-lanterns lit from the glowing candles inside. She pulled her sweater
around her neck and headed down Hawthorne Boulevard, passing the
red-brick Hawthorne Hotel, walking along the thin strip of sidewalk
separating the sides of the road, past the statue of Nathaniel Hawthorne,
Salem's favorite son, then back to Essex Street and Central, around the
Old Burying Point Cemetery, the oldest graveyard in Salem. She passed

that quickly, ignoring the stone-carved headstones. Suddenly, she remembered that the remains of John Hathorne, Hawthorne's ancestor, a magistrate at the witch trials, were buried there, and she understood her sudden chills. Then she laughed at herself. Hathorne is dead and bones, six feet under, while you're walking home where you'll see your dear and loving husband soon. Hathorne can't hurt you now. Besides, when your husband is a vampire and you're a ghost, is there anything left to frighten you?

Sarah didn't wait to be rational. She hurried back to Derby past Pickering Wharf. It was quiet along the dock except for the people eating at the restaurants, some outside under the umbrellas watching the serenity of the night-tide bay. She thought about stopping by the Witches Lair to see if Olivia was there, but it was late and the shops were dark. She wondered if she should get another psychic reading after all. She couldn't live like this, swinging from the tips of dangling nerves, unable to settle until they brought their child home. James was right. It would take time. And Jennifer was right too. Olivia had helped her before. True, Sarah had been frightened out of her wits at the psychic reading, but then, when Sarah was wrought with angst over those chain-filled nightmares that jolted her awake, Olivia had pointed her in the direction of Martha, who had pointed her in the direction of Elizabeth, which was who she had been all along. Maybe she would go for another reading after all.

Maybe.

Back home she was just was as agitated as she was before she left. Looking for something to do, she wandered through the newly remodeled stainless steel kitchen with the modern marble island in the center, though everything was clean and there was nothing to keep her occupied. She saw the wood ladder so she climbed up to the open, loft-style attic. She sighed when she saw everything strewn about, old feather mattresses, silverware, cooking utensils, blue and white Delftware dishes, mugs, rolled up seventeenth century maps. She picked up a pile of moth-eaten linens so threadbare they disintegrated in her hands, but beneath them was a seventeenth century chest with the lock unlatched. She pushed open the top, looked inside, and gasped aloud.

"Hello."

Sarah was startled to see James at the top of the ladder. She was so distracted she didn't hear him come in. Normally, she heard him open the front door, the old-time wood frame creaking like an old man standing from a low chair.

"Hello yourself," she said.

"What are you doing?"

"Keeping busy. It's a mess up here, did you know that?"

"Everyone's attic is a mess."

He stepped onto the attic floor and held out his arms. Sarah pushed herself into him, squeezing him, closing her eyes, losing herself in him. When she stepped back he was intent, looking over her shoulder at the brown material she pulled out of the trunk.

"I didn't know you kept my clothes," she said.

"I kept everything. This whole house was a tribute to you. I left, sometimes for decades, but I always came back. I thought I should sell everything and move on, but I could never bring myself to let go."

Sarah held the dress out, inspecting the stitching, running her hand over the fabric. "It's a little worn," she said, "but it isn't too bad. Maybe I could bring it to someone to restore it."

James took the dress into his hands and held it close to his face, dwelling on the details, intent the way he was when he was reading or taking notes, or the way he looked at her.

"Whenever I missed you, I took this out and held it in my arms as if I were holding you again." His mellow voice cracked. "I'd cradle it, bury my nose in the folds of fabric, aching for any sense of you. It didn't bring back your dark curls or your full lips, but it was something I could hold."

He shook his head as though pressing the sadness away. "I haven't pulled it out for nearly a year now. I don't need it any more." He nodded at the brown Pilgrim-style dress. "You haven't seen this before tonight?"

"I haven't been up here since I moved in."

James nudged her, a playful smile on his lips. "You should put it on. You know, like old times."

"You always hated all the laces and straps."

"I've changed my mind."

Sarah skipped away, then took a book from the chest and handed it to him. "I found this too," she said. "Don't you recognize it?"

James turned the tattered volume over in his hands. The binding was torn and a few pages fell loose. "It's our family Bible," he said. "This was one of the few belongings my father brought with us on our journey from England. I remember how, when we were packing for our trip, my father wouldn't leave without it."

"Tell me," Sarah said.

James smiled as he always did when talking about his father. "I remember standing in our home when he gestured at the fashionable furnishings in our fashionable house in a fashionable part of London. 'Most of this, 'tis not necessary, James,' he said, his hand sweeping across the room. 'The chairs, the tables, even the expensive dishware your mother loved so. They're only things, and when we die we cannot take them with us. Our Lord has no need for them. They shan't come with us to the colonies, either. We'll find new things, whatever things we'll need, right there wherever we are.'

"Then, when he thought I wasn't looking, he slipped this Bible into his bag. When he saw me watching he laughed.

"'Tis that not merely a thing?' I asked.

"'This,' he said, taking the book from his bag, "tis not merely a thing, James. 'Tis our memories. Your mother is in here. Your grandparents, maternal and paternal, and their parents, maternal and paternal. We're fortunate to have such records since most families do not keep them.'

"Already by 1690, the book was old and worn. My father placed a few wayward pages back between the covers and slipped the book into the bottom of his bag. 'We must keep our memories, Son, because as we move on through this life, what else have we?'"

Sarah took the book and flipped the pages, careful because she didn't want the binding to disintegrate in her hands. She saw the listing of James's family back to the year 1579. Some entries were complete, with birthdate and death date, who they married, when they married, and the birthdates of various offspring. Some entries had birthdates but no death dates. Others had death dates but no birthdates. Others were merely an imprint of a long-forgotten name. She saw the date of James's mother's birth, 12 August 1642, and the date of her death, 30 October 1689. His father, John William Wentworth, was listed as born 27 May 1630, and there was John's father's name and birthdate, too blurred by time and ink to make out clearly, and John's mother's too, though all Sarah could make out was an R at the beginning of her name. Sarah found James's listing, his details written in his father's perfectly curled seventeenth century calligraphy—James John Wentworth, son of John and Emily Wentworth, born 19 April 1662. Where the date of his death should have been recorded was, also in John's hand, the word "Dead?"

"Should the night I was turned be listed as the date of my death?" James asked. "After all these years I still can't decide."

"You're still here," Sarah said. "You haven't died."

"A doctor might disagree with you."

"When you're no longer animate, no longer conscious, that's when you die."

"Then I'll never have a death date."

"Is that a bad thing?"

"I would like to have a death date."

"James..." Sarah turned away. "Don't say that."

He sighed, then pointed to the open page in her hands. "My father added you the day we were married."

There she was, Elizabeth Wentworth nee Jones, born 27 November 1669. And there was the date of her death, 13 August 1692. Then the shock of the other name, Grace Wentworth, died 13 August 1692. Their baby. Sarah felt a surge of love for her father-in-law. He always had the warmest, most loving heart of anyone she had ever known, except, of course, for James. She always knew where James's kindness came from. And here was proof, over three hundred years later, that John hadn't forgotten the baby. James brushed her tears away with his fingertips.

She looked through the high window, the sky fully black, the wind whispering memories through the shadow branches on the crooked oak outside.

"What else is in that old thing?" James asked.

Sarah reached into the open chest and removed two more dresses and three white caps, her underpetticoats and half-boned stays. She found more wool, only this wasn't a dress but a garnet-colored coat, breeches, and waistcoat.

"You're right," James said. "Seventeenth century clothing was hideous. Put those away before I start screaming."

Sarah held her dress in one hand and James's old clothes in the other. "I'll put this on," she said, holding out the dress, "if you put this on." She held out the garnet-colored clothing and smiled.

"Never."

She folded the old clothes, laid them into the trunk, then straightened up the books, the maps, and the kitchen utensils, making neat piles along the wall under the window. She coughed from the three-centuries-old dust.

"Why don't you do that another time?" James asked.

"I need to clean up here before the social worker comes for the inspection." Sarah stopped straightening and turned to James. "What do you know," she said. "We were talking about the seventeenth century and you're all right. And so am I. I even walked by the Old Burying Point tonight."

"What were you doing there by yourself, Sarah? You know I don't like you going out at night alone. I can't help you if I'm not there."

Sarah kissed her husband, loving his tender concern for her, as though she were the most valuable thing in the world and only he could protect her. She let her lips linger, but he pulled away.

"What is it, Sarah? You only go for walks when something is troubling you."

She touched his cheek, running her fingers down his neck and passed the open collar of his button-down shirt to his chest. She knew he saw the slightest change in her expression, heard the tiniest halt in her voice. He knew her so well.

"Are you sure about adopting a baby?" she asked. "You're not going to change your mind?"

"I won't change my mind, Sarah. It feels right to me now, as it has to you all along."

Sarah nodded. "Good," she said. "You'll be a great father, James. I know you will." She looked at the seventeenth century memories piled along the walls. "We'll clean that up tomorrow," she said.

James smiled at the closed trunk. "I'll give you one more chance to put on your old clothes," he said. "It might be fun reliving some of those memories."

"Some things are better in the twenty-first century."

James pulled her toward him and pressed his lips into hers. When she opened her mouth he grabbed her by the waist and pulled her toward him, untucking her blouse, unbuttoning her from the top down, kissing her everywhere her flesh was exposed, pulling her clothes away. She dropped her pants and stepped out of them. James stepped back, admiring her.

"I was right the first time," he said. "It's easier undressing you now."

Sarah reached for James. "What are you doing all the way over there? Come here."

James grasped her, clutching her, kissing her. She pulled his button-down shirt off his arms and his gray t-shirt over his head. She ran her hands over his cool blue skin, outlining the contours of his muscles from his neck down his chest to his stomach to the top of his jeans. No matter how many times she saw him, his dead-pale complexion over his sinewy frame, his flat-black eyes glistening, his gold hair stubbornly in his eyes, his smile, she was amazed by him. "I love you more than anything in this world," he whispered in her ear.

"I love you more," she said.

And she closed her eyes and let him take her away.

CHAPTER SEVEN

In November Halloween was gone, ghosts and ghouls replaced by stoic Native Americans holding pies and smiling, buckle-hatted turkeys unaware of their fate. And pumpkins. The trees were bare now, the burst of temporary color gone, leaving their sugar and crimson behind, the leaves raked away. The branches, now naked and spindly, shivered in the poking, colder air. Storm after storm wet Salem, riding out to the ocean on the crashing waves of the bay. Heavier coats were found, scarves and mittens pulled from their summer hideaways, and people walked closer together, huddled in preparation for the real cold to come. It was calmer in Salem after the summer tourists and the Halloween partiers cleared away, and the locals stretched their legs and walked the quiet streets in peace.

Sarah paced the wooden gabled house two steps at a time, rearranging the autumn harvest centerpiece on the table near the hearth, straightening the Happy Thanksgiving banner on the wall. She paced again, now three steps at a time, down to the end of the great room and back, dusting the bookshelves again and back, checking the baking cookies in the stainless steel oven and back. When she heard the squeak of the front door, she sighed with relief. She ran to James and pressed herself into his arms.

"She's not here yet," Sarah said.

"I told you I'd be back in time."

She pushed herself away and paced again.

"Maybe I should have put out some Pilgrims," she said. "What if she notices there aren't any Pilgrims? Everyone has Pilgrim decorations at Thanksgiving time. What if she thinks we're not good Americans? What if she thinks we won't know what to do with a child because kids love Pilgrims at Thanksgiving time?"

"First of all, those Thanksgiving harvest plays the kids do aren't factually correct. If she wants to know why we don't have Pilgrims in our house, I'll explain it to her." He pulled Sarah back into his arms and kissed her forehead. "We are Pilgrims."

"We didn't come over on the Mayflower."

"No, but we were here when Massachusetts was a colony. We'll bring down our old clothes from the attic and show her."

"That's not funny."

Sarah walked back to the oven, checked the cookies with a spatula, decided they were brown enough, and pulled them out, placing them onto an autumn orange cake platter with green and yellow leaves.

"Cookies?" James asked.

"Chocolate chip cookies."

"They smell sweet."

"That's why people love them." She pulled one apart, then licked the melted chocolate dribbling down her fingers. "Do you want to try one?"

"I'd love to, but I can't."

"You can't eat at all?"

"Honey, I haven't eaten solid food in three hundred and nineteen years."

"That's too bad. Life isn't worth living without chocolate chip cookies."

"I think I'm doing all right."

The cauldron in the hearth caught Sarah's eye. It looked like it should bubble, bubble, toil and trouble while the three witches in Macbeth cast spells and foretold the future, hysterical with evil visions and dastardly deeds. She looked inside, checking to see if the heavy black pot could be unlatched and removed, shaking her head when the seventeenth century fastenings held strong.

"I never should have left this," she said. "I should have had it taken out during the remodeling. She's going to think it's a child hazard, and it is." She jumped at the hollow knock that echoed like a loud No! No! No!

James stroked her hand. "It'll be fine," he said. "Relax."

He opened the door, and the social worker walked in, stiff and stoic, underpaid and overworked, an unsmiling woman in an ill-fitting purple jacket with linebacker shoulder pads and a purple flowered skirt. She looked, Sarah thought, like a summer plum. She was slump-shouldered and long-faced, like this was the fiftieth home she had visited that day and it was always the same, smiling faces, fresh-baked cookies, guarantees they would take care of the child whether they would or they wouldn't.

The plum-looking woman entered the great room without saying hello. She didn't acknowledge James or Sarah. "You have a lot of books," she said finally, writing in the spiral notebook in her hand.

"My wife and I both like to read," James said.

Sarah stepped aside as the woman nodded at the flat-screen television and shook her head at the three hundred year-old desk, scratching more notes. James looked over her shoulder, trying to see what she wrote, but Sarah shook her head at him. She didn't want the woman to notice anything odd about James, though his curiosity was human enough. The plum-looking woman stopped in front of the cauldron.

"Are you witches?" she asked.

"No," James said, "but our best friends are." When the social worker didn't smile, James stepped away. "The cauldron came with the house," he said. "We thought it gave the place character so we kept it."

"How old is the house?"

"It's from the seventeenth century," Sarah answered.

"How long have you lived here?"

Sarah and James looked at each other.

"Two years," James said. "We both work at the university."

The plum-looking woman nodded. "If you're approved you'll have to have that thing," she gestured with her pen at the cauldron, "removed. It's a safety hazard."

"Of course," Sarah said.

"Does this place need an inspection? Sometimes these older houses have bad wiring, or improper plumbing."

"The house is up to code," James said. "We made sure of that when we had the place remodeled."

"When was this remodeling?"

"They finished during the summer. I have the paperwork here."

He handed her the forms that said the three centuries-old house met the qualifications of a twenty-first century inspection. She glanced over the paperwork and nodded, writing more notes. She looked around the kitchen, the bedroom, the smaller room in the back. She scowled at the wood ladder that led up to the attic.

"Can that be removed?" she asked.

"We can take it out if it's a problem," James said.

She nodded, scowling more at the cauldron as she walked back into the kitchen.

"Would you like something to drink?" Sarah asked.

"Thank you. Water would be fine."

"We have some cold water in the fridge," Sarah said.

"No need to trouble yourselves. I'll get it."

Before Sarah could protest, the social worker opened the refrigerator and eyed the groceries before pulling out the water pitcher. Sarah dropped into a chair, unable to hide the horror on her face. What if the social worker saw James's bags of blood? But James nodded, pointing to his temple, an 'I've got this' look in his eyes. He pulled a glass from the cupboard, poured water for the plum-looking woman, then joined Sarah at the table, smiling the whole time.

"What do you do at the college?" the social worker asked.

"I'm a professor, and my wife is a librarian."

"What do you teach?"

"English literature."

She sipped her water as she glanced over the application in her manila folder. "I think you're my son's English professor. Levon Jackson. Do you know him?"

"Very well," James said. "He took two of my classes last year, and he's in my Shakespeare seminar this term. He's a bright young man, and a very good writer."

Mrs. Jackson clapped her hands, her mother's love everywhere on her round cheeks. No longer the plum-looking woman, now she was Levon's mother.

"You should hear how he raves about you, Doctor Wentworth. Every day he comes home saying, 'Doctor Wentworth said this,' or 'Doctor Wentworth said that.'"

"It's a pleasure teaching a student who wants to learn," James said.

Mrs. Jackson's round-cheeked smile lit the room. "You've done a world of good for my boy, Doctor Wentworth. I was so worried about him after that back injury meant he couldn't be considered for the NHL draft. Going pro is all he's talked about since he put on his first pair of skates. When that was no longer possible for him, he floundered. He didn't have plans for anything else, and now he wants to be a professor like you. I'm pleased to meet you, Doctor Wentworth."

"Please, call me James. It's my pleasure."

As Mrs. Jackson looked over the paperwork, James winked at Sarah.

"I don't see any problems here, Doctor Wentworth. Everything seems to be in order. Don't worry about a thing. I'll have the rest of the paperwork approved by my supervisor." Mrs. Jackson looked at Sarah. "Mrs. Wentworth, you have a lovely house with a lot of history here. Any child would be lucky to have such a home."

"Thank you," Sarah said.

James escorted Mrs. Jackson to her car, said good night, and waved as she drove away. Back inside, James walked to Sarah, put his arms around her, and pulled her close. She felt the invisible fairy-like thread drawing them together again, only now it was looser, stretching out, over there to where someone else waited, someone they didn't know yet but someone who was loved unconditionally.

Just because, Sarah thought. Whoever you are. We love you just because.

She pointed her chin up, and James kissed her. When she opened her eyes, he was smiling.

"Was that your idea to move the blood bags?" she asked.

"I thought she might look in the refrigerator," he said. "To see how clean we are."

"That's why you're brilliant, Doctor Wentworth."

"I know," he said.

They know. It is just as the trader man said. They are going soon, going West, the direction of Death, they say.

Going...

Going...

Gone.

They go about the night the best they can. The boys play 'a ne jo di' (stick-ball) in the moonlight, which they play with hickory sticks and deer-hair balls. They are families, mothers and fathers, sisters and brothers, aunts and uncles, grandmothers and grandfathers. They laugh and cry. They grow angry and show kindness. One mother kneels near her crying son who has tripped running. Another watches her husband show their son a trick with the hickory stick. As I watch them I am reminded of Shylock's words, begging for his humanity:

Hath not a Jew eyes? Hath not a Jew hands, organs, dimensions, senses, affections, passions; fed with the same food, hurt with the same weapons, subject to the same diseases, healed by the same means, warm'd and cool'd by the same winter and summer, as a Christian is? If you prick us, do we not bleed...

I try to catch the eye of my neighbor, but he is busy with the medicine man while the women and children disappear into their homes. He is old, the medicine man, his face well creviced, his jowls low, though his silver hair is thick and he has the manner of someone who understands much. He nods at me, and I nod in return, thankful because he is the first Cherokee to acknowledge me. The tribal leaders have gathered and I am not supposed to be here, I think, but the medicine man does not seem concerned. I sit on the ground and watch as they begin the Stomp Dance. There are shell shakers wearing leg rattles made of turtle shells filled with pebbles, and the rattles provide a heartbeat-like rhythm as they dance around the red-blazing fire singing a language I do not understand.

The medicine man stands. He stares at me over the heads of the seated men. "Listen," he says. "We are praying to you, our Creator, Unetanv, the Great Spir-

it. Who are we without our lakes and valleys? Our rivers and forests? The copious rain and the good soil?

"Chief John Ross fought our removal in the United States Congress, in the United States Supreme Court. Do not the liberties of the American Declaration of Independence apply to us? 'We hold these truths to be self-evident, that all men are created equal, that they are endowed by their Creator with certain unalienable Rights, that among these are Life, Liberty, and the pursuit of Happiness.' Does that not apply to us as well? But no one in the government would hear him."

The men nod as they stare at the orange flames, at the crackling cinders, at the ground beneath them, at the half-hidden moon, or at whatever phantom images their blank stares show them. The medicine man watches me, a knowing gleam in his eyes. I sense his words are meant for me.

"Listen. This is the creation story of our people. In the beginning, there was no land. Only water and sky. All living things dwelled above the sky. In this time, all beings lived and talked in common. Then the sky vault became crowded with the people and animals. To find more room, Dayuni'si, the water beetle, flew down to see what was there. It dove to the bottom of the ocean and brought up mud that grew and grew and grew until the earth was born. This was so long ago even the oldest medicine man cannot remember. Even I cannot remember, and I am the oldest of them all. Then the earth dried and man was created. A brother and a sister. And we have grown from there.

"They have wanted our land from the moment they arrived. They have the right of discovery over the land, they say. But how do they discover what is already here? We were already here. Did we only begin to exist when they arrived?" The medicine man looks at me as though he knows I was here all those many years before. "They have taken our land as though it was theirs all along. For years they have chipped away at it, pocketing this piece here, stealing that piece there. After they decimated our people with their diseases they wanted more. Now they want it all. But we know the land was meant for us. For all of us. Many of our people converted to the Americans' religion. Were not Adam and Eve expelled from their Paradise because they were not content? Here we are content. We know the wind is our brother. The trees are our sisters.

"Great Creator, hear our cry. We want to be invisible so we can fly away like the birds and then the soldiers will not find us as they have already found others. We do not want to lose our ancestors. They are everywhere here. Where the soldiers want to take us, they are not there. This is what I have said to you."

He sits, his head slumping under the weight of his fears. Everyone is silent, the singing crickets the only sound in the forest night. Then, the medicine man lifts his face and nods at me. He sees I understand.

CHAPTER EIGHT

J ames learned about the new blog post when Jocelyn called him. He heard Billy crying in the background, the baby giving vent to his mother's fears.

"Hempel's doing it," Jocelyn said. "He's naming names. He must know about me since he mentioned dentists."

Steve came home, and James heard him trying to comfort his wife and son. When Jocelyn excused herself to be with her family, James heard the dread in her voice.

"What are we going to do, James?"

"It'll be all right," James said.

He pulled up Hempel's blog on his laptop, but he couldn't bring himself to read it. He paced the ten short steps of his office, remembered the day just eight months before when Hempel sat in that very chair, flipping through these very books, waiting for some sign that James was the undead professor he thought he was. But James had fooled the reporter and sent him scurrying away. Now, if Hempel was ready to do what he hadn't done before—name names—then James didn't know what would happen. If other vampires were made public, how much longer could he stay hidden? When he was too agitated to ignore it any longer, he sat near the computer and read:

As most of you know, after ten years of service to the community, I have been released from my duties at *The Salem News.* But I have so much more to share. I am beginning this blog with the belief that, with the more proof I am able to provide, the more followers I will have. The more followers I have, the more people will be on the lookout for these insidious creatures that go bump in the night.

In the interest of full disclosure, I admit the reports of my having been institutionalized as a teenager are correct. For three weeks at the ages of sixteen, and for another five weeks at seventeen, I was hospitalized because my psychiatrist was convinced I was hallucinating after I explained how my father was murdered by a vampire. I was declared delusional and admitted to the institution though I was quite sane. For those naysayers who insist that I am on psychedelic drugs or mad, I will allow them their foolish beliefs. Those who choose to believe me will find themselves vindicated, and, ultimately, safe. We cannot be too cautious when dealing with animals who hunt and kill at will.

I can prove beyond a shadow of a doubt that those I will name are not living but dead though they walk among us, mocking us, making us believe they belong among respectable society. You may believe me or not, but allow me to ask you this: if you knew your family's safety was at stake, if you knew your next door neighbor was a bloodsucking deviant who would murder without regard for the sanctity of human life, would you allow that neighbor to stay close to those you love most in the world? Would you, like a 1960s placard-wielding hippie, say, "Vampire rights!" and allow them to go on their way in the night, drinking from whomever they please?

Do you know why your dentist keeps late night hours instead of a normal nine-to-five day like everyone else? Do you know who's behind the counter at your local donut shop? Do you know who your night-shift doctors are at the ER? If you notice that those around you at night are unusually pale with an odd contrast of dark eyes, you may want to shake their hands. Colder than you expected? Keep your distance.

I realize I'm making these declarations at a danger to myself, but I believe I was given the knowledge of vampires for a reason: to alert humanity to the dangers in the night. Sometimes we must be willing to take chances to change what must be changed.

James couldn't shut the computer down quickly enough. He stood, kicking his feet, stretching his arms behind him, trying to wake the numbness. Again, he wondered if he should tell Sarah. Again, he decided she didn't need to know. Not now. Mrs. Jackson had pushed their paperwork through in record time, and they rushed to get everything done so they could bring their child home. They took the next available parenting classes (fortunately they had night hours). Their salaries were verified and they had letters of recommendation from their supervisors, James from Goodwin, Sarah from Jennifer. James remembered Sarah's face when she realized they needed to do a criminal record check, along with fingerprints and a doctor's note.

"Do you have fingerprints?" she asked. She pulled his hand close to her face and studied the tips of his fingers.

"No fingerprints, just like I don't have a reflection in the mirror." Sarah didn't hear the sarcasm in his voice. "Of course I have fingerprints, Sarah. I used to be human."

"But what about the background check and the doctor's note?"

"I have current paperwork, honey. How do you think I was hired at the college? I don't think they'd take too kindly to my original diplomas. My degrees are a little old."

"Then how do you have current paperwork?"

"You can buy anything over the Internet these days."

"And the doctor's note?"

"Howard's cousin is a doctor."

They were approved in record time, thanks to Mrs. Jackson. They were ready to find a child to foster, and then, if all went well, to adopt. They were going to speak to Mrs. Jackson the next night about finding a good match. That was what Sarah kept saying.

"We're going to find a good match, James. I can feel it."

And they would. And they would be safe, secure, and want for nothing. They would have their little family, and they would be happy. Even Kenneth Hempel wouldn't stop them. James had decided.

The next night James and Sarah walked into Children's Home. Even a cursory glance through a thesaurus couldn't yield a word to describe the sight of children of all ages, from infants to teenagers, who want a home, James thought. Sarah walked the halls with her shoulders bent forward, her eyes watching her feet, one step after another, as though she were afraid to see the worried young faces that had already seen more than others do in a lifetime, wondering what they had done to deserve a life without a family. How do you explain to someone so young, with such a limited understanding of the world, that they themselves had not done anything wrong? That their parents were foolish or impaired somehow. That some parents gave them away because they thought it was the best decision, that adoptive parents could give the child a better life. But James didn't know if that mattered to a three-year-old without a family.

This wasn't an orphanage like the one Oliver Twist would have endured in Dickens's day. Children's Home was brightly lit, the fluorescent lights casting an unnatural white glow all around, and they passed playrooms with large windows letting in the street lamps and moonlight. The walls were painted primary colors, blue, yellow, and red, and along the sides were short shelves with buckets of toys. It looked like a preschool, with whiteboards with ABCs written in block letters, and watercolor and tempura paintings were hung on a clothesline stretching across the ceiling. The social workers, though tired, were positive, smiling. James could see the compassion in their eyes, though he guessed that no matter how hard they worked there would always be more children, and more children. And then they would work harder for less pay. They nodded at James and Sarah as they walked past. James nodded back while Sarah continued to study the formica floor. James knew she was afraid she wouldn't know what to do, who to choose, why one child was better than another, why this one should have a home and that one shouldn't. How do you walk into a place of children to choose your child and leave the others behind?

James and Sarah were escorted into an office at the end of the long hallway. Mrs. Jackson stood and extended her arms towards them like they were old friends. She hugged Sarah, then pointed to another lady behind a desk.

"This is Sarah Wentworth, Mrs. Mills. She works in the library at the university. And this is Doctor Wentworth. He's my son's professor."

"Just James, please," he said.

The other woman stood. She had short gray hair, eyes hidden behind round owl-frame glasses, and she looked James and Sarah up and down, a staff sergeant checking her recruits before a marching parade. Were the Wentworths suitable parent material? Responsible? Caring? She must have decided they were all right because she stepped out from behind her desk and shook Sarah's hand.

"Very nice to meet you," Mrs. Mills said.

"Mrs. Mills is the supervisor here," said Mrs. Jackson.

"Thank you for staying late tonight," James said. "We're having midterms and I couldn't get away."

"I told you, he's very dedicated to his students," Mrs. Jackson said.

"Good to hear. Good evening, Mrs. Wentworth."

"Good evening."

Mrs. Mills went to her desk, pulled out a manila folder, and checked the papers inside. "Everything seems to be in order. Mrs. Jackson went out of her way to make sure everything was done in a timely manner, which is impressive. If Mrs. Jackson thinks highly of you, you must be doing something right. We're going to get this done as quickly as possible."

"Thank you," Sarah said.

"So what were you thinking?" asked Mrs. Mills. "Boy? Girl? Infant? School age? The infants go first because everyone who adopts wants an infant. Toddler? There are a lot of toddlers here now. Perhaps you'd prefer an older child? They're always the hardest to place. People think the older ones are too damaged and won't form the same attachments to them. It's not true, but it's not easy to sway people from their opinions."

Sarah shook her head. "We want a child who needs a loving home."

"Mrs. Wentworth, all of our children need a loving home."

James put his arm around his wife, brushed a dark curl from her face, kissed her temple. She looked so sad. James knew she would have adopted every child in the place if she could have. *My wife has a heart as big as the sky*, he thought.

"Whoever we find will be perfect," he whispered.

The door was pushed open and a younger woman in blue jeans and a Boston Red Sox jersey stuck her head into the office. "Mrs. Mills, we had a drop off," she said.

"When?"

"Just a few minutes ago."

"How old?"

"The nurse says about six months."

"Six months? Dear me."

Mrs. Jackson rushed out of the room. Mrs. Mills stayed in her chair and covered her eyes with her hand, well chapped from repeated sanitizing, and took a moment to herself.

"What's a drop off?" Sarah asked.

Mrs. Mills wrung her hands as though she could squeeze everything that was wrong for the children of this world out through an imaginary dish towel, their problems nothing more than excess water.

"Hospitals, police stations, and manned fire houses are places where parents can leave their newborns without fear of prosecution. Then there are times when people drop off children of any age. It's not covered under the safe haven law, but often we can't find the parents since they leave no trace so they walk away without consequences."

"Other than eternal guilt," James said.

"We hope they have at least that. But the safe places are the only other alternative some parents have."

"Other alternative?" Sarah asked.

"Times are hard, Mrs. Wentworth. Many don't realize how desperate the situation is for so many children."

James wondered about the new wave of lost children. Not lost boys like those in the Peter Pan story where they went to the magical Never-Never-Land. There they would never age, never worry, never fear. There they would have the frivolity of eternal childhood, an immortality of sorts. But these children were all too mortal, James knew, all too familiar with the wicked, wicked world, left abandoned in a fire station, or a social worker's arms.

Mrs. Jackson reappeared, crumpling into the chair across from Mrs. Mills. The lines in her forehead were deeper, the creases around her mouth craggier, her exhaustion aging her ten years.

"It's a baby girl," Mrs. Jackson said. "She looks to be about six months old, maybe a little hungry, but otherwise in good health. No one saw who left her. She was left in a basket outside the door."

"A baby abandoned in a basket. That's an old one, isn't it?" Mrs. Mills said. "Was there a note?"

"For what it's worth."

"What did it say?"

Mrs. Jackson pulled the crumpled paper from her pocket and flattened it. "It says, 'This is the Grace you have been missing.'" Mrs. Jackson shook her head. "Poor thing won't stop crying. She's holding her arms out, like she knows her mother's close by and won't stop until her mother comes for her. I've been doing this for twenty years, and this might be the most heartbreaking thing I've ever seen."

James nodded. He heard the baby as soon as she was brought in, the painful screams, the short spasmic breath.

"Abandoned by someone who likes crossword puzzles," Mrs. Mills said. "The note doesn't make sense."

Suddenly, Sarah sat up straight, her eyes wide, her mouth moving with words she couldn't quite say. Finally, she asked, "May I see that?" She pointed to the crumpled note.

"Maybe you can make sense of it," Mrs. Jackson said.

Sarah flattened the note on the desk. The words were large, an odd combination of elegant calligraphy and child-like scrawl. She read aloud:

"This is the Grace you have been missing." She said it again, slowly, as though she were making sense of the message one word at a time. "This-is-the-Grace-you-have-been-missing." She took Mrs. Jackson's plump hand in hers and squeezed. "Can I see her? Can I see the baby?"

"Why don't you bring Mrs. Wentworth to see the baby, Lannie?" Mrs. Jackson said. She opened the door and stepped aside. "This way, Mrs. Wentworth."

When Sarah heard the baby cry her hand went to her throat, then her heart. James followed Sarah and Lannie down the hall, Mrs. Mills and Mrs. Jackson behind them. At the end of the hallway a door was propped open by a short stool, and inside was another young woman in a Boston University t-shirt rocking the screaming baby. The young woman looked ready to cry herself.

"I've tried feeding her," she said. "I've tried giving her a pacifier. I've tried singing to her and changing her diaper. She won't stop crying."

"Give her here." But even in Mrs. Jackson's motherly arms the baby wouldn't settle.

Sarah stood outside the door, one foot past the threshold, watching, waiting. Then she walked to Mrs. Jackson.

"Can I see her?"

As soon as Sarah's hands touched the blond-haired baby she stopped crying. The baby looked up with round blue eyes with white flecks around the irises, held out her six-month-old hands, and smiled. Sarah pulled her close, and the little girl laughed. Sarah turned to James, tears on her cheeks.

"This is the Grace we've been missing," she said.

James squeezed his eyes shut, unable to cry in front of the social workers. Sarah sat in the rocking chair, holding the baby close, singing to her, oblivious to anyone else.

"What does she mean?" Mrs. Mills asked.

"My wife was pregnant once," James said. "A long time ago. She named the baby Grace, but the baby died."

Mrs. Jackson watched Sarah and Grace bonding, both smiling and laughing at each other as if they had always known this day would come. Mrs. Jackson leaned close to James and whispered, "I'll start the paperwork. I think we can do this quickly, don't you think, Mrs. Mills?"

"I do," said Mrs. Mills.

Mrs. Jackson watched Grace nuzzle into Sarah's neck. She looked at Sarah and the baby, at James, then back at Sarah and the baby. "How funny," she said. She squinted at James, and he pushed his wire-rimmed glasses back on his nose, Clark Kent style. "Henrietta," she said, "do you see it? Except for his dark eyes, that blond-haired baby looks just like Doctor Wentworth."

"I was thinking the same thing."

"I guess it was meant to be," James said.

"I think you're right," said Mrs. Mills.

James watched his wife and the baby, the Grace they had been missing, and his heart, though unbeating, flooded with love for that tiny blond-haired, blue-eyed girl. He sensed, as keenly as Sarah did, that that baby in her arms was their baby, the one they lost over three hundred years before. He knew it the way he knew vampires were real, along with witches, and werewolves, and ghosts in the form of reincarnations. Their daughter was home, the trio begun all those years before finally complete. After all, he reminded myself, crazier things have happened. And crazier things would happen still.

CHAPTER NINE

"Hush," Olivia said. "I need to listen."

She sat on the edge of the bed in James and Sarah's bedroom while she held baby Grace on her lap, the tiny pink fingers in hers. Martha stood to the side, her black flappers bob swaying in rhythm with her heavy-set form while she held her hands on top of Grace's head and whispered Wiccan prayers. Olivia closed her eyes, her coin earrings jingling with each nod of her head, her body rolling to and fro, her eyes moving rapidly beneath her closed lids, focused on something only she could see. She leaned toward the baby, straining to hear, then nodded. When she sat stone still, a monument to mother and child, Martha stopped whispering. Grace watched them, her eyes wide like new-bloomed flowers.

"She knows who you are," Olivia said. "She's been looking for you."

Martha nodded. "It's true. This is the Grace you've been missing."

Sarah knelt besides Olivia and twisted the baby's golden curls between her fingers. The tears spilled freely down her cheeks. "I knew it," she said. "I told James it was a girl. That's why I named her Grace." She saw James's red-rimmed eyes, his fingers pinching the top of his nose keep the blood from streaking his face.

"If any man ever had a reason to cry, you have one now," Olivia said.

"I don't want her to be afraid," he said.

"She's not afraid," said Martha. "You're her father."

He stepped tentatively toward the baby. He leaned over her, kissed the top of the gold hair that matched his own, except for the curls, which she got from her mother. When Grace smiled James couldn't stop the tears, and the red flowed freely down his face. The baby reached her arms out, and James swept her up and held her close.

Sarah grasped Olivia's hand. "But how can she know us?" she asked. "She was never born."

"We always have knowledge, Sarah. Before we're born, while we're living, after our earthly bodies die."

"That's right," said Martha, her southern accent soothing in its dulcet tones. "We're always connected to our souls. Grace didn't need to be born to know who her parents were. The three of you have always been connected one way or another."

Sarah shook her head, her eyes wide as she stared at her daughter in her husband's arms. "How did we end up at the orphanage when Grace did? I didn't think coincidences like that really happened."

Martha laughed. "My word, Sarah. After moving to Salem and meeting James and Olivia and Jennifer, after going through your past-life regression, after all you've been through, you still believe in coincidences?"

"Einstein said 'Coincidences are God's way of remaining anonymous,'" Olivia said. "That's the universe's hand connecting you to Grace. Be grateful, Sarah. Your family is whole again."

"I will always be grateful," Sarah said. She kissed the top of her daughter's silky gold hair.

James kept one arm around his daughter and slid his other arm around his wife. There they were, the triumvirate of Wentworths, reunited after more than three hundred years. Without a second guess, a single concern, Sarah knew they were right together, like the fluid statues of families where the lines lead toward each other, but then, when you step closer, you see the distinct shapes where before there had only been one. From one there were two. From two there were three.

"This is exactly as it should be," Olivia said.

Everyone important to James and Sarah—Olivia and Jennifer, Howard and Timothy, Martha, Jocelyn, Steve, and Billy, even Jennifer's new beau Chandresh—was in the wooden gabled house that night. Suddenly, a human-looking Howard stepped into the room.

"You guys are hogging the baby," he said. "I want to hold her."

When James handed him the baby, Sarah glanced at the night sky, checking the phase of the moon. Howard smiled.

"No shifting tonight," he said. He looked at Grace, then at James, then Sarah. "She looks just like you, James. You, too, Sarah, with those wide eyes and curly hair. Is it true? Is she yours?"

"Yes," James said.

"What a blessing. Congratulations."

Grace held up her fingers, touched Howard's salted beard, and laughed.

"What a good-natured temperament," Howard said. "She's nothing like you, James."

James laughed. "She gets that from her mother," he said.

Howard looked through the open door at Timothy, who was sitting on the sofa in the great room typing on the laptop on the glass table in front of him, his fingers flying across the keyboard at an inhuman speed, the determination evident in his narrow eyes and set mouth.

"Tim," Howard called. "Come see the baby."

"I've seen her."

"Come on, Tim. Say hello."

"I'm busy."

Howard shrugged. "He's still working on that vampire book." He dropped his voice to a whisper. "I told him I didn't think it was a good idea right now with Hempel on the loose, but he thinks..."

"I can hear you," Timothy said. "Stop talking about me like I'm not here. I'm writing a vampire novel, that's all. Everyone's writing vampire books these days."

"Except it's really your autobiography," Howard said.

"Who's going to know?"

"Timothy's right," Sarah said. "Who's going to know? I think it's a great idea, Timothy. Everyone likes a good vampire story."

She kissed James's cheek and left him in the bedroom with Olivia, Martha, Howard, and the baby. She found Jennifer in the kitchen admiring the new stainless steel appliances and the granite island in the center.

"I love it," Jennifer said.

"I wasn't sure about such a modern-looking kitchen in a wooden house," Sarah said.

"Don't change a thing. It's perfect, like your marriage to James—melding the old and the new."

Chandresh came into the kitchen and kissed Jennifer's cheek. It was the first time Sarah had seen them together, and she liked what she saw. They looked comfortable and content. She looked closely at Chandresh, his soulful, doe-shaped black eyes, his thick black hair—such a contrast to his white-blue complexion—pulled away from his handsome face in a ponytail, his high cheekbones, his shy, boyish smile. Mainly, Sarah noticed the way he looked at Jennifer, with complete attention, as though there were no one else around but her.

"You two look good together," Sarah said.

Jennifer blushed. "It's easy to look good around this guy." She punched Chandresh's arm, so muscular and wide it bulged through his denim button-down shirt.

"You're the one who looks good," he said. As Chandresh stepped away, Sarah grabbed his arm.

"Did you meet James on the Trail of Tears?" she asked.

Chandresh nodded. "James hasn't told you?"

"James doesn't tell me much about his past," Sarah said.

She looked through the bedroom door, saw James with Grace on his hip, and their eyes locked. Of course he heard her.

Chandresh nodded at James. "James should tell you," he said. "But you should know I think your husband is one of the greatest men I have ever known. What he did for my family can never be repaid though I have forever to try. I am always in his debt."

Sarah was moved by Chandresh's words, and Jennifer looked at him as though this was yet one more reason to love this preternatural man. Sarah smiled because she understood.

Chandresh was intent on the conversation between James and Howard, who were huddled close in the bedroom. He disappeared into the room with them and shut the door.

"What was that about?" Sarah asked.

Jennifer looked at the closed door. "I'm sure it's nothing."

A sense of foreboding flooded Sarah and she didn't know why. She had a vague sense that something was wrong, but she didn't know what, so she pretended it was nothing, thinking her instincts were pulling a false alarm as they sometimes did, and she went to Martha, who had taken the baby to the sofa in the great room to watch the fire in the hearth. Looking at her daughter content in Martha's arms, Sarah decided Jennifer must be right. She was sure it was nothing.

After everyone said good night, after he put first his daughter to bed, then his wife, James sat at his desk in the great room looking out at the nighttime Salem sky. The world, that very same world that had been gloomy for oh so very long, was now all brightness and light. For years he thought he needed to justify the space he took, explain his existence, though he managed to quell that ache to a degree by teaching. Now, with Sarah and Grace there in the wooden gabled house with him, he didn't need a reason to be. He just was. And for the first time in three hundred and nineteen years, that was all right with him.

He closed his eyes and leaned his head against his chair, listening to his wife and his daughter breathe. He loved the sound, Sarah's long, slow exhalations, Grace's faster inhalations. Sarah was right. This was right. They were right together.

He wanted to forget his conversation with Howard and Chandresh. He had beautiful, precious things to consider now, and they were both asleep in their rooms. He tried to press Howard's cautious words away, picturing Sarah's full lips or Grace's golden curls instead, but then Howard's tense face flashed behind his eyes, foreboding as he stood near the bed and whispered.

"Hempel's post tomorrow will name names," Howard had said. He turned away, the fatherly love clouding his eyes. "Timothy is on the list. So is Jocelyn. But you're safe, James. You're not on the list." When Chandresh joined them, he added, "I'm sorry, Chandresh, but you're named as well."

Chandresh put his hand on James's shoulder. "You're safe, James."

"For now," James had said.

For now.

James turned on his computer and pulled up Hempel's blog, waiting for some inspiration about what to do when the reality of vampires became public knowledge. As he scanned the words they blurred inside his brain and the letters rearranged themselves on the screen into a single word: YOU. He felt a spotlight overhead, pointing at him like the word on the screen, yelling, "Here he is, the scary undead man hiding before your eyes!"

He tried to shake his paranoia away like water from his ears and he scrolled to the bottom of the page. No one will believe this, he thought. Real and unreal. Dead and undead. And the proof he wanted was right there in the comments which he read first with amusement and then with an odd recognition. What's wrong with this picture, he wondered?

5 Comments

1. crazygurl4u

You lost your damn mind, Hempel. Who believes in vampires in this day and age with science and TV and everything like the internet and stuff? If there are vampires wouldn't we see them? I don't see how vampires can hide. They're not supposed to be invisible or anything, are they?

2. annabellewayne

I bet you still look for the tooth fairy to leave a dollar under your pillow.

3. lvnlifelrg

Get a job, creep! You were fired from the *News* cause your an ass. Quit saying fake shit. No one believes you!

4. AimEE

Just because it doesn't seem possible doesn't mean it isn't possible. Would you believe me if I said I knew a vampire? He's very nice, and well educated too. He wouldn't hurt anyone.

5. crazygurl4u

Good God, AimEE! You're as delusional as the freak who wrote this post. You know a nice vampire? Get your head examined, idiot.

6. annabellewayne

Who else is boneheaded enough to believe this?

7. Janie269

Zzzzzzz

CHAPTER TEN

A December storm broke over Salem, swinging the skeleton branches of bare-backed trees, dropping buckets of snow here and there—along the wide lawn of Salem Common, on the roof tops, covering the wooden House of the Seven Gables, hanging icicles from the Salem Witch Museum and Witch House—leaving Essex County a winter landscape fit for a North Pole postcard. The bay was flat and gray, reflecting the blotted sky and heaving clouds. It was Christmas Eve, and everywhere was decorated with Santas and reindeer and snowmen. Christmas lights, red lights, green lights, blue and white lights, rainbow lights, brightened the storm-darkened streets.

Sarah sat by the diamond-paned window in the great room watching the snow fall. Cinnamon-scented candles burned on the kitchen counter, and pine wreaths with red glass balls decorated the walls. The Christmas tree—Grace's first, and James's too—stood tall and green in the corner near the kitchen, decorated with rainbow lights and garland. The whole house glowed comfort and warm. Sarah thought of her favorite holiday song, "Silent Night," and she hummed it, the lyrics fitting her mood: "All is calm, all is bright..." She thought of Grace, asleep in her crib, her golden curls framing her face like an angel's halo: "Sleep in heavenly peace..." Grace was so like her father. Sarah smiled, and when she saw her reflection in the window she laughed out loud. She could see her own joy reflected back to her.

Life doesn't get better than this, she thought.

The cauldron had been removed, leaving a screened-off fireplace, and a low fire burned, sending warmth into the great room. She turned on the radio and holiday music filled the space, the mellow tones of Bing Crosby's voice lulling her. She checked the basket beneath the Christmas tree and saw that she had wrapped all her presents, for James and Grace,

95

for Olivia and Martha, for Jennifer and Chandresh, for Timothy and Howard, for Jocelyn, Steve, and Billy. She would see them all the next night, Christmas night, when they would gather together in the wooden gabled house to celebrate. She went into the kitchen and checked the apple pies in the oven, then stirred the soup on the stove, crinkling her nose and closing the lid as quickly as she could. She realized she would do anything for her husband. When she heard the squeak of the front door as wood scraped against wood, she smiled. No matter how many times she saw him again, it was special.

"Hello."

"Hello yourself."

She threw her arms around James's neck and pointed up her chin. He kissed her, then brushed a few stray curls from her eyes. She took a step back, examining him, wondering.

"What is it?" he asked.

"I want to know how you know Chandresh from the Trail of Tears. I want to know what happened. And don't you dare tell me another time, James Wentworth. I'll scream loud enough to wake all of Salem if you tell me another time."

"Another night?"

Sarah wasn't amused. "Is it something bad? You shouldn't be afraid of telling me something bad. I'm not that fragile, James. Chandresh told me you helped his family. Tell me how you met him. Tell me what you saw on the Trail of Tears."

"It's a long story."

"We have time."

James sighed. "You win," he said.

"I always do."

He went into the kitchen and made a pot of her favorite tea, Earl Grey. She sat on the sofa, watching him while he moved easily through the slick, modern kitchen. He wasn't concerned when she remodeled, and he wasn't upset when the cauldron was removed. "My life is now," he said when the workers arrived to carry the heavy black pot away. "I don't live in the seventeenth century anymore. We could get rid of it all, Sarah, the house and everything in it, and it doesn't matter. You're my home now." As he brought her some tea, cream and two sugars the way she liked it, she realized she was amazed by him. He was so strong in every way.

She sipped her tea while he paced the great room, to Grace's bedroom, to their bedroom, and back. He often paced when he spoke about the past. Finally, he said, "What would you like to know?"

"How did you meet Chandresh?"

"Chandresh lived near me when I returned to the Smoky Mountains in the 1830s."

"The Trail of Tears happened in 1838," Sarah said.

"Yes."

"I thought you were in London in the 1830s."

"I was, until 1837 when I came back here. I returned to London in 1843."

"That's when you tutored at Cambridge and met Dickens."

James nodded. "When I returned in 1837, I came here to Salem for a while, but it was too hard. I kept wandering to Danvers to see the Rebecca Nurse Homestead, and I'd go to the Old Burying Point to spit on Hathorne's grave. Not that I told Nathaniel I did that, though I suspect he wouldn't have minded very much."

"You knew Nathaniel Hawthorne?"

"I can't say I knew him well. He was so shy he hardly said a word in company. If he said a complete sentence he was talkative that night."

"There's so much I want to know about you. But tell me about Chandresh."

James stood near the window, looking at the mesh-like snowflakes fluttering down from the clouds. "He and his family were pushed off their land with the others." His fingers tapped his legs as though he were typing out frustrated words. "It was more than losing their land. It was the unfairness of it all."

"Unfairness shouldn't surprise you." Sarah patted the sofa, and James sat beside her. He leaned his head against the cushion and closed his eyes. His gold hair fell away from his face, and Sarah remembered why she was so taken when she saw him the first time, the very first time, in 1691. Sitting across from her at the supper table, he looked so thoughtful, so kind. So beautiful. And it was true. He was all those things. She stroked his face from his temple, down his cheekbone, over his lips, to his chin. He opened his eyes and smiled.

"What was I talking about again?" he asked.

"Chandresh."

"Right." He closed his eyes again. "You were here in the 1690s. You know what the Europeans thought of the natives."

"They thought the natives were inferior. Uncivilized."

"European society centered around owning land. The more you owned, the wealthier you were, the higher you were on the social ladder. But the native people didn't believe in owning land. They believed land was meant to be shared. They worshipped nature, and they believed in a great spirit that created all life, and they believed all life was interconnected—the people, the rivers, the animals, the trees..."

"They believe all life is interconnected. They're still here."

"You're right," James said. "Then, the Europeans couldn't understand the natives, their way of life, their way of thinking. The native people lived in the natural world, but the Europeans needed to separate themselves from nature. They built dams, cut down trees, built fences—this is mine, that's yours over there. The native people's creation stories emphasize having respect for all living things, not dominion over them. When the settlers realized the natives didn't believe they owned the land, that made it easier to take it. It took years of wrangling, but finally the United States government got the land concessions it wanted from Cherokee leaders and pushed the people west to Oklahoma in the 1830s."

"Was Chandresh forced to walk?"

"He was, along with his whole family. 'Nunna daul Isunyi,' the Cherokee called it. 'The Trail Where They Cried.' He didn't know me when they began walking. He couldn't see me then."

"He couldn't see you?"

"That part comes later." James sniffed the air. "What is that? Not cookies?"

"Oh no."

Sarah rushed into the kitchen, put on the heavy cooking mitts, and pulled the browned apple pies from the oven. She turned the burner off and moved the soup pot to the cool side. James stood behind her.

"What is that?" he asked again.

"When I was writing the menu for Christmas dinner I remembered making blood soup when we were first married. I made blood pudding then too, but that's a sausage and I didn't think you'd like that as much. I found a recipe online, and…"

"And…?"

"I used some blood from one of your bags and added some spices." She opened the lid and dipped a ladle into the soup. "Can you eat it?"

He leaned over the pot and inhaled deeply. "It smells good. I'm going to try some."

Sarah pulled a bowl from the cabinet and ladled in some soup. She grabbed a spoon from the drawer and set the bowl and the spoon in front of James as he sat at the table. He looked eager to try it, which pleased her. When he brought the spoon to his lips, she watched his face.

James nodded. "It's good, Sarah. The spices are different, but I like them."

"Really?"

"Really. This is the first normal meal I've had in over three hundred years. Thank you."

When James offered her a bite, Sarah wrinkled her nose.

"It's all for you," she said.

"You used to eat blood soup."

"I used to eat a lot of things I find disgusting now."

He ate a few more spoonfuls, nodding at each taste. "It couldn't have been too pleasant making this."

"I'll do anything for you, James. I'll even make you blood soup."

Suddenly, James sat still, his head to the side, listening. Sarah knew his preternatural mannerisms well enough by now to know he heard something she couldn't.

"What is it?"

"A smug, self-satisfied shuffle about five miles down the road." James shook his head. "Geoffrey."

"What about him?"

"He's here."

As if on cue, Geoffrey knocked an offbeat tune on the front door. When Sarah stepped away, James grabbed her arm. "Where are you going?" he asked.

"To let Geoffrey in."

"Why?"

"Because I like him and I'm not leaving him outside on Christmas Eve."

"You like him?"

"He's funny."

Geoffrey's voice boomed through the door. "That's right, James. I'm funny."

"You're not that funny," James said.

"I'm funny enough."

Sarah opened the door, and Geoffrey bowed. "Good evening, little human person. How is the littlest human person tonight?"

"Good evening, Geoffrey. She's fine. She's sleeping."

"Very good. One night I'll come round while she's still awake. I'd like to see her again." He dropped onto the sofa and stared at the Christmas tree as though he had never seen one before. "Bringing the outdoors indoors. And it's all sparkly like. Interesting." Then he sniffed the air. "What's that?" He skipped into the kitchen. "It's... it's..." He stood near the stove and sniffed the soup, closing his eyes while he savored the acrid aroma.

James pulled the bowl toward him. "My wife made it for me."

"What is it? You must tell me."

"It's blood soup," Sarah said. "I made it for James for Christmas. Would you like some?"

Geoffrey sat next to James at the table. "Let's have a go."

Sarah pulled a bowl from the cupboard, ladled some soup into it, then set it in front of Geoffrey.

"You can celebrate Christmas with us," she said.

"Did you really make this for James for Christmas?"

"I did."

"That's rather nice, actually. I forgot how pleasant it was to have a wife, someone soft and warm who thinks about things like Christmas and soups one might like to eat. My wife always went on about little things she could do for my comfort. She was quite the little homemaker she was."

"I didn't know you were married," Sarah said.

"Oh yes. My Becky was plump and pretty, just the way I like them, but it was a very, very long time ago. Nothing to concern ourselves with now, though I seem to be thinking of her more and more these days, especially when I'm here. All the memories..." He looked at James and sighed.

"Try your soup, Geoffrey," Sarah said.

He took a spoonful and nodded. "This is excellent, little human person." He emptied the bowl in two bites and eyed the pot on the stove.

"Would you like some more?" Sarah asked.

"Please."

While Sarah filled his bowl, Geoffrey eyed James with an odd intensity. "When is your birthday, James?" he asked.

"Why do you care about my birthday?"

"I was just wondering when your birthday was, that's all. You needn't be so huffity-puffity over a simple question."

"His birthday is April 19," Sarah said.

"How old are you?" Geoffrey asked.

"Three hundred and forty-nine," James answered.

"Three hundred and forty-nine? God you're old."

"I'm younger than you."

"That's true enough." Geoffrey's eyes narrowed. "How old am I?"

"How do I know how old you are?"

"When were you born?" Sarah asked.

"I haven't a clue. It was ages ago."

"Did anything special happen the year you were born?"

"Don't encourage him," James said.

Geoffrey tapped his temple as though he were trying to jolt open some long-gone memory. "I remember Mother saying she named me Geoffrey Charles because I was born the same day as the future King Charles the First. Then there was something about the East India Company being granted a royal charter the month after I was born. She said she thought of naming me Geoffrey Shakespeare since I was much ado about nothing."

James kept his mouth shut. He opened his laptop and searched the Internet. "1600," he said. "King Charles the First was born on November 19, 1600."

"You're four hundred and eleven," Sarah said.

Geoffrey grasped Sarah's hands and danced with her around the great room, swinging her around, arm in arm like an elegant line dance. "I'm four hundred and eleven!"

He stopped dancing and looked over James's shoulder, his eyes squinting at the words through the glare of the flat computer screen. "What is that with the words on it?"

"It's a computer," James said. "How can you be in the twenty-first century and not recognize a computer?"

"I am in the twenty-first century, James, I am not of the twenty-first century. I came of age in the days when bookbinding was an art. I am appalled at the state of what you call literature these days. In my time, we didn't have electronic doodahs like iPigs or Bumbleberries. I prefer hardcovers that hurt your back when you carry them. *That* is a book. Though I suppose reading on a Snook is better than not reading at all."

"On a Nook, Geoffrey," said James.

"Whatever. It's all nonsense. I'm from a more courteous time when we had eloquent forms of communication."

"Town criers."

Geoffrey turned toward James, his hands on his hips, his eyes slits, his lips pursed in annoyance with his vampling. "Do not mock a perfectly acceptable form of communication. It's a clean, simple way to get information, that. The town crier arrived, said his bit around town, and left us be to act on or ignore the news as we saw fit. You can't pretend you don't know things these days. Information is everywhere. When that story about vampires being real gets out it'll be around the world in sixty seconds, let alone sixty days."

"Who's putting out a story about vampires?" Sarah asked.

James shook his head. "Don't pay any attention to him."

Geoffrey looked at James, at Sarah, then James again. He shrugged and tapped the laptop keys like a little boy trying to play the piano. "So what else does your magic box say about London in the seventeenth century? What else happened when I was born?"

James swatted Geoffrey's hands away, typed seventeenth century London into the search engine, and scrolled through the results.

"Well? What does it say?"

"I don't know," James said. "I haven't gotten there yet."

"Gotten? You haven't gotten? When did you start speaking like an American with that ridiculous accent?"

"What are you talking about?"

"You're British."

"I most certainly am not British."

"You were born in London."

"In 1662. A lot has happened since then, you know, a little something called the American Revolution."

"Oh that."

"Oh that?"

"A little misunderstanding turned into a major blowout because you children couldn't be bothered to pay your taxes."

James glared at Geoffrey. "I think it had something to do with taxation without representation," he said.

"Are you still blowing that old horn?" Geoffrey's frustration showed as two pink spots on his white-blue cheeks. "You know perfectly well that whole taxation without representation shtick was a ruse. You had representation through the colonial legislature, yet you only paid one twenty-sixth of the taxes we paid in Britain. We were just trying to recoup some of our losses. You children were expensive to care for, needing protection from the natives over here and whoever else over there."

"There wasn't enough representation. Our votes wouldn't have counted for anything…"

"Aha!" Geoffrey hopped from foot to foot, pointing at James, the glee everywhere in his bright eyes and wicked smile. "Finally, after more than two hundred years you admit you had representation. Taxation without representation my patooties." Geoffrey paced the great room, propelled by his agitation. "You know the real problem? You didn't care about the tax levied on tea. You cared that we undercut the price of tea from the smugglers. Surprise! Most of the colonial leaders were smugglers! And let's not forget that the British agreed to stop stealing land from the Indians. That wasn't good enough for you greedy, land-hungry colonists."

"Don't you dare call me a land-hungry colonist," James said. He stood to his full height, eye-to-eye with Geoffrey. "I did everything I could to help the people after their land was taken. I even slunk as low as you…" He stopped short, unable to continue. Sarah didn't know.

"I know what you did," Geoffrey said. When Geoffrey saw the shocked expression on James's face, the way James looked at Sarah to see if she noticed anything odd about the turn of their conversation, he backed away. He whispered so only James could hear. "She doesn't know?" James nodded. "You keep a lot of secrets from your little human person." James nodded again.

In a voice loud enough for the neighbors to take part in the conversation, Geoffrey said, "I think you need to write an essay saying how you wayward American children had representation through the colonial legislature, there, Professor Doctor James Wentworth, and get it published in all those boring scholarly journals only academics read. It's about time we get that story straight."

"I think you should go around Massachusetts as a town crier and shout it out at all the public buildings," James said. "You can start at Faneuil Hall in Boston. You can leave right now."

"I think..."

Sarah pushed her way between them, arms out, keeping them on separate sides of the room like a teacher breaking up a fight on the playground. "Boys," she said, "please, let it go. It was a long time ago."

"Listen to your wife," Geoffrey said. "She's smarter than you." He walked back to his corner by the kitchen. "What about you, Missy? When did you start speaking with that ridiculous American accent? Do you say gotten as well?"

"I was born in Boston," Sarah said.

"She's from Massachusetts," James said.

Geoffrey pointed at Sarah's head. "You were born in Boston." He pointed at her heart. "But you were born in England." He looked toward the kitchen. "Can I have more soup?" he asked.

James shrugged. "Help yourself," he said.

After Geoffrey left, James stood outside making sure he was gone. He looked so perturbed, James, like Geoffrey was an unfortunate relation you have to deal with maybe on Thanksgiving and Christmas or Easter, and then you don't think about him the other three hundred and sixty-three days of the year. When James walked back into the house, Sarah took his hands.

"I don't understand why you invited him to our wedding if he annoys you so much," she said. "He thinks you're friends now so he stops by sometimes."

James shook his head. "I don't understand it myself. I'm appalled and fascinated by him at the same time. I hate him for abandoning me after he turned me, yet I feel drawn to him, connected to him, like he has some answer I've been looking for. Perhaps it was the note."

"What note?"

"After he came here the first time he left me a note saying he hadn't abandoned me the way I thought he had. He kept track of me, he knew everywhere I was, everything I did, but since I was doing all right he stayed away."

"Maybe he thought he was doing the right thing. Maybe he thinks creating vamplings is like being a mother bird who pushes her young from the nest—that's how you help them fly."

James shook his head. "There are other ways to help vamplings learn to survive. You help them by being there. Teaching them. Letting them know they're not alone in the world."

"Like being a parent."

James smiled. "Yes," he said.

Sarah brushed some stray strands away from his eyes. "Geoffrey's a link to your past."

"I suppose he is." James looked at the pot on the stove. "How about more of that soup?"

"I can do that." Sarah ladled more soup into his bowl and set it in front of him "Look how normal we are," she said. "A husband and wife together on Christmas Eve, the husband eating soup, holiday music in the background, a fire in the hearth, our daughter asleep in her crib getting ready for her first Christmas. We're just like other families."

"We were visited by Geoffrey and you think we're like other families?"

"All families have a crazy relative. It's mandatory."

"Geoffrey a relative? God help us."

James finished the soup and licked the spoon. "That's one thing Geoffrey was right about," he said.

"What's that?"

"You're smarter than I am."

Sarah smiled. "I know," she said.

CHAPTER ELEVEN

The daycare was two miles past SSU, down Lafayette Street into Marblehead sitting atop a short hill. It was a white Victorian-style home with triangle windows on top and colonial-blue trim. Primary Time Child Care and Preschool stayed open into the night to accommodate university employees like James and Sarah, who stood in front of the door, Sarah clutching Grace to her heart.

"What's wrong?" James asked.

"Maybe this isn't a good idea. She's been doing so well with Olivia."

James took Grace in one arm while he kissed the top of Sarah's hair. "Grace will be fine. She needs to get used to other people."

"But she's only seven months old."

"They have a baby room."

"Maybe I should cut back at the library. Maybe I should quit altogether."

"I want you to do whatever makes you happy, Sarah."

"I know. I love you."

"I love you more."

Sarah opened the door and they walked inside. The friendly looking woman behind the desk was the epitome of a preschool teacher in a boxy applique sweater with apples and ABCs, short curled hair, and a perpetual smile.

"We're the Wentworths," Sarah said. "This is Grace."

"Hello, Mrs. Wentworth. I'm Miss Nancy."

Miss Nancy took Grace's hand. "Hello, Grace. Welcome to Primary Time." With well-practiced hands she swept Grace from James's arms. "No worries," said Miss Nancy. "Miss Linda and I work together in the baby room. I'll call you if we need you, but from the looks of it I think we'll be fine, right Grace? She's a sweet baby."

"She is," James said.

Grace nodded as if she understood every word. Sarah kissed the top of her gold curls and stroked her pink cheek.

"I'll pick you up when I'm done at the library, okay Grace? Then we'll go back to get Daddy. He starts his vampire class tonight."

Miss Nancy squinted. "Vampire class?"

"It's a vampire literature class," James said.

"That vampire show on cable is from a book, isn't it?" Miss Nancy asked. "What's it called?"

"We've never seen it," Sarah said.

Miss Nancy leaned up, watching James. He stepped back, nervous until she turned to Grace. "Your daughter looks just like you, Professor Wentworth."

"Thank you." He smiled at the lady holding his daughter. "You have our numbers in case you need us?"

"We'll all set." Miss Nancy hugged Grace. "Let's go meet your other teacher, Grace." She stepped away, but Sarah stopped her.

"Should I go with you?" she asked.

"You can go wherever you like, Mrs. Wentworth. This is your school now."

Sarah looked at James, and he laughed. "I haven't seen the classroom yet," he said. "Let's go." He clasped Sarah's hand as they followed Miss Nancy into the infant room, painted sunshine yellow with rainbows and clouds on the blue-sky ceiling. They met Miss Linda, another soft-looking, smiling woman, and said good-bye to Grace.

Sarah looked like she would cry as they drove toward campus. "I thought Grace would be a little sad when we left," she said.

"Don't worry, honey. If she hasn't forgotten us in three hundred years, I don't think she'll forget us in a few hours." He kissed her hand. "That school is highly recommended. Martha's daughter has used them for years."

"I know," Sarah said.

She looked miserable, and he hated to leave her in the library but he had to get to class. He groaned to think of it. It was a frigid January night, and it had snowed the day before, leaving slippery puddles and black ice on the ground while the thin branches of the naked trees hunched toward the ground as though still searching for the leaves that got away. The students looked like living bundles of clothes in heavy winter coats, scarves, and hats, and they walked quickly and huddled close, clutching hot coffee in their mittened hands. James marveled at their sensitivity to the temperature. He remembered how he hated the dark winter months in his human days, annoyed by the goose bumps and the shivering, his longing for the warmth of the fire in the hearth, and then, after they were married, for Elizabeth's warmth under the blankets at night. Lost in memories of his first life, he was startled by a human-looking Howard, professorly in a jacket and tie, walking beside him. They stopped near Meier Hall and James looked through the window into the empty first floor room where his class would start soon.

"Starting your vampire class tonight?" Howard asked. James nodded. "Going to teach them how to be a vampire?"

James looked at Howard, saw his friend's wiry salt and pepper eyebrows knitted in a perpetual state of father-worry, not unlike the mother-worry he had seen on Sarah's face at Primary Time. "What is it Howard?"

"What's going to happen after Hempel names names?"

James shook his head. "I don't know, but meanwhile that new post with the names isn't up yet. Perhaps accusing people isn't as easy as Hempel thought it would be. You should see the comments on his blog. People think he's an idiot."

Howard nodded, but the pain on his face was tangible. James felt it two feet away.

"Where will we go, James?"

"It'll be fine," James said. He clutched Howard's shoulder, hoping to comfort his friend, but Howard's face was long, his dark eyes staring at the moon overhead.

"In two weeks I can tear Hempel to shreds and no one would know it was me." There was a growl-filled undertone to Howard's voice that made James shudder.

"But you'd know. You could never live with yourself if you ended it that way."

"Too bad, right?"

As Howard disappeared into the campus lights he glanced wistfully at the sky and sighed. Suddenly, James heard voices inside Meier Hall. He looked through the window and saw students filing into his classroom. He watched them, shook his head, and walked inside.

He nodded at the students as he entered the room, recognizing a few familiar faces from previous terms. He pulled out his class roster and put his book bag in the bottom drawer of the instructor's desk. In a matter of moments every seat in the room was taken. Too bad, he thought. He was hoping most of them would drop and they'd have to cancel the class.

"Hey, Doctor Wentworth. Your favorite student is here!"

Levon Jackson rushed into the room, nearly tripping over a classmate in his haste.

"Are you taking this class?" James asked. "Last year you had to cover your ears whenever anyone said the word vampire."

"I need the units so I can graduate in the spring. Besides, it's make-believe, right? And I can suffer through any class of yours, Doctor Wentworth."

"Thanks a lot," James said.

Levon sat in his usual seat, front row center, and he nodded to familiar classmates. "My mom says hi," he said to James. "She said to tell you not to forget her appointment next Tuesday night. She needs to check up on you, make sure you're all right." Levon grinned. "She likes you, you know, so I wouldn't worry."

"I like her too," said James. "And I suppose you're all right as well."

James looked at the clock on the wall. Class time. Two more students rushed in, shivering and stomping winter wet from their boots. They smiled at James as they took the last seats in the back row. All eyes in the classroom turned to him, and suddenly James felt like he had a flashing neon-pink arrow pointing at his head, freak show style: "Step right up, step right up ladies and gentlemen, to see for yourselves one of the garish creatures of the night. See the angry three-hundred-and-forty-nine-year-old vampire monster-man who wants to drink your blood!" But the students didn't hear any carnival barkers. They watched him, waiting for class to start, and he smiled at the fresh young faces staring back at him while he called role. Everyone who signed up for the class was there. Damn. That never happened. There was even one student who hadn't signed up, sitting in his usual spot in the back closest to the door. James checked his role sheet again, and he was right, Timothy's name wasn't there. James could tell by the way Timothy glanced around that he was listening to every conversation in the room. Levon and Timothy together in a vampire literature class. This should be interesting, James thought.

There was one student who stood out in particular, a young man named Brent Wilson, about twenty years old with dyed jet-black hair, black eyeliner, and black clothing. He wasn't painted white, though he seemed pasty for a human, like he stayed out of the sun. James wondered briefly if Brent was one of his kind, but he looked, listened, and knew, no, the boy is human. He may want to be one of us, but he isn't. James wanted to take the boy aside and tell him the truth. This life might seem exciting, but there are so many problems. Stay human, James wanted to tell him. Stay human the way I wish I could have stayed human.

James passed out the class syllabus, then began with a simple question: "What do you know about vampires?"

He looked at Levon, expecting the well-built, athletic-looking young man to slap his large hands over his ears the way he had before.

Levon smiled. "Not a thing, Doctor Wentworth."

"I guessed as much. Anyone else?"

A blond-haired girl sitting by the window raised her hand.

"Yes?" James said.

"They sparkle."

James sighed. "Anyone else?"

A burgundy-haired girl raised her hand. "They come out at night. They drink your blood."

"Yes, those are common beliefs. What else?"

"They turn into bats."

James looked at the clock on the wall. Ten minutes into class. This was going to be a long term.

"Some people believe vampires turn into bats," he said. He looked at a young man to his right. "Yes?"

"They're dead, but they come back to life at night."

James nodded. "That's another common belief. Does anyone know when the first vampire story was told?"

"The movie with that Russian guy," said a bearded young man. "The one wearing the black cape with that weird accent you can hardly understand."

"His name was Bela Lugosi, and he was Hungarian. The movie version of *Dracula* you're referring to was made in 1931, but vampire stories were told thousands of years before that. The earliest vampire stories go back as far as 4000 B.C.E. to the Sumers in Ancient Mesopotamia." The students began scribbling in their spiral notebooks or typing into their laptops. "The Sumers spoke of a vampire known as the Ekimmu, which they believed was created when someone died a violent death or wasn't buried properly. The Ekimmu were believed to be rotting corpses roaming the earth searching for victims to torment. In early Hebrew tales, Lilith was depicted as a winged demon. She is believed by some to be the first wife of Adam, and since she considered herself his equal—heaven forbid a woman should consider herself a man's equal—she was banished to the demon world. Some say the mark of Cain is the mark of the vampire. Eastern Europe was, and is, a hotbed for vampire legends. Stories of the undead have been told all over the world, and every culture has their own version. Some are merely ghost stories, but others grew from a need to explain misunderstood anomalies before science could explain them."

"Like what?" Levon asked.

"Like porphyria, a hemoglobin issue that causes extreme sensitivity to sunlight. Another is catalepsy, a suspension of animation where the person appears dead but then appears to come to life again. In 1730s Serbia, murders of people and farm animals were attributed to the undead. A number of corpses were exhumed and found to be rosy-cheeked with fresh blood in their mouths."

"That creepy dude with the accent comes from there."

James looked at the bearded boy. "He comes from the area," he said.

"Who has a funny vampire story?" Levon asked.

"The Greeks. Andilaveris isn't a scary vampire, only an annoying one. At night he roamed into villages and dined off the villagers' food and smashed their plates and glasses. One night he stood on the roof of a church and urinated on anyone passing below." The class laughed. "He had to stay in his grave on Fridays, so one Friday a priest, a sexton, and a few others opened his tomb, captured him, and sent his body to a deserted island, Daskaleio, where he was trapped and never bothered anyone again."

Levon nodded. "I like that one, Doctor Wentworth."

"Me too," James said.

"What about the Native Americans?" asked a dark-haired young woman. "They have vampire legends too. What about the Kalona Ayeliski?"

James nodded, keeping it casual. There was nothing odd about the question. This was simply more information he could impart to his curious students.

"For the Cherokee, the Kalona Ayeliski, or Raven Mocker, is a powerful evil spirit, so powerful other spirits and witches fear it. The Raven Mocker tortures and torments a dying person to hasten their death. After the person's death, the Raven Mocker consumes the heart to bolster its own life force. Raven Mockers add a year to their lives for every year their victim would have lived."

"Don't they appear as old men or women?" the dark-haired girl asked.

"They can."

"Why are they called Raven Mockers?" the bearded boy asked.

"The Cherokee believe that when the Raven Mockers hunt they make a sound like a raven's cry. People feared the sound because it meant someone would die soon. Only the medicine men could see them, and the medicine men would stand guard over the dying to prevent the Raven Mockers from stealing their hearts." James shook his head, forgetful of the forty young people sitting there. "They didn't know," he said. "They didn't understand."

A student near the back coughed and James came back to himself. He scanned the faces of his students and realized he had a captivated audience. Even Timothy dropped his pen to listen. In all his years of teaching he had never seen anything like it. He had taught Shakespeare, Dickens, the Romantic Poets, the Harlem Renaissance writers. He had taught contemporary American masters like Morrison, Oliver, and Walker. But here, in this vampire literature class, he had their attention unlike ever before. They were so engrossed in the discussion that most of them stopped taking notes or typing. They watched him the way Grace watched him when he told her bedtime stories—wide-eyed and mesmerized.

"So now we have some background information about early vampires legends," he said. "What else do you already know about vampires?"

"They're real."

James turned to the student who had spoken, the pale-skinned boy in black. Other students laughed. Some rolled their eyes. A few muttered obscenities under their breath.

"Freak," a blond-haired boy said.

"Vampires are real," Brent said. He stared into James's eyes. "Isn't that right, Doctor Wentworth?"

James looked at the floor, at the clock on the wall, around the room at the other students. He smiled. Did Brent know? He sighed, a big display sigh because at that moment, with all eyes on him, the word vampire in the air, hanging over him like that neon arrow he imagined, he needed the students to see his chest move.

"Who believes vampires are real?" Levon asked. "Besides that fool with the blog and that idiot over there."

James looked at Brent. The black-haired boy was firm, his arms crossed in front of him, his eyes disappointed and small.

Suddenly, from the side of the class, James heard, "Hey, Doctor Wentworth, you're pale and you only teach night classes. Maybe you're a vampire."

"Right," Levon said. "Doctor Wentworth's a vampire. Next you're going to tell me his wife is a werewolf."

"Actually, she's a ghost," James said.

Levon laughed. "But you still haven't said how vampires get to be vampires in the first place. Where do vampires come from?"

The bearded boy faced Levon. "You see, first the mommy vampire and the daddy vampire meet and fall in love, and then they…"

"I'm serious," said Levon. "What makes a vampire, Doctor Wentworth?"

"They're cursed," James said. "It's the only explanation."

"Can a vampire ever break the curse?"

"I'm not familiar with any way to break the curse."

James sat on the edge of the instructor's desk while he gathered his thoughts. These young people, so curious, so vigorous, so alive, had no idea what it meant to be cursed. If they knew his truth would they come to his class then? Would they run away screaming in the halls? He settled his worries and continued his lecture about early vampire legends, with no further interruptions from Brent, while the students took notes and asked questions.

"James?"

Sarah stood near the door, a sleeping Grace asleep in her arms. "Class was over twenty minutes ago. We were waiting for you in the library."

"I'm sorry, honey," he said. "I lost track of time."

"We all did," said Levon. "You're a good storyteller, Doctor Wentworth. Especially that Raven Mocker stuff."

"Thanks, Levon. All right everyone. Your assignment for next week is to research an early vampire legend, not the same ones we talked about here tonight, and bring in some information about the legend to share. I'll see everyone next week."

The students said good night and filed away. At first, James thought they were tip-toeing around him, though he knew it was his paranoia brought on by Hempel's blog and Brent's questions. Timothy was gone. A few students peeked at Grace as she slept in Sarah's arms. One blond-haired girl smiled at James. "She's cute, Doctor Wentworth. She looks just like you."

"Thank you," James said.

Levon said good night to James and Sarah and smiled at Grace before he left. When the room was empty and only Sarah and Grace remained, James put his arms around them, holding them close while he kissed the top of his daughter's silk-like curls. He closed his eyes, clearing his mind.

"How did it go?" Sarah asked.

"It's a vampire literature class. How do you think it went?"

"Was it that bad?"

"I'll survive."

"It looked like a full class."

James kissed Sarah's forehead. "It was," he said. "It was."

I smell the charred timber, the dry smoke, the acrid ashes, their putrid fear. I step outside my cabin and see burning everywhere, fires like fiendish eyes blazing in the corn fields or smoldering my neighbor's home while he helps his mother-in-law, wife, and two small daughters to safety away from the smoke and the flames. Nearby forest trees are charred tar-black, and he runs back inside his house to salvage anything he can grab that won't singe the skin from his bones, but all he can find is a blanket and his rifle. Every possession he had in the world is gone. Ashes to ashes, dust to dust. His face is gray with soot, and his tears streak his cheeks white. His sunken head and slumped shoulders show his defeat, and when the soldiers return to lead them away they will leave. What is here to hold them now?

I hear the women's sobbing as close as if they sing their sadness into my ears. To the left, to the right, back and front, side to side I see the soldiers with their pointing rifles and piercing bayonets loitering in the darkness as they spread across the night to other homes, knocking on doors here, making loud declarations there. The blue-suited men wander freely in and out as if these houses were their own, setting aside what possessions they like for themselves, collecting everything else to cart away and sell. They leave nothing untouched, and when there is nothing left to confiscate they set the remaining houses on fire and leave, their damage done. I hear the crunch of their boots on the dried cornstalks as they retreat. For now. One last slap in the face remains.

CHAPTER TWELVE

When you have a story to tell, you must tell it. No matter how you are laughed at, belittled, berated, mocked. No matter what others whisper about you behind your back. No matter the naysayers. Despite the frustration of speaking loudly and no one caring. Whether you get one-star reviews or five, whether you have word-of-mouth, marketing support, a respected platform, massive numbers of followers to hang on your every word or not, you must tell that story or else always wonder what could have been, forever hold your peace.

It was a clear, cold Monday night at the beginning of February when Kenneth Hempel appeared on Channel 16, Salem Access Television. Now everyone could see him telling his story.

"They're here," he said to the camera. He brushed his thinning hair to the side, then tugged at his tightly knotted tie. "Whether we want to believe it or not, whether we can believe it or not, they're here, and we're not safe if we continue to allow them to roam free. Not all of them are a threat to society, but some are, and until we know which is which we must guard ourselves against all of them."

The reporter, a college-age girl with her white-blonde hair cut into a newscaster's bob, looked like she wanted to laugh out loud. She suppressed a sarcastic grin. "You said you were going to name names," she said. "Do you have the names of those you believe are vampires?"

Hempel cleared his throat and read from the paper in his hands. "The vampires currently living within Essex County are: John Edward Lewis. Nancy Bates. Christopher Banning. Jocelyn Endecott. Chandresh Mankiller. Timothy Bryston-Wolfe. And Anthony Davies. I'll explain what proof I have against these individuals in a blog post I'll publish next week."

"There was an article in the *Salem News* this morning that suggested you're trying to recreate the terror of the Salem Witch Trials by falsely accusing innocent people. What do you say to that?"

"In 1692, the people who were accused were innocent of witchcraft, but now the accused are what I say they are." Hempel turned a determined gaze onto the young reporter, his back straight, his head high. "I'm not trying to accuse innocent people. I simply want the truth to be known. I want people to be safe from nighttime predators. If the vampires will willingly come forward, then I won't need to pursue this route of outing them. People have a right to know the truth."

James turned off the TV. He looked toward the bedroom, saw Sarah sleeping, her expression peaceful. The moonlight streamed through the open blinds and illuminated her face in a golden glow. He heard Grace's short, full breaths and he smiled. He walked into his bedroom and sat on the bed, watching Sarah. He wanted everything to stay as it was, his wife and daughter content, his little family happy. But he could feel the cold storm creeping toward them, darkening the sky above their heads, stronger, harder, faster than the most brutal nor'easter ever to strike the shore.

He crawled into bed, spooning Sarah, pushing every other thought from his mind except the one where he felt awash with gratitude because he had her there, with him, in his arms. He held her tightly, trying to meld into her, make them each a part of the other. She opened her eyes and smiled, though James saw the uneasy flicker within her. She threw her arms around his neck and kissed his lips.

"As long as we're together everything will be all right," she said.

"Whatever it is, we'll get through it," he said.

He took Sarah's hand and held it to his chest. He kissed her fingers, her lips, the top of her head. He made love to her with an intensity he hadn't known since the first night they were reunited, as though he needed to reassure himself, and her, that they would always be that way.

Latest Headlines—Most Popular

Reporter's Death: A Homicide, Says Detectives

Leap Day, Wednesday February 29, was a violent day in Danvers, Massachusetts, where former *Salem News* reporter Kenneth Hempel, 47, was found brutally murdered outside his home near Interstate 95. Police believe he was attacked in his home office, his body then dragged outside and left discarded in his front yard. Inside the house, splattered blood stains the rug, and the room where Hempel worked has been destroyed, his laptop computer smashed, filing cabinets emptied and tossed aside. It looked, one officer reported, like a tornado had blown through, leaving Hempel's home office in ruins.

Hempel's remains were first seen by Mrs. Elsie Anderson, who has lived next door to Hempel and his family for the last seven years. Mrs. Anderson was walking home from her Wednesday Afternoon Ladies Musical Auxiliary Society meeting when she noticed a lump of what looked like red mud near her lawn. She followed the trail and found Hempel's bloody corpse. Neighbors heard her scream and called police. When asked what she saw, Mrs. Anderson said Hempel's neck was pierced as though he had been bitten.

"He seemed like a nice enough man, a good family man, but I didn't know him all that well," Mrs. Anderson said. "I never believed him about the vampires. Now I don't know. His neck was bludgeoned, I could see the teeth marks on him, and he was covered in blood. That's what vampires do, isn't it? Bite you and suck your blood?"

Detectives are cautioning the public from jumping to conclusions. "The perp, or perps, meant to make it look like a vampire committed the crime," Detective Chase Peters told reporters. "There's no reason to start believing in vampires."

Hempel found notoriety due to several provocative blog posts where he asserted that vampires are real. On a local television appearance earlier this month he named several residents of Essex County as real-life vampires and he stated he had evidence to prove his assertions. With Hempel's death and the destruction of his home office, that evidence, whatever it was, may not see the light of day.

Hempel is survived by his wife, Lynne, 42, and a son, 9, and a daughter, 6.

CHAPTER THIRTEEN

Two nights later Geoffrey arrived. He was quiet and sullen, which annoyed James more than his usual smugness. He shrugged at James as he walked into the wooden house.

"I assume you heard the news about your friend," Geoffrey said.

James looked at Sarah's reaction, but her face stayed set. She had seen the report about Hempel's murder on the news earlier that evening. She hadn't said anything about it, but James knew she was upset. He could see it in her eyes. He knew her so well.

"He wasn't my friend," James said. "Yes, I heard." He looked again at Sarah, whose chocolate-brown eyes watched him, waiting for answers.

"Was he killed by vampires, or was it a human with a sick sense of humor?" she asked.

"Neither answer is good," Geoffrey said. "Both bring their own problems."

"Who was it, Geoffrey?"

"Vampires."

"The ones who were watching him?"

"Who else?"

James colored red with rage. He waved his arms, first in front of him, then behind, venting the horror loitering a thought or two away. "How could they put us in jeopardy like that?" he yelled.

"They're not like you, James. They don't have human feelings let alone attachments. They believe they have the power of a thousand moons and puny humans are no match for them. They were trying to make a point."

"A point with my life," James said bitterly. He closed his eyes, wrangling his anger, his fear, into a more rational line of thought. "What can we do about them? Where are they from?"

125

"They live in a clan in Delaware, and there's around twenty of them. They shun human society, feed when they can on whomever they can, rationalize their actions with their own warped beliefs. A rather rude group, if I do say so. I don't know what we can do about them. How do you handle those who don't care?"

James watched Sarah, her eyes fixed on the dwindling fire in the hearth, her arms crossed over her chest, her shoulders slumped. James would have handed back every ounce of his immortality to Geoffrey and become every bit of the three hundred and forty-nine year-old man he was to brush that frightened look from her face. She looked too much like she did when he told her Rebecca Nurse had been arrested. He couldn't bear to see her look that away again.

Geoffrey sat on the sofa and looked thoughtfully toward the baby's room. "You're doing quite well for yourself, James. A daughter is a grand thing. I had one once, a plump and pretty little thing like her mother, and a son. One son, who was the light and joy of my life. He was a fine boy, thoughtful, highly intelligent, of course. He was my son, after all." Geoffrey smiled at James. "For years I wondered what sort of man he had become."

"Didn't you know?" Sarah asked.

"I'm afraid not. I was turned into what you see before you when he was only a very little boy."

"Did you ever see him again?"

"Once, many years later, but he was quite a grown man by then with a wife and son of his own. I couldn't bring myself to go round and say hello though I wanted to. I didn't want to frighten him, being as I hadn't changed in thirty years. But I was as proud of him as any father could be in his son. I could see the strong and steady man my good boy had become, and by then my good boy had a good boy of his own."

"You should have gone to see him," Sarah said. "I'm sure he would have accepted you, even as you are."

"The saddest part of this story, my dearest little human person, is you're correct. He would have accepted me even as I am. Only I learned that too many years later." Geoffrey looked towards the baby's room again. "Did you say her name was Grace?"

"That's right," Sarah said.

"Very good. We could all use more grace now."

"Would you like something to drink, Geoffrey?" Sarah asked.

"Yes, thank you." Geoffrey watched James follow Sarah to the refrigerator. "I still don't understand, James," he said. "Here's a perfectly nice little human person who likes you well enough. Why don't you drink from her? Jocelyn drinks from her human person. You don't have to kill someone to drink from them."

James was horrified. He thought of decapitating Geoffrey right there, a clean break, snapping the annoying vampire man's skull clean from his spine and discarding the no longer immortal remains in the woods near Danvers. But he remembered that's where Hempel was found, near his home in Danvers, and he supposed that wouldn't work after all, though the thought of it made him smile. He grabbed an unopened red-filled medical bag from the refrigerator, sliced the top with a knife, and poured blood into two coffee mugs. He put the coffee mugs into the microwave and set the timer. He looked at Sarah, who was wondering, he was sure, why he had never told her that Jocelyn drinks from Steve. The microwave beeped, and James put a warmed mug in front of Geoffrey, who squished his face and crinkled his nose.

"It's all...piecy," Geoffrey said.

"It tastes fine," said James.

"Smells like pig urine."

"It's donated from the blood bank."

"Donated from the blood bank? Is that how I raised you, to be a little beggar vampire? Please, sir, I want some more..."

Geoffrey made a sad little boy face, his cupped hands out, a perfect picture of Oliver Twist asking for more gruel when the morsel he received wasn't near enough.

"You didn't raise me at all," James said. "You left me alone."

Geoffrey shrugged. "I'm so sorry, Sarah. It seems James only knows two songs: 'You Didn't Raise Me at All' and 'The You Left Me Alone Blues.'"

"What on earth did you..."

Sarah held up her hand. "James, please." She shook her head at Geoffrey and sighed. "Sometimes I feel like a mother with two boys instead of one little daughter."

Geoffrey pointed at James. "He started it."

"Geoffrey was just leaving," James said.

"Hmpf." Geoffrey drank his blood in one gulp while his eyes popped and his lips pulled and he grimaced as he swallowed. "Very well, James, I'll leave you to your life drinking revolting donated blood. But be warned. Others of our kind will begin to come out of the shadows of the night, and the human people will know."

"No," James said. "It's not too late to fix this. If people think deranged humans murdered Hempel then they'll keep laughing at the vampire stories."

Geoffrey shrugged. "I don't know, James. Too many are too angry."

"But Hempel is dead," Sarah said.

"I don't know if Hempel himself matters any more," Geoffrey said. "This 'Vampire Dawn' has taken on a life of its own."

"Vampire Dawn?" Sarah asked.

"That's what they're calling it on that talking box you have over there."

"The television?" James said.

"That's it."

That night James was alert to conspicuous shadows. He watched the nearby houses and wondered what the sleeping families inside would think if they knew a vampire lived there, had lived there on and off for more than three hundred years. Would they believe that though his house, the old wooden one with the two peaked gables, had once been haunted by the specter of memories from the Salem Witch Trial days, it was all right now, she was home, they were together again, their daughter in their arms, their family intact. Would they hate me, he wondered? Throw stones? Chase us with pitchforks and torches? Would they even care?

Inside Sarah sat on the rocking chair in Grace's bedroom, resting her head against the side of the crib while she watched their daughter sleep. Grace was an angel in every way, he knew. When Sarah saw him through the window she smiled that smile he loved to see, that sweet, beautiful smile, and he could tell by the determination in her eyes that she had come to the same conclusion he had. They would see this through together.

James walked into Grace's bedroom as Sarah kissed the baby's gold curls. She pulled the blanket to Grace's chin, then extended her hand to James. He pulled her near him, holding her head to his chest, and they stayed close until she sighed. They walked from Grace's room hand in hand, and Sarah shut the door behind them.

"You never told me Jocelyn drinks from Steve," she said.

"I didn't want you to be afraid I wanted your blood."

"She doesn't get blood from the hospital?"

"She used to, but after she and Steve were married they decided she would drink from him."

"Doesn't it hurt?"

"It doesn't hurt the vampire at all." James smiled weakly, then shrugged. "It must hurt some. You have to pierce the skin to get to the blood."

Sarah pointed her chin up, and he kissed her.

"If you want to drink from me, you can," she said. "It might not be safe for you to get blood from the hospital now with everyone thinking about vampires. If you drank from me you wouldn't need to go there anymore."

James stepped back, stunned by her words. "Absolutely not, Sarah. Don't ever bring it up again."

"It can't hurt that much if Jocelyn feeds from Steve. She loves him. She would never hurt him."

"I will not drink my wife's blood."

"That's right—I'm your wife and I love you. My blood must be better for you than anyone else's."

"Sarah, I don't want to drink anyone's blood, but I have to and the donated blood is the best way for me." He pulled Sarah toward him. "I want to take my wife out to dinner and eat pizza and drink beer like everyone else, but I can't so I have to feed myself the best way I can. The best way doesn't include making a meal of my wife."

Sarah didn't look angry, but she wasn't happy, either. She was quiet a long time, her brow furrowed, her arms crossed, lost in thought. Finally, she said, "You knew Hempel was at it again."

James bowed his head. "Yes," he said.

It began to rain, and the tap-tap-tap of the water hitting the wooden house added a hollow tone to their conversation. Sarah took a spatula from the counter and waved it at him in rhythm with the raindrops.

"When are you going to understand I'm not that fragile?" She put the spatula down and dropped her head into her hands. He could see the pain in her eyes when she lifted her head to look at him. "I need to know what I'm dealing with, James. I need to know what we're facing. What else do you know? What other secrets are you keeping from me?"

James put his arms around her waist and kissed the top of her dark curls. He smoothed her creased brow with his fingers. "That's it, Sarah. Now you know everything I know."

"It needs to stay that way, James. You need to be truthful with me. If something is wrong, you need to tell me."

"I will," he said.

And when he said it, he meant it. But he also knew he wouldn't sit idly by this time while everything around him became unsettled and unsure. This time he would make sure his wife and daughter weren't consumed by the madness. Whatever it took, he decided, he would protect them. If they had to flee at a moment's notice, they would. This time they wouldn't stay behind until the madness was too all encompassing to escape, and he took some comfort in that.

It has begun. It is night, and still they are swept from the land like dust from a porch. Soon, you will never know they were here.

They do not want to leave. This is their land. Their trees. Their crops. Their father's fathers, their mother's mothers, their grandparents as far back as history recalls, all of them are here by this rock. There by that river. Every-where your eyes see. But they must go. When the President of the United States will not uphold the agreement that keeps Cherokee land in Cherokee hands, they must go, if not of their own free will then by the force the musket-bearing soldiers are happy to provide.

Some of the people are stoic as they begin to walk, their faces stone-hard. The soldiers are impatient, shouting, pointing, pushing him here, shoving her there. The women scream for their children, but the soldiers are careless, sepa-rating the small ones from the big ones in their haste. This is all the people hear now...hurry.

All the seven clans are here, Long Hair and Blue, Wolf and Wild Potato, Deer, Bird, and Paint. I recognize the medicine man from the Paint tribe (most medicine people are from the Paint tribe since medicine is 'painted' onto the person in the healing ceremony), the one who eyed me so readily at the Stomp Dance last week. He sees me watching through my cabin window. I walk outside to offer my help to his family, but he turns away abruptly, as though suddenly he is afraid of me. I see the way he talks to my neighbor, and though I don't understand their words I see the familiarity between them, the resemblance in their features. I realize my neighbor is the medicine man's son.

I watch in horror as my sturdy, straight-backed neighbor, with biceps the size of a normal man's thighs, stands helplessly nearby while soldiers point bayonets at his family. His mother-in-law refuses to leave her home, whatever was left after the fire, and she sits stubbornly, cross-legged on the floor. My neighbor yells at her in their language, but she folds her arms and turns away like an annoyed five-year-old. Two soldiers push past my neighbor, lift his mother-in-law by the arms, carry her outside, and drop her hard on the ground. My neighbor moves to help her, but the soldiers shake the sharp end of their bayonets in his direction. The medicine man is able to approach the older wom-an, the soldiers do not see him, and he soothes her with his soft-spoken words. My neighbor's pretty wife, with a screaming toddler on her hip, rushes back inside to grab whatever was left unscorched by the fire, and she returns with the blanket my neighbor saved that night. My neighbor grabs his musket from the doorway. All around frantic people call out in cracked voices, seeking family and trying to stay together in the chaos.

I want to help them, Lizzie. The fear you can hold in your hands like sharp-edged razors—can you feel it? The wails of the mothers as they're dragged from their children—can you hear it? Do you see the downcast heads of the fathers as their families are yelled at, pushed at, poked with the sharp ends of bayonets? I recognize their contorted faces, their slumped shoulders, the weight that pulls them all the way down. They look the way I felt when I watched the constable drag you away. This is torture, Lizzie. No other word will do, and I must help them.

The wagons are moving. The walking has begun.

CHAPTER FOURTEEN

James paced the ten short steps of his office replaying the newsreel of Hempel's murder in quick-time scenes behind his eyes. Here is the still of Hempel's whitewashed house. There is the mug shot-like photo of Hempel, his thinning hair brushed to the side, his tie knotted perfectly, his small, nervous eyes. There the blood stains the rug, and there the red ooze trails outside. The more James tried to force the images away, the more brightly they burned and blinded him.

He wanted to leave campus, go walking around Salem, through Massachusetts, across the continent. It would take three thousand miles to ease the anxiety he felt like an itching under his skin. It was a strain, this flat-faced ache. He was done teaching for the night, but Sarah had another hour in the library. Needing to keep busy, he logged into his SSU account and checked his e-mail. At the top of the screen was a link from Howard. James groaned aloud. He didn't want to see it. He opened his office door, ready for his cross-country walk. He got to the elevator, but when the doors opened he couldn't go inside. He had to see what Howard sent.

He walked back into his office and clicked the link, which directed him to a clip from WCVB Channel 5. He stared at the young woman on the screen, her coffee-brown hair leveled in a blunt cut, her beige suit blending into the mess of Kenneth Hempel's home office. That's what Kansas looked like after Dorothy was swept away, James thought. Confusion everywhere. The camera panned to the filing cabinets tipped on their sides. The desk was turned over, and pencils, files, newspapers, and books littered the floor. A yellow line of police tape prevented the reporter from stepping directly into the room.

"This is the office of Kenneth Hempel, the former reporter for the *Salem News* who was murdered in his home office last week. His wife, a teacher for the Salem Public Schools, was gone with their two young children to visit her family in Beverly. Police believe Hempel was murdered here in his office, as indicated by the bloodstains on the floor and the wall, and his body dragged through the back door where his corpse was left in the yard. After neighbors called authorities, police arrived to find Hempel dead, apparently of vicious wounds to the neck. A coroner's report is expected to be released to the public as soon as it becomes available. This is what Sheriff Mannion had to say about Hempel's death…"

Cut to a portly, red-faced sheriff stretching his short neck over the podium lined with microphones. He strains his Boston accent to the limit to be heard over the drumming banter of the reporters. The sheriff's hands jump nervously from his belt buckle to his thinning gray hair.

"We're unable to comment on the exact cause of Mr. Hempel's death until we receive the coroner's report. All we can say for certain now is the perp, or perps, broke into his home some time after 8 p.m. that night."

"How do you know it was after 8 p.m.?" a reporter asked.

"According to Mrs. Hempel, she called her husband at approximately 8 p.m. to ask if he'd like to go out for pizza with the children when they arrived home."

The reporters shout their questions at once.

"We're as troubled by this as the citizens of Danvers," the sheriff said. "We're doing everything we can to solve this quickly and bring the murderer to justice."

"Do you have any leads?"

"We know Mr. Hempel accused certain individuals of being vampires. We have that list of names. We'll be contacting those individuals shortly."

"They're not suspects?"

"Not at this time, no."

"As you just stated, Sheriff, Mr. Hempel accused several people of being vampires on Salem Public Access television. There have been reports that there were more lists with other names. Is there any truth to those reports?"

"Most of Hempel's files were destroyed when the room was vandalized."

"Most?"

"Yes."

"Were others named?"

"We have no further information on that at this time."

A seasoned, older voice spoke out above the crowd. "There are some amusing stories being circulated on the web these days, Sheriff Mannion. Can you verify whether or not Mr. Hempel was killed by vampires?"

Everyone in the room laughed but the sheriff, who blotted the wet from his forehead with his sleeve.

"No comment."

The sheriff nodded and walked away.

Cut to the reporter by the yellow tape outside Hempel's office. "From inside Kenneth Hempel's home in Danvers, this is Kara Kennington for WCVB Channel 5."

The nice-looking gray-haired anchorman nodded at the camera. "Kara, since you're in Kenneth Hempel's home, can you tell us how his wife and children are doing?"

"They're heartbroken, as you would imagine, Bill. Mrs. Hempel declined to be interviewed on camera, but she told me before we went on the air that she didn't know why anyone would want to kill her husband. When I asked if she thought his controversial statements about vampires had anything to do with his murder, she said she wasn't sure. She said she never took his vampire talk seriously, and she didn't think others did either."

"Very sad. Thank you Kara."

James sat at his desk unmoving for the longest time. It might have been an hour or a minute. A century or a year. The physical time didn't matter. It only mattered that it had begun. He thought of Jocelyn and

Timothy. He thought of Chandresh. Oh my God, Chandresh. Now will you think of me differently? Now will you think I hurt you instead of helped you? James remembered the night the mean-mouthed soldier stood outside Chandresh's home, ignoring the Cherokee man as though he were less than the mud that scuffed his officer's boots, and he wondered if this experience with the police would be more of the same.

James worried for his friends, but he worried for himself too. Someone had access to the files the police salvaged from Hempel's office, and James guessed that his name was somewhere in those files. It had to be. Hempel had pursued him with such narrow-minded purpose for seven long months, taking notes on that damned yellow legal pad, researching, asking questions, spying. James saw it in his mind, his name on a list somewhere in Hempel's office spelled out in mismatched magazine clippings like a ransom note from a madman.

"This is absurd," he said aloud. "You heard those reporters laugh. Timothy, Jocelyn, and Chandresh will be fine. We'll all be fine." He unlatched his window and pushed it open, letting the sharp March night air into his office. This too shall pass, he thought. By next week everyone will have forgotten about Kenneth Hempel. I already have.

James heard the lighting-quick flash and Timothy stood by the open door. "Did I hear my name?" Timothy looked around the office. "Why are you talking to yourself? Don't you know only crazy people talk to themselves?"

"They're only crazy if they answer," James said.

Timothy sat in the empty chair near the bookshelf while James closed the door. "What were you saying?" Timothy asked.

"I was just hoping that everyone was going to be all right after the police interrogation."

"I wouldn't call it much of an interrogation. They stopped by last night and asked where I was the night Hempel was murdered. It was easy enough to answer since I was here in calculus class. The professor takes roll so they can verify it if they need to. They didn't seem too concerned. They said thank you and left."

"Do you think that's it?" James asked.

"I do, and so does Dad."

James nodded. Perhaps this would blow over even more quickly than he hoped.

Timothy didn't look pleased. His face was puckered as if he had just eaten a bagful of sour gummy worms. He crossed his arms over his chest and his legs at the ankles. "Aren't you going to ask me what's wrong?" he asked.

"Is something wrong? You always look that way."

Timothy pulled a three-folded business letter from his backpack and waved it in the air. "All those half-assed vampire books out there and they turn *me* down! It's bullshit!"

"What are you talking about, Timothy?"

"I finished my memoir and sent queries to some editors saying it was a vampire novel. They all turned me down!" Timothy shoved the letter in James's face. "This one editor said I wrote the most unbelievable vampire story he ever read, so I called him and told him I'm really a vampire and it's all true."

"Timothy!" James yelled so loudly the window rattled in its frame. "How could you do that after everything that's happened? Don't you have any sense in your head?"

"Relax, James. The editor didn't believe me. He laughed and said writers are all alike. Whenever someone criticizes our work we claim it really happened."

James slumped into his chair and turned toward the open window. He leaned his head outside, allowing the night bay breeze to cool him. "It's for the best," he said finally. "We need to stay as far away from the word vampire as we can right now."

"I just wanted to share my story," Timothy said. "I don't understand a lot about the world, James, especially now, and writing helps me make sense of things, you know?"

James nodded. "I know, Timothy. But there's no rush. This madness will blow over, all madness does, and then you can try again. And you still learned about yourself from your experience writing the book. You don't lose that wisdom."

As Timothy left, James looked at the time on his cell phone and saw it was library closing time. He went to turn down his computer and saw a new link from Howard. What now, he wondered? When he saw the comment on the *New York Times* blog he blinked once, twice. But it was still there. Even if he sent the screen crashing through his office window to smash on the pavement outside the words would still be etched into his brain, tattooed, leaving their imprints. Forever.

I've read the posts from the haters bashing Kenneth Hempel saying he was a loser who deserved to die for the stupid stuff he said. Here's my two cents. My sister is an orderly at Salem Hospital and she says she's been providing blood for a real vampire for over a year now. When she first told me that I freaked, but then she said how she got him donated blood from the blood bank and he never hurt her, not even a bit. Never tried to sneak a bite, I asked? Not once, she said. She was very casual about it, like it was no big deal, he was no big deal, yeah he's a vampire, whatever, and that's that. My sister is smart (she goes to college and everything) and if she says vampires are no big deal then I believe her. Suck on that haters!

After they arrived home and put Grace to bed, James showed Sarah the clip about Hempel's murder and the comment on the *New York Times* blog. She watched and read, nodding at nothing in particular, trying to absorb it all. James kissed her forehead and watched her with all his intensity.

"Perhaps I shouldn't have told you," he said.

"Yes, you should have. Everyone everywhere is talking about vampires. In the grocery store. In the doctor's office. Every book on vampires has been checked out of the library, and there's a waiting list two months long. Every computer I walk past someone is on a vampire website. Every conversation I hear in the halls is about vampires."

James stroked her face from her temple to her chin. "Let them talk. The police questioned Timothy for ten minutes and left. No one is taking this seriously."

Sarah nodded. She wanted to be convinced, but then she felt the slithering iron chains lurking behind her as though ready to snap at her like a King Cobra. She hadn't seen the chains since the past-life regression, but for a moment they were there again, mocking her, ready to drag her away. James lifted her chin with his hand and kissed her frown away. She closed her eyes, straightening the words out in her mind. Finally, she said, "You can't get blood from Salem Hospital anymore."

"No."

"And you won't drink from me."

"No."

"Where will you go?"

"Jennifer knows someone at the General Hospital."

"She's also the one who found Amy."

"Amy's sister didn't mean any harm. She was trying to say vampires were all right."

"She was a little too specific."

"Perhaps. But there's no reason to connect her comment to me."

"I know."

James shook his head. "You don't believe me."

"I do...I want to...I just..."

"I know, honey. I know."

Grace cried from her crib and James carried her into the great room, sitting with her on the sofa, rocking her, soothing her. When Sarah joined them, Grace smiled, yawned, and patted her father's shoulder. James held her close and kissed her cheek. Sarah put her arms around them both, struggling to control the shaking that rattled her bones from her marrow to her joints. A whisper, an incoherent mumble, words of caution she couldn't quite make out—what were they saying? She thought she was being warned, about what she didn't know, but she guessed from the way James avoided her gaze he felt it too.

It's midnight. Do you know where your favorite celebs are?

Tom Hardison, star of the movie *Every Damn Way*, has been spotted at night, every night, and only at night. One of our reporters cornered him outside his favorite club at three a.m. this morning.

"Out late again, huh, Tom?"

"Yeah. Whatever."

"You've been looking kind of thin and pale lately. When's the last time you've eaten? And you're only out at night."

"What?"

"We never see you during the day. Do you sleep during the day?"

"Yeah, dude, I'm a vampire like everyone says."

Hardison is just one more name in the new trend to "out" certain celebrities as vampires. According to sources close to his latest film, when Hardison wasn't on the closed set of the soundstage he demanded all exterior windows be covered with heavy curtains during the day, claiming it was hard on his eyes. Others stated that Hardison was never seen with the cast at lunch, always choosing to stay in his darkened trailer, alone.

"He was always so pale, and when I touched his hand he was so cold," said one source. "I don't know. Maybe with all the talk about vampires these days people are expecting them to be real. He might be a vampire for all I know."

What do we know about the guy? Based on what we've seen, he's either a vampire—or stoned. Maybe it's hard to tell the difference.

CHAPTER FIFTEEN

Marissa Tillis.
Manny Santiago.
James Wentworth.
Ned Zuckerman.
Rachael Morgan.

There it was. His black-word name on the white-paper list released by who-knows-who, someone with access to the yellow legal pads in Hempel's closet. The reports did state that Hempel had no plans to go forth with these names. For whatever reason, Hempel was less convinced about these individuals than the ones he made public. When James saw the look on Sarah's face as she scanned the newspaper and saw his name, he realized he didn't know what to say to soothe her. He had been so careful for those long three centuries, moving on whenever he had an inkling anyone found him odd. He had become mistrustful after he was turned, taking great pains to hide his preternatural truth from nearly everyone. But now wherever he went he felt eyes on him, that neon arrow he imagined hovering a foot above his head, pointing him out in flashing lights. Bloodsucker. Monster. Villain. Evil.

Vampire.

When word started getting around the university, others stepped around the topic. They didn't believe it the way they didn't believe the accusations against anyone else, and James realized they felt sorry for him.

"But Professor Wentworth is a nice family man," neighbors said to inquisitive reporters. "He's married to a lovely young woman, a librarian, and they have a new baby. He's been at the college about two years now. I hear he's well respected there."

One neighbor, a retired man, went on the local news standing in front of the wooden gabled house. "I used to think this place was haunted because it's so old," the neighbor said, "but now I know Mr. Wentworth is just a regular guy with a family and a job at the college."

On campus, James made a conscious effort to remove the bulls-eye he felt nailed to his forehead. He had to put the flashing neon sign aside. If a student on campus yelled, "Hey Doctor Wentworth, someone called you a vampire. Isn't that crazy?" he'd nod and agree. If another professor said, "Look out, Professor Wentworth's going to bite your neck!" he'd laugh.

But as the nights passed he felt the shift. When he walked the corridors of Meier Hall, he'd hear students whisper, "They say Professor Wentworth is a vampire." When they saw him they'd stop talking.

Two weeks after his name was printed in the paper his Shakespeare seminar was half-empty. He brushed it off as midterm blues and taught as usual. As he walked back to the library, he looked at the students, many rushing past to their next class, deep in their conversations or solitary and absorbed in the music blasting from their earbuds. He thought they wouldn't look him in the eye, but he dismissed that too. Not everything is about you, James, he thought. They're too busy living their lives to worry about you. In the library he passed a few professors, and where normally they'd exchange pleasantries, the usual 'How are you? I'm fine. How are you? I'm struggling along, you know,' that night they hurried past, their eyes focused on the other end of the hall.

The night after his Shakespeare seminar James let himself into his office, and he relaxed when he smelled strawberries and cream wafting down the hall. Sarah peeked around his open door, her eyes ringed red from tears.

"What's wrong, honey?"

Sarah walked into the office, looked down the hall, and closed the door behind her. "I think I'm becoming paranoid," she said.

"What happened?"

"I think Miss Nancy is suspicious of us."

"Miss Nancy?"

"I'm sure she gave me a strange look when I dropped Grace off tonight. She sounded all right, but there was something odd in her manner. Then she took Grace and walked into the classroom like she always does and everything seemed fine. Am I going crazy? Miss Nancy has never been anything but wonderful to us."

"We're both hypersensitive to this accusation thing."

"I know, but I made a decision tonight. I want to quit the library, James. I want to stay home with Grace."

"Whatever you want, Sarah."

"You don't mind?"

"Mind? I think it's the best decision for us right now."

Sarah smiled. Her shoulders lowered from her ears and she breathed easier. She threw her arms around James's neck and kissed him. "I knew I had the best husband in the world." She kissed him again. "I'll give Jennifer my two-week notice when I get downstairs." She kissed him again. "I love you."

"I love you more."

Sarah nearly skipped away, she looked so happy. James sat at his desk looking out at the wet night. The spring was new, yet even under the damp sky in the streams of moonlight he could hear the whispers of budding grass. He left for his vampire literature class, wondering if it would be any fuller than his Shakespeare seminar.

He walked into a full class and exhaled loudly, not for show but with relief. He heard two girls sitting by the window laughing at what idiots people could be.

"How can anyone believe Doctor Wentworth of all people is a vampire?" said the girl with short blond hair.

"How can anyone believe vampires really exist?" said the girl with long blond hair. When they saw James walk to the instructor's desk everyone stopped talking. James thought they looked at him the way Kenneth Hempel had, waiting for the one reaction that would prove once and for all the professor was of the paranormal persuasion. He scanned the faces and didn't see Timothy. That's probably for the best, he thought.

"Hey, Doctor Wentworth," Levon called. "I was afraid you wouldn't show."

"I have no reason not to come. I have a responsibility to do my job, and my job is teaching this class."

"Can you believe how gullible some people are?" said the bearded young man. "Now everyone is looking for vampires."

"I know too well how gullible people can be," James said. "Where did we leave off last time?"

"We were talking about the Eastern European vampire legends and how they contributed to Bram Stoker's writing *Dracula*," Brent said. He was no longer white-looking. He wore a long gray t-shirt under a sky-blue t-shirt instead of black on black. His hair was no longer dyed jet black but a natural chestnut hue.

"You look different," James said.

"I decided it's not much fun being a vampire now. Isn't it true, Doctor Wentworth? It's not much fun being a vampire now?"

James looked at Brent, his face hard, unwilling to let the young man see the fear he sparked. The others held themselves still like curious statues, afraid to breathe lest they miss the professor's response.

"Brent," James said, "you know there's no such thing as vampires. That's what this class is about, studying the literature that's come from the mythology."

"You have pale bluish skin like the cadaver we dissected in science lab. Black eyes. No one sees you during the day. Every other professor I have comes into class with their coffee cups."

"Are you saying I'm not human because I'm pale and have dark eyes? Because I don't like coffee?"

"You were on that list for a reason. No smoke without fire."

"You're so wrong about that," James said.

"He wears glasses," said Levon. "How many vampires do you know who need glasses?"

"Anyone can put on a pair of glasses," said Brent.

"Someone needs to knock some sense into that fool," said Levon. "This dude is seriously nuts." Levon stood, his athletic frame strong and powerful, and he pointed at Brent. "Haven't you seen Doctor Wentworth's wife and daughter? He's a college professor. How many vampires do you know who teach for a living?"

James put his hand on Levon's shoulder. "It's all right," he said. "Let him be."

Another student, a young lady wearing a blue hoodie with SSU in orange letters on the front, raised her hand.

"Yes, Rachel?"

"I was reading about some of the earlier vampire legends and I saw something about the Lilu but I couldn't find much information about them. Were the Lilu vampires?"

James could have kissed the girl for changing the subject. "Stories about the Lilu date from Babylonian times," he said. "The Lilu were believed to be female demons who killed pregnant women and newborns. One demon, Lilitu, was adapted into Hebrew demonology, and she's called the mother of all vampires."

"I'm doing my presentation on Ancient Egyptian vampires," said Levon. "Sekhmet was an Ancient Egyptian vampire who slaughtered humans for their blood. That's where the idea that vampires could be killed by a stake through the heart came from."

"Can a vampire be killed by a state through the heart?" Brent asked.

"That's what the legends say," James said.

"The name of this class is 'The Curse of the Vampire.' Do you believe vampires are cursed?"

James wouldn't back down. He had walked through the fire, barefoot to the other side, when he braved the sunlight to beat back one vampire hunter. He wouldn't be swayed by the petulant boy in his classroom.

"Every vampire legend is based on the idea that the undead are touched by evil," James said. "That's how the legends explain the vampire's strength, agility, ability to live after they die."

"You didn't answer my question. Do you, Doctor James Wentworth, believe vampires are cursed?"

"If vampires were real, then yes, I believe the only way they could live as they do would be if they were cursed."

"Are they cursed by Satan?"

"Let's hope not."

"Cursed by evil?"

"I don't know."

"So vampires aren't evil? What's the curse then?"

"Wait..." Levon held up his cell phone. "I just looked up the word 'curse.' It means to swear an oath or wish evil on someone. It also means an evil prayer, an invocation of evil or misfortune, or a formula or charm intended to cause harm."

"Girls used to call their periods The Curse," Rachel said.

The class laughed.

James scanned the young faces, some of whom would never believe the truth about vampires—it was too impossible, they'd say—but others would believe too readily. He wanted Brent, the list with his name, this whole mess to go away. He wanted to shout, "I have a wife, the light of my life, whom I love, whom I have loved every night for over three hundred years! You cannot imagine how I love her. And I have a daughter, also my daughter for over three hundred years, and she is our family's glue. I would never hurt you!"

But James saw the problems that would come from such a confession. He saw compassion in some faces, understanding in others, but he also saw concern, perhaps even distrust or fear in a few. Could they see the confusion Brent's prodding had brought on?

James didn't notice the student filming him on her cell phone. Even with his pinpoint instincts he didn't see the camera pointed at him or the flashing red light. The next day Jennifer e-mailed him the clip she noticed over a student's shoulder as she watched it on YouTube in the library. The caption said 'Vampire Teaching at Salem State University.' The video itself was not particularly incriminating. He was teaching, that was all, but there he was, his pale-as-death complexion, glaring white against his hunter green button-down shirt, his eyes too dark even under his wire-frame glasses, and there, for all the world to see, is the clear concern everywhere in his face from Brent's persistent questions.

I am a vampire, James thought. And now all the world knows it.

He was a nice-looking young man, sandy-blond hair, pleasant smile. He was also a dead-looking young man with an ice-blue tone to his ghost-white complexion, and his death-black eyes looked wrong against his boyish features. He sat straight in his chair, his broad shoulders firm, looking the interviewer in the eye as he spoke. He had a calm, earnest voice with the hint of authority that comes with living a long time. He wore a brown jacket over a white button-down shirt. He was fresh-faced and handsome, like a young Hollywood actor come to promote his newest film. He explained how he was turned into a vampire when he was twenty-eight years old.

"You're trying to tell me you're one hundred and twenty-two years old?" the interviewer asked. The interviewer had been around awhile and looked past the century mark himself.

"I am," the young-looking man said.

"And how were you made into…into…?"

"A vampire?" The young-looking man laughed. "I was turned in 1918 when I was returning home from serving in World War I. I was staying with friends in Massachusetts until I returned to my family in Kansas. I was outside smoking a cigarette when suddenly I was attacked."

"How were you attacked?"

"That part of the legend is true, I'm afraid. He bit my neck and fed from my blood."

"So you were attacked, and then what happened?"

"Then I fell unconscious. When I woke up I was as I am now."

"And the family you were returning to…"

"My wife and three young sons."

"And you never saw them again?"

"No, sir. I didn't think I should impose myself on them, being as I am. I didn't want my boys to suffer because their father was so changed."

"Were you afraid you were going to hurt them?"

"No, sir. They were my family. Contrary to popular belief, we don't have to hurt anyone, especially our own families. But things were different then."

"How so?"

"People were...not as accepting of differences as they are now. I was afraid bad things would happen to my family if they harbored someone like me."

The interviewer pressed his square-shaped glasses against his nose and shuffled the papers in front of him. "So you, Martin Helms, a man who appears to be in his late twenties, wants me to believe he's a vampire who's one hundred and twenty-two years old who didn't return to his family because he was afraid of what would happen to them if people found a vampire in their home?"

"That's right, sir."

"If you're really as old as you say you are, I ought to be calling you sir, not the other way around. So why are you going public now? What's changed?"

"People are learning the truth about my kind. They're afraid and they don't need to be. Everywhere I look these days I see people debating the pros and cons of vampires, the truth and consequences, some still wondering if we're real or not. I want people to understand they don't need to fear us. We're contributing members of society. We're doctors, lawyers, writers, dentists, teachers, bankers, actors, police officers, professors. We own homes. We pay taxes. We're law-abiding citizens. Many have families, and some have even intermarried with humans. Most of what people know about vampires is fiction and should be treated that way."

"Do you really believe people are more accepting now than they were then?"

The vampire thought before he answered. "I hope so."

"How have you and others like you managed to stay secret all this time?"

"We haven't been all that secret. Many of the legends sprang from some kernel of truth that's been twisted and turned over the years. For whatever reason, God has decided that now is the time for everyone to learn the truth."

"God or Kenneth Hempel, the murdered reporter."

"God. Kenneth Hempel was simply His instrument."

"Do you believe in God?"

"I do."

"How could you? Don't vampires work for the Devil?"

"I hope not, sir, because I've never met any devil, though I've met enough devilish humans to last all my lifetimes. But I feel God in my life every day."

"You're telling me vampires aren't Satan's spawns?"

"I'm no one's spawn, sir. I'm only me, Martin Helms, and I am what I am, and that's a vampire. I'm here with you tonight because I want people to know I mean them no harm. I come in peace and love, to bring understanding between our peoples."

The interviewer crossed his arms in front of his chest, looking at Martin a long moment before he spoke. The tension spilled across the studio, through the cameras, into the eyes of the millions watching.

"Have you ever killed anyone, Mr. Helms?"

"I'd prefer to not answer that question."

"It's a simple yes or no answer."

"I'd prefer to not answer that question."

"By refusing to answer you're implying that you have killed people."

"I do not recollect killing anyone."

"Then how do you find blood to live? Is that another myth about vampires, that they need blood to live?"

"No, that is another myth with basis in truth. We do need blood to live. However, it doesn't have to be human blood. And many vampires find humane ways to feed."

"Such as?"

"Such as donated blood."

"From the hospital?"

"That's one place a vampire can find donated blood."

"Where else?"

"It's hard for me to say. It's different for each vampire."

"You must have a place where you get blood."

"I assure you I feed myself without hurting anyone in the process."

"Can vampires hypnotize people into giving their blood?"

"No, sir. That's on television."

"You said many vampires find humane ways to feed. Does that mean other vampires don't find humane ways to feed?"

"I can't speak for all vampires in the world because I don't know every vampire. Just as you can't speak for the humanity of every person in the world. I can only speak for the vampires I know, and I can say unequivocally they harm no one to feed themselves."

"Do some vampires murder humans for their blood?"

Martin Helms paused. "That's not for me to say," he said.

"So there are some vampires we should fear?"

"Sir, I was a sergeant overseas during World War I. You wouldn't believe the horrific sights I saw. Trench warfare is ugly. Read Wilfred Owen's poem 'Dulce et Decorum Est' if you don't believe me. If you look at human history and see man's inhumanity to man, I think a few rogue vampires…"

Martin stopped midsentence. In the flash of a flicker of white concern in his black eyes he showed the world he knew he said too much.

CHAPTER SIXTEEN

The next night James walked into the great room to see the blinds still drawn, the blackout curtains closed, the room left in eerie shadows that echoed the darkness outside. Sarah sat on the sofa, her eyes darting from James to the front door to the window and back to James, a quiet but alert Grace in her arms. Olivia, Jennifer, and Chandresh stood along the wall glancing uneasily at each other while Timothy hovered close to Howard.

"Here's James," Sarah said. "Oversleeping as usual."

She tried to smile but her lips quivered. James stopped midstep, his head tilted, listening until he made out the footsteps, the voices, and the clicking cameras outside.

"What is it?" he asked. No one answered. "Sarah, what's wrong? Who's outside?"

"Everyone," Olivia said, the weariness weighing down her voice. She slapped her hand in the air like she was shooing them all away. "Reporters. Photographers. Tourists. Busybodies."

"They want to see the vampire's house," Jennifer said.

"This is ridiculous," James said. "I'm telling them to leave."

"Don't," Sarah said. "When I opened the door to let Olivia in they rushed the house, shouting questions, snapping pictures. She barely made it inside."

"How many are there?" James asked.

"Not that many," said Howard. "Maybe fifty."

"Only fifty? What a relief." James paced to the door and reached for the knob, his hand hanging midair until he dropped it. His agitation shimmered outward and he quaked. "They can't stay there," he said.

"Sarah's right," Olivia said. "If you go out you'll only make it worse."

"Look at the mess Hempel made," said Jennifer.

153

Chandresh took her hand. "This is what he wanted, and he wasn't going to stop until he got it. Now we have to figure out how to make this right."

"Can this ever be right?" Howard asked.

"You'd be amazed at what some people can overcome," Chandresh said. "Not only overcome, but rise above and become better afterward."

Jennifer smiled at her strong-armed, doe-eyed man, and he kissed her cheek.

When no one left the wooden gabled house by midnight, the crowd dwindled away. Timothy peeked around the blackout curtains as the last of the lookie-loos disappeared.

"Maybe we should just confess," Timothy said.

"Why can't you understand, Timothy..."

"No, James, listen. I wanted to confess to Hempel last year, but you talked me out of it. I wrote a book about being a vampire that was turned down by every publisher and you told me it was for the best. But what if you're wrong? What if we add our voices to this new vampire song everyone is singing? Everyone's talking about the Vampire Dawn. We should too."

"And then we'll sit around the campfire singing 'Kumbaya' and join hands and swear eternal friendship." The sarcasm stretched James's voice thin. "That's not how it works, Timothy. We haven't seen the repercussions from this Vampire Dawn because it's too new. But it will come, and the humans won't be as accepting as you keep wanting to believe."

Timothy's pale cheek flushed hot with frustration. "Guess what, James—your way didn't work. Your name's in the paper, and so is mine, and so is Chandresh's, and so is Jocelyn's and there was just a crowd of people outside your door. We can't hide any more. We need to help people understand they don't need to fear us."

"Listen to James, Timothy," Howard said. He put a fatherly hand on his son's shoulder, but Timothy shook him away.

"No, Dad, I've been listening to James and everyone still found out about us. Every night more of us are coming out, and it's time to join them."

"Who else is coming out?" Olivia asked.

"There's that television show tomorrow night," Jennifer said. "A vampire is submitting himself for a medical examination in front of a live studio audience. It's been all over the news."

James dropped his head into his hands. "Doesn't he know the problems he's going to cause for us after he's proven to be dead?"

"We were human once," Chandresh said. "We have the same foibles and weaknesses. We want to feel important. We want recognition as a way to feel like we matter."

"Now is their chance to get the attention they've had to deny themselves," Olivia said. "All the world will be watching."

"That's what I'm afraid of," James said.

The event boasted more viewers than the Academy Awards or the Super Bowl. Millions were glued to their television sets or their computer screens as one vampire, a two hundred and ten year-old named Justin, who looked around nineteen with longish hair the color of the setting sun and eyes like intense coals, sat on the examination table. Justin had agreed to medical tests in front of the world. This was it, the commercials had promised. If you want to know once and for all if the legends are true, then watch—8:00 p.m. tonight, 7 Central.

As promised, Thursday at 8 p.m. three medical doctors from Yale, Harvard, and Johns Hopkins University hooked Justin to hospital monitors so they could tests his heartbeat, his breath, his temperature, his pulse. One camera closed in on a gray-haired, gray-bearded doctor with Justin's wrist in his hand.

"There's no pulse," the doctor said. He spoke loudly, as though he needed to hear his own words.

"There's no heartbeat," said another doctor. His words sounded like a question.

The third doctor, the oldest of the three, his wisdom in his benevolent smile, said, "There's no doubt in my mind that this man isn't alive, at least not in any traditional sense. Look here." He gestured at the flat-line monitor. "He has no breath, no heartbeat, no temperature and therefore no warmth to his skin." He shook his head, his hand on his cheek, and the camera close-up caught a line of sweat beads on his upper lip. "These results prove beyond a shadow of a doubt that this man's body is dead. As a man of science, I never believed this day would come. This is truly miraculous."

"Are you declaring this man dead?" a reporter asked.

"This man is dead, yet he walks. It's impossible, but it's true."

A close-up showed the monitors and their wires, as though the news director needed to prove that everything was plugged in, the power came from the electrical socket in the wall, the ends touching Justin. No editing tricks here. This man was dead. There was even a live studio audience, and random people were chosen to listen through the stethoscope, touch Justin's wrist, watch his unmoving chest. As people became convinced of Justin's preternatural condition they ran away screaming, or burst into tears, or quivered in their seats. Others expanded like puffer birds, unafraid. One woman in the audience stood and said, "I'm not afraid. He looks like my grandson." Another woman said, "This is the work of the Devil. Only Satan could conjure something so hideous." Someone else shouted "What's so hideous about that baby-faced boy?"

An elderly man yelled at Justin. "Why are you here? You don't need to parade what you are for all the world to see. Why don't you keep it to yourself and let the rest of us live in peace?"

"There's nothing wrong with what I am," Justin said. He didn't look annoyed. He looked the elderly man in the eye.

"What you are is an abomination before God."

"The truth is, sir, I don't know why I am the way I am, or even how I came to be this way. But I cannot change my nature. I am what I am."

A woman pointed at the boyish-looking vampire. "I see the coldness, the murder in your eyes," she said. "All you want is my death."

Justin looked at the floor, his eyes small in concentration, his hands folded in his lap. He would find the right words. Finally, he shook his head.

"I don't wish for your blood or your death, ma'am. I know this is hard to accept. The existence of my kind doesn't seem natural. I wish you peace, ma'am. That's all."

"Dead is dead," another man said. "They should be buried six feet under and left to rot with the other corpses."

"The whole world has gone mad," a woman said to the television camera. "If you believe vampires are real, I have some oceanside property in Kansas I want to sell you."

The cameras pulled back, and the doctors crowded Justin, hands stretched out, grasping as though they were the mortally ill needing the faith healer who might fix them. They asked questions, and the young-looking man answered as well as he could. He didn't know the answers to all their questions himself. Finally, he said, "It's magic."

A woman shouted "Hallelujah!"

Fade to black.

Suddenly, people weren't hiding their fear. It was all too familiar to Sarah, who had felt the same nail-chewing friction in 1692. The same kind of far-reaching fear. She saw it in the way people's eyes darted left and right in the grocery store. She saw it in their tapping legs and high shoulders in the post office. She even saw it in the library, where people avoided her entirely. She had given her two-week notice to Jennifer, and she would be leaving soon anyway, but it hurt her, this sudden invisibility among people she had been friendly with for over a year.

Even before moving to Salem, Sarah had never revealed much of herself to anyone. She always had friends, but she never felt a part of anything. She kept her own counsel, and she gave nothing away so others would have nothing to reproach her with. Not that she didn't have a caring, loving heart, but she spent most of her life hiding it, keeping it safe in the locked cage of her chest, where no one could take it away or break it. Since the past-life regression the year before, she realized her cautious nature as Sarah was a result of her experience as Elizabeth. When James came into her life again her walls came tumbling down, only now she wondered if she needed to erect them again.

Sarah comforted herself with the thought that she was paranoid, that's all. They're thoughts in your head, she'd say to herself, problems you're creating in your own mind. And then someone, then someone else, and someone else again, would pass her with eyes straight ahead, staring at something that wasn't there, not acknowledging the space she occupied. They no longer held the library doors open for her. One librarian, a scowling, dark-haired elf in glasses and permanently collapsed lips, not only wouldn't acknowledge Sarah when they arrived at the same time but she walked faster so she could get into the library without worrying about such niceties as polite greetings. Normally, the elf managed at least a terse nod when Sarah said good morning. Again, Sarah tried to convince herself she worried too much, but she also decided she should be ready for anything. She would hope for the best and expect the worst. She wouldn't be caught unprepared by the madness ever again.

Her last night in the library was quiet. It was Spring Break, and the library echoed with the absence of bodies to fill the space. She sat behind the librarians's desk and looked around at the industrial-style space with large windows and overhead beams, the bright fluorescent lights, the gray and blue chairs scattered around the computer terminals or the study desks, the stacks of books stretching wall to wall. The library would always hold a special place in her heart. This job prompted her journey across the country from Los Angeles to Salem. This was where she saw James the first time after their awkward encounter in front of the wooden gabled house. This was where they became friends, he sharing tales about Salem in 1692 and she only too pleased to listen. This was the very desk where she sat where he presented her with a book of Anne Bradstreet's poems and they recited "To My Dear and Loving Husband" together. Sarah frowned when she thought how it was just above this room, in James's office on the third floor, where he confronted Kenneth Hempel in the full light of the spring sun.

Jennifer came out from her office and sat in the swivel chair beside Sarah. "What's wrong?" she asked.

"Your witch's intuition," Sarah said. "When I first met you I always wondered how you knew what I needed before I knew I needed it."

"My mother is better at it than I am."

"I know."

Jennifer followed Sarah's gaze across the empty room. "Feeling nostalgic?" she asked.

Sarah nodded. "This library has been the center of my life as long as I've lived here."

"Now the center of your life is in your home with your husband and daughter."

Sarah felt the deep-seeded joy flush her cheeks hot. "Yes," she said. But the joy fled and left her cold at the thought of what was happening in the world outside. "What's going to happen, Jennifer? How is this going to end?"

Jennifer looked away, and for a flicker Sarah thought she saw fear in her friend's hazel eyes.

"What is it?" Sarah asked. "What do you know?"

Jennifer shook her head. "I don't know anything, Sarah. I'm as worried as you are."

"Did Chandresh tell you something?"

"Chandresh hasn't told me a thing. He's as close-mouthed as your husband. Come on, Mrs. Wentworth." She took Sarah's hand and led her out from behind the librarians's desk. "Cough up the keys. They're no longer yours."

Sarah took the blue and orange Salem State University lanyard from around her neck and handed it to Jennifer. She felt like she was giving away a piece of herself. Jennifer unhooked the keys and handed Sarah back the lanyard. "Keep this," she said. "A memento."

Sarah clasped the lanyard in her hands. "I'll cherish it, but I do have other mementos. I have you, your mother..."

"And James."

Sarah smiled. "And James."

Jennifer looked at the time on the clock on the wall. "We better go. We don't want to be late to your celebration."

"Celebration?"

"Didn't I tell you? We're having a get-together at Jocelyn's tonight. You know how we Wiccans like to celebrate the solstice and the equinox, the autumn harvest and the winter moon. Now we're celebrating your New Spring, Sarah. This is your time."

"My time for what?"

Jennifer flipped off the lights, set the alarm, and locked the door as they walked outside. "We'll have to see," she said.

They walked arm-in-arm down Lafayette into Marblehead toward the childcare center, their conversation dotted with the shrieks and giggles of girlfriends.

"I'll never forget the look on your face when you saw James looking at you through the window in the library that first time. You looked like you'd seen a ghost."

"I thought I had seen a ghost. Here I am minding my own business getting ready for a seminar and suddenly there he was staring right through me. I felt like he knew everything about me."

"He did."

"I didn't understand it at the time. I only knew I felt drawn to him."

Sarah clutched Jennifer's arm tighter. She shivered in the evening air, the heavy breeze from the bay still adding a nip in March. There were buds and blooms ready to sprout, spots of color here, more green there. They crossed the street and walked up the short hill toward Primary Time Child Care and Preschool.

"Should I call James and tell him to meet us at Jocelyn's?" Sarah asked.

"He already knows."

"So everyone knew but me?"

"Exactly."

"Is your mother cooking? I love your mother's cooking."

"You don't think I'd let Jocelyn take care of the meal for us, do you? I don't think she's cooked in over fifty years."

As Sarah opened the door to the Victorian-style house she saw Miss Nancy by the front bay window staring out as though she were looking for someone. When her eyes lit up Sarah realized Miss Nancy was waiting for her.

"Miss Candice," Miss Nancy called, moving her eyes from Sarah to scan Jennifer. "Mrs. Wentworth is here. Bring Grace and her belongings, please."

Miss Candice was a large woman with short arms and cascades of black hair who appeared with Grace in one arm and a pink backpack in the other. Grace wasn't crying, but she looked upset somehow, or worried, or...Sarah wasn't sure. She clutched Grace to her heart, stroking her daughter's gold curls from her topaz eyes, kissing her forehead. Grace clutched Sarah's neck and buried her face away. Miss Candice held the pink backpack out as though handing month-old laundry to the maid who didn't do her job. Jennifer took the bag and wrinkled her nose at Sarah.

"What's wrong?" Sarah asked.

"We put children first at Primary Time, Mrs. Wentworth. We're concerned for the welfare of the children."

"What do you mean?"

Miss Nancy looked at Miss Candice, who nodded. Miss Nancy paused as she considered her words. "We think it would be best if Grace didn't come back. We don't believe we're the best place for a...child of her kind."

"How could you ask this little girl to leave your school?" Jennifer asked. "What has she done?"

"She hasn't done anything. Yet."

"Yet?" Jennifer was yelling now. "What do you mean yet?"

"She means," Miss Candice said, "she may bite the other children."

Sarah shielded Grace from the impossible women and backed toward the door. "My daughter doesn't bite," she said.

"Now you listen here..." Jennifer glared at the women, trying to cut them with the bilious look in her eyes, but they were haughty in their self-righteousness. Sarah touched Jennifer's arm and shook her head. She knew they weren't worth the energy it would take to find the right words, but even as she walked away she wanted to knock some sense into them. She wanted them to understand how special Grace was, how far she had come to find her way home. She wanted to make them feel as small as she felt. She wanted to scream. She wanted to rage. She wanted to bring the fury of the heavens down on them, but their smugness stopped her cold.

She held back the tears until they crossed the quiet road. Jennifer followed, holding the pink backpack, the anger still etching lines between her brows. At Jocelyn's yellow house Sarah saw everyone through the window, and as soon as she saw them she knew something was wrong. At first, she thought they knew what happened to Grace, but that couldn't be right—there was no way for them to know. Steve opened the door, and Sarah saw his red-rimmed eyes. Chandresh stood behind him, and he looked worried too.

"Oh no," Jennifer said. "What's wrong?"

"Come here, Grace," Olivia said as she took the baby into her arms. "Let's go into the next room and see Billy. He has a wonderful new ball we can play with." As they walked away, Grace began babbling, nonsense syllables as babies do, but it sounded to Sarah like she was trying to tell Olivia what happened at Primary Time. Maybe Grace can explain it better than I can, she thought. Then she saw James's shadow before she saw him. At first, she thought she was seeing things, a dark silhouette moving on its own accord with a life of its own, a blank space shaped like her husband only he wasn't there. She shuddered at the thought of emptiness where her husband should be, and when he stepped into the light she sighed with stilted fear. He was there, it was all right, but she had a sudden fear that the next morning she would wake up in an empty bed, no dear and loving husband beside her. James took her into his arms, but even as she pressed herself into him she was afraid she was dreaming him. When her tears soaked his shirt through he bent down so he could see into her eyes.

"What is it, Sarah? What's wrong?"

"They won't watch Grace anymore."

"Who won't?"

"Primary Time. They said they're afraid she's going to bite someone."

James looked at Jocelyn, who was sitting at the dining room table, her shoulders slumped, her head bowed. Sarah looked at the pretty red-haired vampire, a wife and mother who went nights to the poorer areas around Boston fixing the teeth of those who couldn't afford dental work, and she realized her friend had been crying, her cheeks stained red with sadness. Steve held his wife's hand while he brushed her heavy tears away with the back of his hand.

"Jocelyn," Sarah said. "What happened?"

James shook his head. "Things are wrong all over."

Olivia came into the kitchen with Grace on one hip and Billy on the other, her eyes watery. The coins of her gypsy-style earrings clinked, adding a dancing sound mismatched to the somber mood.

"Some horrible person threw a brick covered in blood through Jocelyn's office window," she said. "She was filling a patient's cavity when the glass shattered and the brick landed at her feet."

"Oh my God," Jennifer said.

"I heard the footsteps outside, but I didn't pay attention," Jocelyn said. "There are restaurants nearby so there usually are people around at night. I had just turned the dental drill on when the brick crashed through and nearly hit me. It looked like a downpour of glass splinters."

Jennifer took a cloth from a drawer, ran it under the tap, and wiped the blood from Jocelyn's face.

"I've been a dentist here for four years," Jocelyn said. "Patients who hadn't been to the dentist in decades came to me, frightened, but they came because someone told them I would take care of them. Maureen was the first client I've had in two weeks. After the brick nearly hit her she jumped out of the chair, grabbed her bag, and ran away." The fresh blood tears streaked her white complexion pink. Steve smoothed his wife's hair and kissed her cheek.

"Steve said there was a message taped to the brick," James said. "What did it say?"

Jocelyn shook her head. "It doesn't matter."

"Did they threaten you?"

Steve forced a smile that looked wrong on his unshaven cheeks. "'No vamps allowed,'" he said. "Not so bad, right?"

Chandresh hovered near James, whispering, intent. As James listened he paced the floor of the narrow kitchen, the rubber soles of his black Converse shoes squeaking on the hard wood floor. Sarah watched his fingers tap a quick-time tune on his blue jeans while he nodded in response to Chandresh's words.

"What will you do, Jocelyn?" Olivia asked.

Jocelyn shook her head. "Leave Salem?"

"And go where?" James asked. The overtone in his voice made Sarah think he had considered the question himself and hadn't found a suitable answer.

And go where, Sarah wondered? To Boston? California? Singapore? Brazil? Where could they go to make a new home if they couldn't stay in this one any more?

They walked home in silence, James and Sarah holding hands while James clutched Grace close with his other arm. The final winter chills were finally blowing away from the bay. It was a clear night, the sky black, the stars white, the neighborhood silent, the houses dark. The grass, the bushes, the leaves were budding every shade of green again, but nothing looked real to Sarah. She looked at the familiar surroundings, and the historic buildings, the museums, the restaurants were unreal, like she was dreaming them too. She felt the strength of James's heatless hand as it wrapped tightly around hers. He must have sensed she needed to walk, or he needed to walk too, and he led her past Derby Street toward the Essex Street Pedestrian Mall, past the Artists Row, long closed for the night, down the small streets of gift shops, the pharmacy, the center for the Peabody-Essex Museum, the main stop for the red trolley car she took around town when she first moved there. This was where she visited the Farmer's Market on Thursdays during the warmer months to buy her produce and bread. This was where she stopped for frozen yogurt with her mother when she visited from Boston. Across the street, on the other side of Route 114 was Lappin Park, the landscaped corner where the bronze statue of Elizabeth Montgomery as the Bewitched Samantha sat. That was where she had walked with James on the first steps of their journey together.

She needed to hear the soothing tones of his voice, so just as she had always done, she asked him questions to get him talking. "What was Chandresh saying to you at Jocelyn's?" she asked.

"He said this situation reminds him of the Trail of Tears."

"How?"

"Whatever story is repeated most often, that's the story people believe. People wanted to believe the Cherokee were bad because that made it all right to take their land. The Cherokee assimilated to American ways, and they did it successfully, but no matter what they did the propaganda against them was so strong there was little they could do to sway public opinion."

"Does Chandresh think public opinion is going to sway against the vampires?"

"It already has, honey." Grace stirred, opened one eye, saw her father, and went back to sleep. James pressed her jacket closer around her little face. "I want to show you something when we get home," he said. "You might find it interesting."

They continued through the Pedestrian Mall, then crossed New Liberty Street, passed the houses of the Peabody-Essex Museum and Armory Park, turned around the imposing statue of Roger Conant standing tall in the intersection between Brown Street and Washington Square North as he stared over Salem Town like the proud Puritan he was when he founded Salem in 1626. His squinting eyes and his set mouth reminded Sarah of a strict schoolmaster eyeing a classroom of unruly boys. She hadn't known Conant himself, he was seventy years before her time, but there was something about his condescending look that made her shudder. Sarah peeked at Grace, who was still sleeping, oblivious to her parents' midnight jaunt.

"We should take her home," Sarah said.

They headed around the green lawn of Salem Common, deserted in the night, then continued around Washington Square North to Essex Street to Bentley Street to Derby Street then home.

Sarah followed James into Grace's room where he gently removed the baby's shoes and jacket. Sarah took the clips from Grace's gold curls and laid her down on her back. She kissed the top of the curls, and James kissed the cherubic cheeks. Grace didn't stir.

"She sleeps as well as her father," Sarah said. "Nothing wakes her."

"A baby who sleeps well is a good thing."

They slipped into the great room. Sarah looked out the window into the darkness of the waning night. She yawned, it was after one a.m., and James kissed her lips. "You should go to sleep," he said. "It's late."

"What did you want to show me?"

"Of course you remembered."

He took the antique-looking key from his keychain and unlocked the bottom right drawer of his seventeenth century desk. Sarah peeked over his shoulder while he flipped through some files and saw the time-worn papers with his old-fashioned, calligraphy-style handwriting.

"Is that where you keep letters for your girlfriend?" she teased.

James grinned. "Yes. These are letters for my girlfriend." He found what he was looking for—a newspaper clipping—and handed it to Sarah. "Read this," he said.

It gives me pleasure to announce that the benevolent policy of the Government, steadily pursued for thirty years, in relation to the removal of the Indians beyond the white settlements is approaching to a happy consummation.

The consequences of a speedy removal will be important to the United States, to individual States, and to the Indians themselves. It will place a civilized population in large tracts of country now occupied by savage hunters. It will separate the Indians from immediate contact with settlements of whites; free them from the power of the States; enable them to pursue happiness in their own way and under their own rude institutions; will retard the progress of decay, and perhaps cause them gradually, under the protection of the Govern-

ment and through the influence of good counsels, to cast off their savage habits and become an interesting, civilized, and Christian community.

Doubtless it will be painful to leave the graves of their fathers; but what do they do more than our ancestors did or than our children are now doing? To better their condition in an unknown land, our forefathers left all that was dear in earthly objects. Does Humanity weep at these painful separations from everything, animate and inanimate, with which the young heart has become entwined? Far from it. It is rather a source of joy that our country affords scope where our young population may range unconstrained in body or in mind, developing the power and facilities of man in their highest perfection. Can it be cruel in this Government when, by events which it cannot control, the Indian is made discontented in his ancient home to purchase his lands, to give him a new and extensive territory, to pay the expense of his removal, and support him a year in his new abode?

And is it supposed that the wandering savage has a stronger attachment to his home than the settled, civilized Christian? Is it more afflicting to him to leave the graves of his fathers than it is to our brothers and children? The policy of the General Government toward the red man is not only liberal, but generous. He is unwilling to submit to the laws of the States and mingle with their population. To save him from this alternative, or perhaps utter annihilation, the General Government kindly offers him a new home, and proposes to pay the whole expense of his removal and settlement.

Andrew Jackson
President
United States of America

Sarah read the name a second time to be sure she saw it correctly. "The President of the United States wrote this?" she said. James nodded. "Our President would never say anything like this. Would he?"

James shook his head. "I don't know if we've come as far as we think we have, honey." He took Sarah into his arms and held her close a long time, resting his chin on top of her hair, inhaling deeply and basking in the sweetness of strawberries and cream, running his fingers through her curls. She yawned again, and James kissed her forehead. "You should go to bed," he said.

Sarah nodded, too tired to argue. She left James staring out the window, as though he were watching for a torch-bearing mob waving pitchforks, screaming and flashing their fists. She stopped in Grace's room where the baby slept without a care in the world. She sat in the rocking chair and closed her eyes, swaying back and forth. She breathed out deeply, then stilled her breath, concentrating, slowly in, slowly out. She wanted to pray, but she didn't know how. She was born in Boston to lapsed Catholic parents. She wasn't raised in the church. She never went to services. Did she believe in God? She wasn't sure. In her entire life, all thirty-three years of it, she had never thought much about Him, whoever He was. She never considered angels or miracles. She never even considered the reality of past lives—that is, until she learned of her own. When she found James, he became her miracle. That she was his wife Lizzie reborn—to Sarah, that was simply the means through which she found her end—James. She waited, eyes still closed, for the prayer to come. If you need a favor from someone you hardly know, what do you say? How do you ask? But she was desperate. She needed to think there was help out there somewhere. After all, how did she find her way back to James, and how did Grace find her way back to them?

She remembered her life as Elizabeth. In the seventeenth century, you believed in God, and heaven help you should you forget Him for a moment. The Bible was ingrained into your DNA, and everything you did from dawn until dusk was for the Church. Your entire life, from the moment you awoke until you closed your eyes at night, was geared toward following the Bible's word, to do whatever you could to win His favor and hope he would send you to Heaven for the ultimate reward. But life was different now, and it wasn't so easy to believe.

Sarah stared at her daughter, her rose-like cheeks, her angelic face, her tiny bud-like lips, her fists clenched as if she were keeping her innocence tight to her, and she fell asleep with her head against the rocking chair dreaming of a quiet life with her husband and daughter by her side, hoping the words to pray with would come soon.

CHAPTER SEVENTEEN

James carried Sarah from the rocking chair near Grace's crib into their bedroom, and now she was sleeping in their bed. He looked out the window, wondering what Sarah saw when she stared outside with such intensity. He meant to ask her, but she had gone into Grace's room and fallen asleep, and she needed the rest. He felt antsy suddenly, his muscles tightened, his senses alert. He opened the front door, stepped outside, looked up and down the deserted road and heard nothing. He walked to the end of the block, turned toward the bay, looking toward the horizon where the dark water met the line of lightless sky. He wanted to see farther than the horizon, out into the future, where he would still be there with his wife and daughter. He didn't want attention. He didn't need recognition. He didn't need anyone but Sarah and Grace to know his name. But he was nearly three hundred and fifty years old, and he knew nothing stayed the same, no matter how much you wanted it to.

He stepped close to the bank of the bay, breathing in the salt of the low-tide sea, needing to feel human for a moment. There were times when he found such peace in the seaside, but tonight the nerve-filled worries kept him itchy. He walked towards Pickering Wharf, wishing Olivia were there, wanting to hear her motherly voice tell him everything was going to be all right. She was a psychic, after all—she would know. He thought of calling her, but he didn't want to wake her. She had been with Jocelyn most of the night, he knew. He walked toward the street and stopped near the U. S. Custom House, the stately Federal-style brick building with white trim and matching Corinthian columns, the wide stairs leading up to the door. He remembered how Nathaniel Hawthorne worked in that building from 1847 to 1849. In fact, Hawthorne had written *The Scarlet Letter* there, even using a tour of the Custom House itself as an introduction to the sad story of Hester Prynne and her mark of sin. James had been rereading *The Scarlet Letter* and *The House of the Seven Gables* for the Hawthorne seminar he was going to teach next autumn. He thought of the local tributes to Salem's favorite son, its touch of literary genius, and he was looking forward to introducing his students to Hawthorne's work. He headed back toward his own wooden gabled house, stopping outside, watching it as though he had never seen it before. The house seemed pensive, he thought, contemplative, considering something too big for words.

James opened the green front door and stopped. He heard the footsteps running, running, then pausing, then running again. The sound continued for a minute, and his senses screamed when he realized the footsteps turned down his street. He spun around, ready to pounce. Suddenly, Levon Jackson turned the corner, his eyes scanning the houses until he saw the wooden gabled one. He stopped when he saw James.

"Doctor Wentworth!" Levon hunched over, his hands on his knees, panting for breath.

James ran to him. "What is it, Levon?"

Levon tried to talk, but his empty lungs failed him. He straightened himself and took James by the shoulders, shaking him as if trying to wake him. He was wide-eyed, Levon, crazed-looking, so unlike his usual friendly self. James felt a jolt like static when Levon's wide eyes settled on him.

"You have to go, Doctor Wentworth," Levon said, his words barely audible over gasps for air. "Grab your wife and baby and go." James stared into Levon's worried face. "They're coming to take her. Your daughter. My mom got a call from Child Services saying they needed to take Grace away."

"Why, Levon?"

"Because of what they're saying about you. You need to go, Doctor Wentworth. In case they come to take your baby."

"They're going to take Grace?" Sarah said. "James?"

James saw her there, her hands on her face, the tears in her eyes. He took his weeping wife into his arms. "No one is taking her," he said.

James reached out to shake his student's hand, but he stopped himself, afraid of the repercussions if Levon knew the truth, especially now. Levon clasped James's shoulder with a firm grip.

"It doesn't matter what you are, Doctor Wentworth. I know who you are."

"It doesn't matter to you that I might be a vampire? Last year you said vampires were villains."

"I was wrong." Levon started at a noise in the street. "You better go, Doctor Wentworth."

"Thank you, Levon."

Levon smiled, a flash of white brilliance. "Any time, Doctor Wentworth." And then he ran away.

When James turned around he saw Sarah with Grace in her arms, two large canvas duffle bags and the meowing black cat in her carrier on the ground by the door.

"I packed the bags last week," she said. "We even have a place to go."

"We do?"

"Olivia's cousins in Maine. Olivia said we could go there if we needed to get away."

James stopped, certain he heard footsteps nearby. He half-expected to see Levon turn the corner again, but there was no one. In his mind's eye he saw a crowd storming the wooden gabled house, an angry, seething mob ready to burn down the place, ready to drag Sarah and Grace away and decapitate and quarter him. But there was no one there. Then he thought he heard a car driving toward them. He took Grace from Sarah's arms and brought her to the Explorer by the curb, strapped her into her safety seat, and helped Sarah in. He grabbed the bags and the cat and put them into the back of the car. He stopped, listened, and knew for certain he heard a car accelerating in the distance. He ran back to the gabled house, turned out the lights, locked the door, and drove away, checking his rearview mirror, expecting to see flashing red lights behind him.

"Are they coming?" Sarah asked.

"I don't know, honey, but I heard a car and I don't want to take any chances."

Sarah nodded. She closed her eyes and leaned her head against the high back of the car seat. She opened the window, shivered, then closed it again while the Salem sights passed by in a blur. James was driving fast along the narrow, deserted streets. Everyone else was safe in their dark homes, warm in their soft beds, with their families, which was where they should have been too, James thought bitterly. He searched everywhere, looking for anyone who might notice them, straining to see the flashing lights, but they weren't there.

Damn you, Hempel, he thought. This is all because of you.

He drove down Derby Street, past the Custom House he had been looking at moments before. He sped past Pickering Wharf and the Salem Waterfront Hotel, down Hawthorne Boulevard to Charter Street, past the Salem Witch Village and the Witch Trials Memorial and the Old Burying Point. He turned right down Route 114, past Lappin Park, where he nearly kissed Sarah when they walked the Salem streets together that first time. Sarah was so nervous about him then, as she should have been. After all, he did jump out at her from the shadows the first time he saw her. He turned left down Bridge Street, back to Route 114 where he could take Route 128 toward Danvers and Peabody, where they could head towards Olivia's cousins in Maine.

Leaving was nothing new for James. He lost track of how many places he lived over three hundred years. Istanbul. Tokyo. Sydney. British Columbia. London seven times, not including the first twenty-eight years of his life. Germany. France, Italy, and Switzerland. All over the United States. Salem, too many times to count. He didn't feel strange leaving his house behind since he had left it many times before. What troubled him was the pain in his wife's eyes. She wasn't used to leaving in the middle of the darkness. She left, once, when she was Elizabeth, when the pock-faced man took her away. If James found any solace it was in knowing that that night was different. That night they left before anyone could catch them.

He worried about Grace, dragging her along on this midnight ride, but the baby didn't seem to sense anything was wrong. Grace, as was her way, was babbling her nonsense syllables, clapping her hands to the words she understood herself well enough, and she even made herself laugh a few times. Soon, the rolling car lulled her to sleep, which is how she stayed for the remainder of their drive to Maine. James checked her in the rear view mirror as she slept, her rose-colored cheek resting against the soft green mesh of her car seat, her gold eyelashes fluttering like butterfly wings. He marveled, perhaps a bit proudly, that his daughter looked more like him than Sarah. She had parts of Sarah, certainly, her full lips, her curls, her thoughtful gaze. But she had his gold hair, the blue eyes he had before he was turned, and his ability to sleep through anything.

Sarah pulled her cell phone from her bag, then put it down again. "Can't they track our phones?" she said. "I wanted to call Olivia."

"You're not the only one who has brilliant ideas, Mrs. Wentworth. Check beneath the seat." Sarah pulled out a small black cell phone, an older flip-top model. James smiled, pleased with himself. "Use that. It's not attached to either of our names."

"Where did you get this?"

"You can get anything over the Internet these days."

"What if Olivia doesn't recognize the number and won't pick up?"

"She knows the number. She's the only one who does."

Sarah turned away from the window and closed her eyes as though she were dizzy from the flash-fast speed as James's extrasensory reflexes kept them moving along the highways and byways toward Maine. He could see her fighting the tears away.

"You were planning for something like this," she said.

"Yes. And so were you."

Sarah nodded. She held herself together, but he knew her face so well. Every frown, every grimace, every squint, he knew them before they appeared fully formed, before she was conscious enough of them to try to hide them. He had known every feature of that face for over three hundred years. Even when she wasn't there for him to take into his arms he knew that face, dreamed of it, imagined he kissed it during his loneliest hours. And at that moment she had the same strained look she had had as Elizabeth when they accidentally stumbled upon their friends as they were hung from an ugly tree on Gallow's Hill. She pressed Olivia's number into the keypad on the cell phone, put the phone to her ear, and waited.

Theresa and Francine Silvers lived in Herrick Bay, Maine, nestled close to the islands in the Gulf of Maine near the Bay of Fundy by New Brunswick and Nova Scotia. A drive that should have taken five hours took two with James behind the wheel. There were no strange looks from the half-awake attendant when they stopped for gas. No police cars followed them. They left Salem after midnight, so the I-95 North to Salisbury/Portsmouth New Hampshire was deserted, and Exit 52 to the I-295 to the Maine Turnpike to Exit 113 very nearly so. They drove through small northeastern towns bordering deciduous forests, passed farmhouses, curious horses, and rural roads. When they arrived in Maine they drove toward their destination in Brooklin, along Route 175, Reach Road, which became Bay Road further along. Finally, they arrived at Flye Point Road along Herrick Bay, the water just feet away, and James drove past the tall, spindly trees, the sprouts of forest green waving at the nervous-looking newcomers as they passed the cleared-out driveway toward the one-floor tan cottage with white trim, a reconverted carriage house.

Sarah studied the note in her hand, her handwriting scrawled from writing in the fast-moving car, and she searched the house for some clue they were in the right place. It was nearly three o'clock in the morning, and it would be terrible to knock on the wrong door though that must have been the place since there were no other houses around. When she saw two red-haired women, obviously mother and daughter, peeking at them from behind red-gingham curtains and nodding, she knew they were in the right place. James stopped the car in front of the house, but the older woman came outside and pointed to an open whitewashed garage out of view of the road.

Theresa and Francine walked to the garage while James parked. After he stopped the car they helped Sarah lift the baby from her car seat and the cat in her carrier. The women's friendly smiles were as wide as their open arms. The older woman embraced Sarah, and the younger woman held Grace.

"Welcome James and Sarah," the older woman said. She peeked under the blanket draped over the younger woman's shoulder to look at the baby. "And this pretty little one must be Grace. I'm Theresa." She nodded at the younger woman holding the baby. "This is my daughter Francine. Don't worry. You're among family here."

Theresa looked like Olivia, James thought. She had the same wisps of gray in her red hair, only her tone was more burgundy, shoulder length and pulled into a ponytail. Francine was younger, college age. Her dyed orange-red hair hung down her back, and she wore black eyeliner and a black Irish-knit sweater over black jeans. Though she should have been intimidating looking, like a goth, she showed the same kindness her mother did, the same friendliness James had known from Olivia and Jennifer, from their whole family back generations. Theresa clasped her hands together, a very Olivia-like gesture, and took Grace from Francine's arms. Grace woke up, her blue eyes tired but curious as this stranger woman hugged her close and kissed her cheek. Grace smiled at the woman, babbled her greeting and patted her hair.

"You are the most precious thing," Francine said. "Mom, isn't Grace the most precious thing?"

"She is." Theresa touched Grace's ringlets. "Look at those gold curls and those big blue eyes. She's like a little doll with her cheeks and lips painted pink." She looked at James, then back at the baby. "She looks just like you, James."

James opened his mouth but said nothing.

"It's all right," Theresa said. "We know who you are. We know about Elizabeth," she nodded at Sarah, "and we know about Grace too.

You have nothing to fear from us. We're Wiccan, like Olivia and Jennifer, like our family all the way back. You know, James. Your secrets, and all of you, are safe here."

"Hush, Mom." Francine looked around to be sure no one overheard, but there were no neighbors for miles. James felt as though he had driven to the end of the earth and they were the last five people left in the world. The thought suited him fine.

The old carriage house was larger inside than it looked from the road. Outside it looked like a casual, modest bungalow, similar to other homes that populated the sparse, rural land. Inside it was spacious, with high ceilings and rooms that stretched toward the sea. It was simply furnished, with red and white checkered curtains, red overstuffed chairs and a matching sofa, light wood furniture. The windows were large and framed by light wood, overlooking the spindly feathering trees and the rocky coast of the jagged bay.

The women allowed their houseguests a few moments to acquaint themselves with their surroundings. Finally, Theresa said, "Olivia said to tell you that Jennifer and Chandresh have gone to Oklahoma. Steve, Jocelyn, and Billy left for Canada since Steve has family in Montreal. They'll be here to see you as soon as they think it's safe."

"Were they going to take Billy away?" Sarah asked.

"Olivia didn't say."

Theresa showed James and Sarah to their room off the side of the kitchen. "You'll find us to be gracious hostesses," she said. "James, you've known my family for over three hundred years, which means we consider you part of our family, which makes you and Grace our family as well, Sarah. I can't believe we're just meeting now for the first time, James. I insist you treat this like your own home. Take off your shoes, put up your feet. If you want something from the fridge, take it. We'll take care of you too, James, don't worry. We're very informal here, isn't that right, Francine?"

"If you guys need anything, just let us know. My room is down the hall on the right."

"We'll leave you to rest," Theresa said. "It's been a long night."

Sarah kissed both women on the cheek, and James shook their hands, grateful for their hospitality, silently blessing Olivia for being Olivia. When Theresa closed the door behind her, he saw the square room with white walls, a four poster bed of light wood and a beautifully carved antique-looking crib pressed against the wall with freshly washed linens and a small stuffed brown bear inside. He sighed, believing they could wait out the madness in this comfortable home in Maine, then go back to their wooden gabled house when sanity returned. He looked for the window and realized it was already covered, four quilts thick, to keep the daylight outside. He nodded. For that moment, everything was all right.

Sarah was overwhelmed with appreciation for the kindness of these women who were virtually strangers to them. She didn't know what she would do without her wonderful Olivia and her loving family. She took a sleeping Grace from James's arms and set her down inside the crib. Sarah stroked her daughter's gold curls from her eyes but then she was overwhelmed by the weight of it all. She turned from Grace, she didn't want her daughter to see, and she crumpled over and wept. James caught her in his arms and pressed her close, her head to his chest, his hands on the small of her back, his lips on the top of her hair.

"We're safe here," he said. "It's all right."

Sarah relaxed into his arms. She exhaled loudly, as though she held her breath the whole drive from Massachusetts to Maine. She was too tired to struggle so she let James take care of her. Theresa and Francine had thoughtfully left a bottle of rose-scented bubble bath on the rim of the bathtub, and Sarah watched as he poured the pink liquid under the hot running water and she watched the foamy bubbles form under the tap. She let him undress her, one piece of clothing at a time—first her cardigan sweater, then her t-shirt, then her jeans, then her bra and pant- ies. When she stood naked in front of him he kissed her, everywhere.

There was something urgent in his kisses, she thought, something that needed her. The idea crossed her mind that he was worried they might not have much more time together. She shuddered the thought away.

She felt the heat between them flush her cheeks pink, and she undressed him, too, piece by piece, and he joined her in the bathtub, letting his hands wander her body. It was perfect, she thought, the man she loved beneath her, his skin against hers in the comforting warmth of the bubble bath, his hands on her breasts, his lips kissing the back of her neck. As he rubbed his hand between her thighs and she knew she couldn't wait for him any more, she straddled him and she kissed him and she knew everything was going to be all right.

When she saw him sleeping in the dawn she was envious. Sleeping like the dead had its advantages, she thought. She laid down next to him and watched him in his stillness, taking comfort in his strong arms and extrasensory perception. She closed her eyes, tried to still her breathing, counting backward from one hundred, imagining her family in the comfort of their wooden gabled home, but she couldn't settle herself enough to sleep. Wearily, she pulled herself out of bed, she was so exhausted, and turned on the small tube television on the whitewashed dresser. As soon as she saw the headline flash across the screen, "Attacking the Pro-Vampire Factor," she knew she should turn the television off, but she didn't.

We've been hearing a lot about the vampire problem facing our country, and some vociferous cuckoos are saying it's fine for vampires to be out and about in the world. After all, they argue, vampires have always been around, and we've survived. Have we? How many murders have been committed in the night by these bloodsuckers? Do we really need to worry about vampire rights? What about our right not to be attacked while out for a nice dinner with the family? Who's protecting that right?

The President said the American people are generous enough to accept the vampire as our neighbors and friends. He said there's no reason to be frightened by vampires when they've given us no reason to be frightened except in scary movies. Once again he's off his nutter. He can't see what's right before his face: the American people are outraged at this blatant display of death. Hasn't the President seen the reports of people rallying in the streets shouting anti-vampire curses and wearing garlic ropes around their necks and waving wooden stakes and rifles loaded with silver bullets? A Congressional committee has come together to write a bill that would require all vampires to register with the government. That's the most sensible thing I've heard in years. I don't want a violent criminal in my neighborhood, and neither do you. Vampires are murderous blood drinkers, and they need to stay far away from my neck of the woods.

The Americans I know prefer to operate on facts. Here are the facts:

1. Vampires drink blood. Where do they get blood? From us, that's where. We're not talking about borrowing a cup of sugar here, people. We're talking about piercing someone's skin to get to the blood underneath. Grossed out yet?

2. Vampires live forever. What pack did they sign with the Devil so they could do the impossible? Even with all the studies being done at major universities around the world we still have no idea how a vampire's body works. To me, that makes them frightening.

3. Vampires procreate. How? According to what some have said, those old *Dracula* movies have it right. They bite, and feed, and, with some black Satan's magic, abracadabra, new vampire. Pretty creepy if you ask me. And I wonder...do they ask if you want to be a vampire first or do they grab people at random? And they might be living right next door to me, or to you. Scary.

Tonight I have Doctor Joshua Allen Trichter, a professor from New York University, here to discuss the vampire problem. Thank you for joining me, Doctor. You're a scholar in the realm of anthropology, is that correct?

Yes, that's right.

And that makes you a vampire expert?

I've been studying the vampires who have come forward in the last few months, so I'm as much of an expert as one can be at this time. You must realize, this is a very new field.

First of all, you've gone on record saying there's no reason for people to panic with the confirmation of the existence of vampires, is that right?

That's correct. I don't think there's anything to be afraid of. Humans and their preternatural counterparts have coexisted for thousands of years.

You just said "I don't think there's anything to be afraid of." Sounds like speculation to me, Doc. As you say, this is a very new field. Vampires have long been dismissed as myth, and now here they are and I'm supposed to accept your unproved theory that an undead, blood-drinking freak is perfectly acceptable in my neighborhood?

You might be surprised at how comfortably you could live next door to a vampire. More than likely, you already have an undead neighbor. Many of us do.

What about the blood drinking? How can you explain that away?

I don't need to explain it away. They do drink blood. Scientists are trying to understand how blood helps the vampires stay animated. But as strange as it seems to us now, people around the world have always known about vampires. The longer our society has existed, the more technologically advanced we've become, the more detached we've become from the spiritual, fantastical elements, but they've always been there. There are many cultures throughout the world still innately in tune with the spiritual realm and they're not at all surprised at the emergence of living vampires.

They're not living. They're dead.

Technically their bodies are dead, yet they're animated and have consciousness as we do. Don't forget, vampires were human once, and they have the same emotional lives we do. They feel joy, and fear, and worry. They fall in love. Often they create pair bonds as we do when we're in monogamous relationships.

Do vampires feel anger?

Of course. We all feel anger.

And they have a harder time controlling their anger.

I wouldn't jump to that conclusion. There's no reason to assume...

And traditionally the vampire is a symbol of violence and horror.

That's correct.

Don't they still represent violence and horror? Your argument lacks compelling evidence, I'm afraid. I'm going to ask you again. What about the blood drinking?

Many of the vampires we've been studying are just as others have said, professional and family-oriented. They've found creative ways of feeding themselves that is as noninvasive as possible.

The idea that there are nice ways to get blood is ludicrous, don't you think? What are those noninvasive ways to get blood? I'm looking at my hands and there's no blood there, that is, unless you pierce the skin. Can you pierce my skin without causing me pain? Or fear? Can you?

I didn't think so. Thanks for watching. Good night.

Sarah turned the television off, crawled back into bed, slid her arms around her husband, and held on.

CHAPTER EIGHTEEN

The Wentworths lived quietly in Maine, comfortable in their nook at the edge of the water. The Silvers' reconverted carriage house sat alone within a tree-studded, peace-filled woods which bordered the rugged shoreline where canoers and kayakers paddled the placid gray water. You could walk outside, turn in all four directions, see the trees and the birds and the flowers on three sides and the rocky shore of the bay on the other, and not see another person anywhere. You'd see soaring eagles and red squirrels scampering across the yard, but otherwise, no one for miles where their closest neighbors were organic farmers, artisans, musicians, and outdoorsy types. The solitary house in the chirp-filled woodlands perched alongside the isolated bay was, Sarah thought, idyllic.

As far as Olivia knew, as far as anyone could tell, the Wentworths had fled Salem without being trailed. Olivia heard nothing about a hunt for James, and Martha and her other Wiccan friends were on the alert for any news and they had heard nothing. Sarah called her mother using the extra cell phone, and her mother was her usual preoccupied self, listing her ailments, noting the wrongs of the world and how she meant to right them because she knew the answer to everything better than anyone. She didn't say anyone had tried to contact her about Sarah's whereabouts. She didn't hear the strain in Sarah's voice as Sarah struggled to sound light and happy. Maybe she and James had been paranoid after all, Sarah thought. Maybe she and James had panicked. But it was for the best that they left Salem, she decided. They couldn't take a chance that someone would come to take Grace. And how she loved Maine.

To pass the long daytime hours, Sarah helped Theresa with the mid-April gardening, content to dig in the dirt, plant seeds, weed away the dead leaves, water the ground. It was still nippy in Maine in April, around fifty degrees, but Theresa was a master gardener and knew when to plant and weed and sow. Although Sarah loved how the house sat on the edge of the rocky shore, most of all she loved the wild, loose garden coloring with signs of life. Columbines, blue cohorsh, and Jack-in-the-Pulpits budded here and there. The birch trees and dogwoods were waking, and Sarah imagined the lush blues, yellows, and reds that would brighten the bay when the sun shined on the northeastern shore. Grace crawled on the springy green grass, laughing at the songbirds, pulling herself into a standing position with her mother's help. Sarah also helped around the house however she could, cooking, cleaning, vacuuming, borrowing Francine's lime-green Volkswagen Bug—they didn't want anyone noticing the black Explorer with its Massachusetts plates—to travel to the nearest grocers, the general store fifteen miles away. She begged Theresa to take some money for the trouble—and expense—of having the three Wentworths there, eating her food, using her electricity, taking her space. But Theresa refused.

"James has helped our family for generations," Theresa said. "This is the least we can do for him."

"Every time I ask James about his earlier years he says 'Another time.' I'd like him to tell me about his past for a change."

"I know it seems like he's keeping secrets, Sarah, but I think when you've lived as long as James has it can seem burdensome to have to think back over hundreds of years. Especially when he's happy now."

Sarah smiled. "That sounds like something Jennifer or Olivia would say."

"Olivia and I are first cousins. Our mothers were sisters."

"I didn't know that." Sarah looked at Theresa, recognized the same friendly, motherly gaze she saw in Olivia. Where Olivia's eyes were steel-gray, Theresa's were darker, like thunderclouds on a stormy day, like the Maine sky when it rained. She decided it was safe to ask Theresa. She was Olivia's cousin after all. "Do you know how James became involved with your family? He told me your ancestor helped him first, in 1693."

"That story has been passed down for ten generations. James met our ancestor when he was a newborn vampling. She helped him understand what he was, and he protected her from some who meant to do her harm. Without him, she wouldn't have survived and none of her future generations would be here."

Grace crawled to the shrubs, too close to the prickly rose bushes for Sarah's comfort. Sarah picked her up and stopped to watch as the pink sky and blue clouds of the sunset reflected off the pink-blue water of the bay while the light dropped and grew darker. It looked too perfect to be real, Sarah thought, like it was painted with short feather brushstrokes and pastel watercolors, a Monet scene for the taking.

"The days are long here," Theresa said. "The sun rises before six in the morning and doesn't drop until after seven in the evening."

"It's hard waiting for James," Sarah said.

"I know," said Theresa.

As the darkness settled, Sarah carried Grace back to the wooden lawn chair near the edge of the embankment. She watched the moon shiver over the water in the bay, over the rocks and peaks, and she thought the scene was more perfect in Maine than Massachusetts. It's colder later into the year here, she thought, but she could bear it. Maybe they could settle there. Maybe James would stay.

Theresa brought out a steaming pot of Chai tea and two porcelain cups with a tin of sugar and a decanter of cream. She sat on the wooden lawn chair next to Sarah and took Grace into her arms.

"Will you tell me how James met your ancestor?" Sarah asked.

"I will," James said. He opened the screen door, walked outside, and leaned over Sarah, his hand on her head, his fingers in her curls.

"I don't mind telling you anything you want to know," he said. "I don't mean to make excuses every time you ask me, but I worry that one day I'll tell you something that will make you change your mind about spending your life with me. We had to flee our home in the middle of the night because of what I am, Sarah. Sometimes I think you'd be better off if we weren't together. If you have to suffer for what I am, that would be the worst curse of all."

Sarah felt the salt sting her eyes. "James, if you don't know my place is with you, wherever, whenever, then I don't know what else to say to convince you. You're my dear and loving husband. I will never leave you ever."

"And I promise you the same."

Theresa tugged on Sarah's sleeve, handed her Grace, then slipped silently into the house. James took Grace and held her to his chest with one hand, Sarah's arm with the other, and he led them past the white-washed fence of Theresa's property out to the edge of Herrick Bay. It was colder now that the sun had dropped, but Sarah felt brave. The house was just steps away if she became too cold. She took off her shoes, rolled up her jeans, and she did the same for Grace. Grace's feet were in the edge of the rocky sand where the water touched the shore. Taking her daughter by both hands, Sarah stood her on her small bowed legs. When the low-tide wave washed toward them, wetting their feet, Grace squealed with delight.

"She's like me," James said. "She's used to the cold."

"Come on, Gracie," Sarah said. "Show Daddy how you can walk like a big girl."

Holding tightly onto Sarah's hands for support, Grace took her first steps, babbling in explanation the whole time. "That's it, Gracie," James said. "That's my girl." Sarah heard the joy in the softness of his voice. He dropped his head until he contained his tears, and he bent over the water and washed the red away.

"You don't need to hide," Sarah said. "She loves you as you are. Like I do."

James dried his hands against his khaki pants. "I don't want to scare her," he said.

"She's not afraid of you."

James dried his face with his shirtsleeve. Suddenly, he stood still, his back straight, his head turned, his eyes closed in concentration.

"What do you hear?" Sarah asked.

"It's the strangest thing. I could have sworn I heard..."

"Is someone here? Do we need to leave?"

"No, no. It's...Geoffrey."

"Geoffrey is here?"

James stopped, listened, and Sarah hardly breathed while she waited.

"Nothing," he said. "I must have imagined that smug, self-satisfied shuffle coming this way. What would Geoffrey be doing here anyway? No one knows where we are."

"He'd come over if he was here," Sarah said. "He has no reason to hide from us."

They stepped away from the water, finding a dry place to sit at the edge of the sand. It was fully dark and windy now, but Sarah didn't feel cold. She found the water's mist soothing. They sat silently, the only noise the ebbing waves sleeping at the edge of the shore and Grace's bursts of giggles as she slapped her hand on the sand. As Grace settled down, her gold eyelashes drooping over sleepy eyes, James picked her up and held her close, rocking from side to side as she fell asleep. Who could be afraid of this man, Sarah wondered?

"I wish we could stay here," she said.

"Why can't we?"

"What about Salem? What about our house?"

"It's just a house, Sarah."

"But it's our home."

"As long as we're together, anywhere we are will be home. For now, this is home. No one is looking for us here. We'll stay as long as we need, and longer if you want to."

Sarah took Grace into her arms and held her daughter close. "But how long can we afford it? Neither of us are working any more."

"Damn," said James, looking distracted suddenly. "I still hate how I had to call Goodwin like a thief in the night to resign." He walked back to the edge of the shore, his hands clasped behind his back as he pondered the winking stars. "I liked it at SSU. I liked the students there."

"You didn't have a choice. Grace..."

"I know, Sarah. No job in the world comes before you and Grace."

"But we have no more salary coming in."

"Are you worried about money?"

"Aren't you? I know we have some savings, but I don't know how long that will last."

"You don't know?" James kneeled in front of Sarah and looked into her eyes. "We were married so long ago the first time, but I assumed you remembered."

"Remembered what, James?"

"Don't you know who my father was?"

"Your father was John Wentworth."

"And what was special about him?"

"He was good and kind and he had a warm, loving heart. And...and..."

"And wealthy. Good, loving, and wealthy. When he died he left everything to me, plus I have the money from the land I sold." He took her hand and kissed her fingers. "I've been living off my professor's salary, so that money has been saved, invested, and reinvested for hundreds of years. We have enough to support ourselves for the rest of our lives, and Grace for the rest of her life, and her children, and probably even her children's children and their children after them. We have a lot of money, Sarah."

"But your father knew you were turned. You told me about the night he found you in the woods."

"He knew, but he didn't care. He still left me his heir."

"Did you go back to Salem to collect your inheritance?"

"No. Father returned to England after I left him. He was too heart-broken to stay in Massachusetts."

"After you left him?"

James sighed. "After he found me in the woods I didn't stay with him long. I didn't feel safe there, for his sake. The witch trials were over, but the madness hadn't gone. People still eyed each other warily. They still whispered behind other's backs. And if there had been any reason to suspect anyone, I'm sure the hysteria could have broken out again easily enough. I couldn't subject my father to that."

"When did you leave?"

"I stayed with him about a month. I slept during the day, protected from the sun by the quilts he pinned over the window. When I woke up my father would be sitting in a chair by the hearth, staring at me like he still hadn't reconciled himself to the specter I had become, like he had to remind himself every night that I was no longer myself."

"How did he take your change?"

"You knew my father. His love knew no boundaries, even for his preternatural son. He loved me as he always had. He gave me a place to stay. He kept me away from the sunlight. He even found blood for me to drink."

"Where?"

"From Mr. Eggleston after he slaughtered the hogs. Father explained his cook needed it for blood soup. He claimed blood soup was his very favorite meal, though in truth he couldn't stand it."

"Your father loved Indian pudding," Sarah said.

James laughed. "Yes, but Mr. Eggleston didn't know that. After a few weeks he must have realized my father was eating an extreme amount of blood soup, even for someone who claimed to love it so much. Then he and his sons began sniffing around my father's house. One night the Egglestons came by, and Jonas, the younger son, asked my father if he was there alone. I was hiding behind the house, not wishing to be seen, but staying close in case my father needed me. Luke, the older son, saw me loitering and started as if in fear.

"''Tis merely my son, James,' my father said. 'Surely you know him. He's been gone some time now but, blessed be God, he's home.'

"My father waved me inside, and I walked as close to the men as I dared. They refused to look at me, and I saw their memories of you in their downcast eyes. My father laughed heartily. 'You Egglestons look white as specters.'

192 | MEREDITH ALLARD

"The men quivered in their chairs, visibly nervous at being compared to the very thing that could have seen them hanged months before. And still they wouldn't look at me, though they were reconciled that I was the unknown presence in my father's house. They nodded at my father and left and didn't come back. Yet I knew I was still a danger to my father. Every time I told him I must go, he begged me to stay."

James's voice cracked, and his eyes searched the water, barely visible in the darkness, as though he wanted to see his father again.

"Is that when you left?" Sarah asked.

"The following night I awoke and my father was sitting at the table as usual. He was slurping on a bowl of gruel, watching me absentmindedly, his thoughts somewhere far away.

"'I must go,' I said. ''Tis too dangerous for you now with me here.'

"'You cannot leave me,' my father said. He knelt besides me, grasping my hands, imploring me to stay.

"'I must go,' I repeated. 'I am leaving tonight.'

"Even though this demon blood was still new in my veins, I felt very human then. I was a son abandoning his beloved father, and every ounce of my being felt broken because of it. 'Those men will return eventually,' I said, 'and next time they may not be too ashamed to see me. They will step closer, look into my face, into my eyes, and they will know I am not myself. Then they'll notice I do not appear in daylight, or they'll question again the amount of blood you ask for.'

"'Is there no other way you can eat?' my father asked.

"'Aye, but you do not want to know what it is.' My father shivered. 'You are afeared,' I said. 'You know what I say 'tis true.'

"'The fire is not lit, and I am but a human and 'tis growing colder.'

"I looked at the unlit hearth, then glanced through the window at the night sky. I saw the beginning traces of winter as frost in the air. My father threw some timber in the hearth and lit a fire. The flames exploded into reds and oranges and I felt the heat against my skin. It was wonderful. I had become so used to cold that the warmth of the fire made me feel human. For a moment I weakened and thought I should stay. Perhaps living with my father, finding blood from unobtrusive sources, keeping his company and his counsel, was possible even as I was. I looked at my father's face, saw the undying love in his eyes, how he would be there for me, that night and every night we were together. I knew he would do everything he could to make this life as easy for me as possible. Then I realized, like a slap on the face, that it couldn't be done. I was what the witch hunters had been searching for—a demon presence in Salem.

"I walked close to my father, leaned over him, and he wasn't afraid. He knew I drank blood, and he knew he had blood aplenty in his warm human body, and he never once shrank from me in fear. I kissed the top of his balding head and grasped his hands.

"'I love you dearly, Father,' I said, the blood streaking my cheeks. 'I always will. I will never forget you.'

"My father grasped my hands again. 'No, James. No! I cannot let you go.' He broke down in heartrending sobs. 'You cannot go. You cannot...'

"I released his hands and flashed away as fast as any demon running wild in the pits of hell. Even when I was miles away I heard him weeping and murmuring my name.

"'James... my boy...come back...my son...come home.'

"I couldn't stand the sound of his anguish and I nearly turned back, but I saw a vision of those innocent women hanging from the ugly tree on Gallows Hill, and I remembered the terror on your face as the constable dragged you away. I couldn't go back to him."

James shuddered as the pain from so many years before wrenched through his preternatural body. Sarah stroked his arm with short caresses, trying to comfort him.

"Poor John," she said. "Did you ever see him again?"

"No. Just two months later my father abandoned Salem and returned to London. He lived there for another year until he died."

Sarah shuddered, the colder nighttime air and her wet feet finally prickling her. She looked at Grace, whose eyes were fluttering under feather-like lashes.

"I'll tell you what you want to know," James said, "but I can see you're cold. Let's get you both dry and warm inside."

In their bedroom, James dried Grace's feet with a towel and changed her into her nightshirt and set her down in her crib. Sarah changed into her flannel pajamas, grateful that Theresa had left the pot of untasted tea on a hot plate on the dresser, along with a platter of homemade bread and fresh cheese. With Grace put to bed, Sarah poured herself some tea and sat on the bed next to James.

"Was John sick when he left Massachusetts?" she asked. "Why did he die?"

"I think he died of a broken heart." James could hardly say the words. "After I left my father I disappeared into the woodlands again. Sometimes I forgot where I was or why I was there. Then one night as I stumbled along I saw a woman near a low-burning fire outside a thatched hut of branches. She had wild red hair and an unwashed face, and she sat on the forest floor barefoot and cross-legged. At first I thought I would hunt her, but when I approached her she turned to me so casually I had the feeling she had been waiting for me, though how she knew I was coming I didn't know. I didn't know I would be there myself. I can sneak up on my prey unnoticed and unheard, but somehow she knew I was there. She smiled at me and nodded.

"'Tis about time,' she said. 'What took you so long? Have you been dallying on your way to me?'

"I thought she must have me confused with someone else. I couldn't guess her age since she looked both young and old. She had a feathery billow of red-brown hair, which made her look young, but the straggly rags she wore were hardly stitched together and made her look old. She walked toward me with strength in her bearing, then stopped a foot away and crossed her arms in front of her chest as though she were challenging me."

"I've seen that look from Jennifer a hundred times," Sarah said.

"Exactly the same. Beneath the dirt on the woman's face I could see she was young since she had smooth skin. Her eyes were bright and steel-gray."

"Like Olivia."

James nodded. "'You're late,' she said.

"'What do you want?' I shot back. 'I know you not.' I turned away, but she grabbed my arm and held me more tightly than I would have thought possible from someone of her diminutive size. She came no higher than my waist.

"'Ah,' she said, 'but I know you. You're the one I'm waiting for. You're the one who will go on.'

"'What nonsense do you speak, woman?' I said. 'How can you be waiting for me?'

"''Tis the prophecy,' she said. 'Someone tall, strong, and golden-haired, a man with skin as white as snow and as cold as the winter wind, will come. You will help him as he will help you and your future genera-tions.' She gripped my hand more tightly. 'That golden-haired man is you. You are part of my fate, as I am part of yours. After you will come the man who will be the continuation of my bloodline, and we are a strong bloodline as far back as blood goes. But you know all about blood, do you not?'

"I stepped away, suddenly afraid of her. 'Be not troubled,' she said. 'I have no visitors here. You are in no danger from me. I have secrets of my own.'

"She turned toward the fire, waving her hands upward as though she beckoned the flames to rise and they obeyed, growing higher and hotter at her command. She turned to me and smiled.

"'I am special,' she said, 'and so are you.'

"'If you know I am special then you know more than I,' I said. 'I know not what I am.'

"'Do you know how you came to be this way?' she asked. I still wasn't sure what to make of her, this ragged, dirty young woman living alone in a hand-made shed in the middle of the forest, but she already knew about me, so I told her about that night with Geoffrey outside the jail, and when I finished speaking she brushed my words away with her hand.

"'You're to stay with me,' she said. 'For a while.'

"'According to whom?'

"'According to the prophecy.'

"'What prophecy?' I demanded. 'What the bloody hell are you talking about?'

"'I can read the prophecies. All my kind can.'

"'Your kind?'

"'Aye. Haven't you been bothered enough about witches to recognize one when she stands afore you?'

"I laughed bitterly. 'Very well then,' I said. 'You're the one they've been searching for. Come with me, woman, because I know some people down Salem way who'd like to show you their special tree. They searched for you so hard my wife died of it.'

"She threw up her hands as if she were annoyed. 'No one looks for me, boy,' she said. 'I am good enough at my ways that no one alive knows I'm here. I've harmed no one. I help, not hurt. I use my potions to heal, not poison. I cannot thwart, only thrive. That foolishness down Salem way had nothing to do with my kind. It was because of human weaknesses—pettiness and fear and blackmail.'"

"She was right," Sarah said.

"Yes, but I wasn't willing to admit it at the time. 'You said no one knows you're here,' I told her, 'yet I know you're here and you were expecting me.'

"'Caught that, did you? No one alive knows I'm here. You aren't alive now, are you?'

"I slumped under the weight of her words, and her voice softened. 'Come,' she said. 'As I said, you're to stay with me.'

"I didn't have the will to argue or flee, and it was going to be dawn soon, so I followed her into her hut. It was a tiny one-room structure, and I had to bend over to walk inside. There was a small cauldron hanging over a lit fire in the hearth, pots of herbs and liquids on a roughly chopped wooden table with three stumps for chairs and two beds of rags on the floor. She gestured to one of the beds. 'There,' she said. 'You see I've been expecting you.'

"'Are you certain no one lives here but you?' I asked.

"'No one.'

"'There are three chairs,' I said.

"'I am expecting another. Soon.'

"The windows were already covered with quilts, in preparation for my presence there during the day, I presumed. Along the back wall, hidden in the shadows, so much so I didn't notice them until I was standing there, was a short, wide shelf stacked with books."

James brushed a stray curl from Sarah's cheek. She looked at Grace, who had pulled herself upright in her crib, standing silently, as enthralled in her father's story as her mother. She wouldn't be going to sleep again any time soon. James took the baby from her crib, her tiny hands clutching his t-shirt in her fists. Grace didn't take her eyes from her father's face, and Sarah thought Grace must understand every word he was saying. Grace tugged again on James's t-shirt and murmured.

"I think she wants you to go on with your story," Sarah said.

"I think you're right." James sat on the bed near Sarah, propping Grace in a sitting position between them. "The witch gestured at the shelf. 'You're a reader,' she said. 'You will stay as long as it takes to read these books. Not a moment longer.'

"I relented and nodded. Besides, I had nowhere else to go and I thought reading might help to ease the pain of being away from my father, and from you, so I stayed.

"The woman and I hardly talked during the nights. She talked to the stray squirrels who came to eat the nuts and berries she left for them, she scribbled strange drawings and words in a language I didn't recognize with her colored inks on paper, she chanted late into the night and bubbled concoctions in her cauldron.

"'How did you get so many books?' I asked her once. 'I don't see many bookbinders in the forest.' She swatted my words away since she always found my questions annoying.

"'I haven't always lived here,' she said.

"'Then why did you come?' I asked.

"'Because I wanted to live as I wanted to live. I cannot conform to foolish ways. My father tried to marry me off too many times, finally to an elderly widower who stank of spoiled fish and lived in room no bigger than a boot. I wouldn't hear of it, and my father despised my stubbornness. But I wouldn't obey. I knew of my abilities from the earliest age. My mother had them. She taught me all she knew before she died.'

"'How did she die?' I asked.

"'My father turned her in for witchery while we lived in England yet. They burned her at the stake.'

"Burning convicted witches? I wanted to vomit at the thought. The hangings were horrible enough, the dungeon where you died too dreadful. But to burn them alive? The witch shook her head. 'I know you're suffering from the hunts,' she said. 'I have no right to speak such ways.'

"She sat on the dirt floor in front of the fire. I didn't know how that meager hut stayed upright, it looked so haphazard, like sticks in a mud pie, and I wondered how it didn't burn down whenever the fire was lit. I half-expected the cinders to catch the walls and burn the place down the way the fiery sparks caught the wood when they burned the living people alive.

"She watched me a long time, saying nothing, pulling her knees to her chin as she sat cross-legged on the ground. 'You do not like what you are,' she said finally. 'You will need to make peace with it. You're going to be this way a while.'

"'Make peace with it?' I said. 'I would gladly make peace with it except I know not what I am.'

"'You truly do not know?'

"'I know I am unhuman. Horrid. Despicable.'"

"'You are those things only if you choose to be. Otherwise, you are vampyre.'

"'Vampyre?' I wasn't even sure I knew the word. 'What on earth are you saying, woman?'

"'I'm saying you're magic, vampyre. You will never age beyond what you are now. You will never grow infirm or sickly or weaken. You will always have the strength of one hundred mortal men and the speed, sight, hearing, and reflexes of the most refined hunters in the wild. Your living body is dead and yet you still walk and drink. Blood. The living force in blood is what moves you. You will live forever.'

"'Surely you jest since you cannot mean forever,' I said. 'Tell me truly—when will this be over? When will I be able to sleep in peace?'

"'I jest you not. Once you are infected with the magic, you cannot escape it, that is, unless you find magic more powerful than the one that turned you in the first place.'

"I jumped over to her, knelt by her side, shaking her shoulders. 'Where?' I begged. 'Where is this magic more powerful than the one that turned me into this accursed thing?'

"'I cannot say. It is too rare and to my knowledge it has never been done. But you never know what you will find once you begin looking.'

"'So I am trapped like this? Dead and alive? Without my Lizzie? Forever?' I slumped over as I realized there was nothing I could do to release myself from this curse and I would wander the nights missing you, hiding from the daylight, searching for blood to drink for the rest of time. I closed my eyes, wishing there were some way I could end myself because the thought of existing that way for eternity was too dreary.

"'Be not mournful, vampyre,' she said. 'There will be better nights ahead for you.'

"'My name is James,' I said.

"'Very well, James. 'Tis about time you introduced yourself properly. I was beginning to wonder where your manners were. I am Miriam.' She grasped my hands and didn't flinch from my dead-cold skin. 'Hear me, James. There will be a night when you'll be glad you are what you are. You must believe me, or else every night from now 'til then will be a lonely, useless burden.'

"'When will that be?' I asked bitterly. 'When will I be glad for the blessings of this curse?'

"Miriam shrugged. ''Tis not as if I know the date of every event ever to happen in the history of the world. Things happen in their own time. You'll find what you're looking for when it needs to be found. That is all.'

"That sounds like something Olivia would say," Sarah said.

"Yes."

"Was she more pleasant to be around after that?"

"Miriam became an invaluable friend to me. She showed me how to live more comfortably this way. She taught me how to use my instincts to their best advantage. She showed me where I might find willing donors if that was how I wanted to live—without killing. She taught me how I needed to make peace with myself because I wouldn't get any farther along until I did.

"'There's nothing you can do to change what you are,' she told me. 'You can't go back and change that night. You can't tell the bad vampyre man to leave your human neck alone. You can't bring your wife back to life. You are what you are. Vampyre. Since there's nothing you can do to change it, you might as well accept it and learn to live with it for as long as it lasts.'"

"Theresa said you saved Miriam from people who wanted to harm her," Sarah said. "What happened?"

"About a month after I arrived I was woken up by voices. I pulled the quilts back from the window and saw five men surrounding Miriam, grabbing for her, pulling her arms, tugging at her skirts, taunting her, making rude gestures at her. They were very drunk, I could smell the liquor on them, and they were very dirty and ragged, as though they had been traveling for some time. Miriam held herself with dignity, and she didn't seem afraid, though she looked toward the house to make sure I was there.

"'There he is,' she said, 'the one who will save my life and take yours.'

"The oldest of the men laughed the loudest. 'Him?' the man said. 'He can't take one of us, let alone all. We shall take you as we want you...'

"'And do we want you...' said a leering black-bearded man, who licked his lips to emphasize his point.

"'...and then we'll knock your friend's brains out because we can.' The face of the oldest man was well lined, like a map of the underworld where every evil intention was marked. He grabbed Miriam's wrist, dragged her to the ground, and kicked her in the back before I pounced on him. The others charged toward me but I flipped them off as easily as if I were flicking flies away. I made a show of the older man, snapping his back and biting his neck and feeding until the others disappeared into the maze of the trees..."

James stopped to watch Sarah's expression. "It's all right, James," she said. "Keep talking."

"Miriam was all right, just some scrapes and bruises. She wasn't all that concerned. 'You see,' she said. ''Tis the prophecy. You were here to save me from those wretches. You are serving your purpose well, James.' Then, just two weeks later, the moment I read the last word of the last book there was a knock on the slab of wood she used as a door.

"'At last,' she said, 'he is here.' She opened the door and there was a red-haired, dark-eyed young man who smiled when he saw her.

"'James,' Miriam said, 'I'd like you to meet my husband. What is your name, husband?'

"'Matthew,' he said. Matthew stepped into the hut and looked at her like he had known her all his life. He hardly acknowledged me, he was so consumed by staring at Miriam. She opened the door wider for me to pass.

"'Good-bye, vampyre. You will know my children, and their children, down the generations. They will help you find your way.'

"'Thank you,' I said.

"'You needn't thank me,' she said. 'I was merely fulfilling the prophe-cy, as you will fulfill your end as well.' Miriam took my hand. 'We are intertwined, you and I. We will always be connected, even when I am gone and you are still here.' She stepped aside so I could pass. 'Blessings on you, James John Wentworth. Peace be with you. And always re-member...you will return, James. You will.'

"I stepped outside and she closed the door behind me. Even as I flashed away I heard her kissing the man who had appeared out of no-where. He must have been the third chair, I thought, though we weren't in the house together long enough to use them. There were years when I struggled to make sense of her words. They were hard to accept at times."

James smiled. There was such joy in his eyes, such love, that Sarah's heart swelled at the sight of him. "And now here you are," he said. "Both of you. Miriam was right—I have returned."

"Now I understand why you and Olivia and Jennifer are so close. Miriam helped you find your way then, as they help you now. As they've helped me. And now Theresa and Francine are helping us."

"We're fortunate to have such friends."

"It's in the prophecy," Sarah said, "and I've learned not to second guess prophecies. They usually come true."

"And what is your prophecy for us?"

"That we'll live happily ever after. Whether it's here, in Salem, or Sydney, Australia, it doesn't matter. Whether people like vampires, don't like vampires, think you're a vampire, think you're not a vampire, it doesn't matter. As long as we're together, everything will be fine."

"I think that's the best prophecy I've ever heard," James said. "Let's make it come true."

The lines of weary, broken-hearted people stretch down all the miles of the road as far as I can see, and I can see far now, Lizzie, I can. They are everyone. They are the elders, the wisest and the most respected, with gray in their hair and bends in their frames. They are the youngest, from newborns clutching their mother's chests to toddlers who can barely walk on their own, to smaller children who are wailing, echoing the fear they see in their parents' eyes. The young men ride their ponies until the ponies are confiscated and they are forced to walk alongside the rest. The young women catch the lewd glances of the blue-suited soldiers who do not hide their delight at the sight of the pretty raven-haired girls. The walkers are husbands and wives, fathers and mothers, sons and daughters, uncles and aunts, nephews and nieces, cousins, friends, neighbors, and anyone else you ever knew from the day you were born. They walk across the rough terrain of the heavy forest, wagons passing at a slow pace on either side. Some call for family members they cannot find. Most say nothing, staring at the back of the head of the person in front of them, stumbling over a rock here or a dip in the dirt there. Some watch their feet as though their numb legs have become detached from their torsos and they wonder how they move forward. Those too weak to walk are hauled in the wagons transporting food and blankets. Though it is a summer night and the sky is shimmers and the stars wink, there is a storm-like gloominess in everyone. They look on in bewilderment as though they hardly know how they got here.

Those at the front have stopped to put up their camps for the night. Fires crackle and burn in the open air. People call for their family members again, hoping to find them now that the walking has stopped. There is a surprising stillness in the camp for the number of people here, the soldiers's horses, the livestock. As families settle together, they whisper if they need to talk, hunching away from the soldiers who aren't shy about butting someone in the head with a musket because they can. The blue-suited soldiers patroling the camps notice me, I am obvious with my blond hair and dead-pale skin, but I am not the only white man here who is not a soldier. There are others here too—some of whom are walking as a show of support, but there are also teachers for the children, doctors to care for the ailing, preachers to preach the Good Word, and missionaries thinking now is as fine a time as any to convert the heathens. Many of them will live with the native people in their new home.

Here is the conversation of two soldiers:

"I heered Gen'ral Scott don't like the expenses of all this," one says, a freckle-faced boy of perhaps twenty. He gestures at the supplies, the horses, the wagons.

"He said for every thousand injuns taken," says the other, "at least half are strong enough to march twelve to fifteen miles a day, and the exercise would be good for 'em too."

The first soldier scans the clusters of people who are visibly exhausted and looking for the food and water rations they haven't yet received. "I don't know, Bill. None of these ones looks like they're gonna last another day at this, let alone three months."

"No matter. The more that dies the less we got to worry about transporting. Who needs to move them anyhow. Leave 'em here to rot, that's all I got to say."

Their conversation sickens me to the core and I leave them, searching for some way to be useful. I bring food and water to as many as I can, what little there is. I want to shake some sense into the soldiers, or at least rattle their brains a bit. They will succeed in their quest, I think bitterly. The Cherokee will die if these meager rations are all they're given to subsist on for such a long journey. I put the food, if you call stale cornbread or roasted green corn food, and the drops of water in the ration cans down near those who need them most. The water supply won't be replenished until they come to a creek or a river, and there isn't one near the campsite tonight. I remember seeing a river miles back, and I can run there and back a number of times before dawn. I say to the gray-haired man next to me, smacking his dry lips, his mouth open as though trying to suck in moisture from the air, "I will get you water." He doesn't acknowledge me, but I don't mind. I understand his pain. I will find water for as many of them as I can, Lizzie. You will be proud of me.

CHAPTER NINETEEN

The next night James awoke to the sounds of pots and pans clanging and clashing in the kitchen. He dressed, opened the bedroom door, and saw Sarah stirring something in a pot on the stove. The house was dark except for ten pillar candles burning on the countertop, giving the house a romantic glow. He heard the low, mellow music from the CD player in the living room and grinned at the sight of Sarah in a flowing black dress and strappy gold heels. She nodded when she saw him.

"Happy birthday," she said.

"Happy birthday?"

"It's April 19. You're three hundred and fifty years old today."

"I don't feel a day over thirty."

"You look good for your age."

"You're not so bad yourself, Mrs. Wentworth." He kissed her lips, running his fingers over the softness of the black silk dress, then glanced around the carriage house. "Where's Grace? Where's Theresa and Francine?"

"They took Grace to visit their friends in Bangor. I told them they didn't need to leave their own house to babysit our daughter and we could celebrate your birthday together, but Theresa insisted we should have the place to ourselves for a while. That's their present for you. They said to wish you a happy birthday and they'll see us later."

She dipped a spoon into the pot and brought it over to James. "I made you more blood soup," she said. "Geoffrey isn't here to steal it from you this time."

James shook his head. "I wouldn't be so sure. After last night, I still expect him to jump out from behind a tree any minute now."

"But he's not here now."

"Right."

"Which means we have the house to ourselves."

James grinned. "What did you have in mind?"

"First, we're eating dinner. You're having blood soup and I'm having the pasta I made for myself. After that?" She smiled. "We'll have to take it from there."

"I like that plan."

After dinner, while Sarah washed the dishes in the sink, James wandered into the living room and turned on the TV.

"Typical man," she said. "Can't wait to get the television on."

"I'll turn it off as soon as I have some company." He flipped past one station, then another. When he couldn't find a Red Sox game, he settled on the news. He saw the topic flash across the bottom of the screen and sighed. He used the remote control to lower the volume so Sarah couldn't hear.

To quarantine or not to quarantine—that's the debate started in Congress today. For the safety of the American people, Congress says, they want to send vampires of American descent to internment camps similar to the ones we saw in this country when Japanese-Americans were unlawfully detained during World War II, and, to even more horrific effect, in Europe when the Jews were sent to death camps. The ACLU is fighting vigorously against the round up, stating that according to the laws of the land you cannot arrest law-abiding citizens out of whim or whimsy, and that's all Congress has right now—unproved theories about why vampires should be separated from the rest of us.

This is America, and we do not round up people for kicks. We have things like laws and a Constitution, and the idea of arresting people for no reason, removing them from their homes, their lives, the people they love, because yes, vampires, like you and me, have families they love, is just wrong. Think of the uproar over Guantanamo Bay when people were suspected and arrested, sometimes for cause, sometimes not, many of them left in jail indefinitely without charges brought against them. Many linger there still. Will we see an uproar of indignation when our friends and neighbors are carted away, to who knows what circumstances, simply because some people have rationalized the need to sequester them—a rationalization, by the way, not based on any research or fact?

There are those in the Anti-Vampire faction combing horror films for proof that we should be afraid of vampire people. Hey you, they say, they're going to turn into bats and flutter outside your window at night and drink your blood for dessert! They say we humans are made in the image of God, and the vampire isn't human; therefore, they must be in cahoots with Satan. Only Satan's magic can make the dead live, they say. But didn't Jesus bring Lazarus back to life after death? Do we need to be afraid of a few vampires because they happen to be alive after they die? I don't know about you, but I'm keeping an open mind. When Reverend Doctor Martin Luther King Junior said he hoped his children would be judged on the content of their character, not on the color of their skin, that sentiment could refer to anyone who's seen as different. I'm not judging anyone of vampire descent until I meet them, know them, and have some sense of who they are. I'm just saying.

I know I'm going all Pollyanna here, but I still believe this is a country of tolerance. True, that tolerance is often hard won, but ultimately rationality will win. People from all over the world have come to this country seeking freedom—every kind of freedom. Freedom of speech. Freedom of religion. Freedom from an oppressive regime. Freedom to be straight or gay or somewhere in between. And now, openly for the first time, freedom to be dead. It makes me proud to see that, at every protest against vampires there's an equal number of people out in support, cheering for the vampires, dressed as traditional Dracula vampires, holding "Love all God's creatures" and "I Heart Dracula" and "No Vampire Ever Hurt Me So I Won't Hurt Them" placards. If we can accept people of all creeds and religions, then certainly we can accept people who are dead.

Surely we've learned a thing or two since the 1940s when thousands of law-abiding Japanese-American citizens, many of whom were born in this country, were imprisoned in internment camps for no reason other than their ancestry. I know these days it's popular to go along with the angry ones because they shout the loudest and make a funny show, but many of us are logical, thoughtful, and willing to give people who are different than us, however they are different from us, a chance.

As for the claims that vampires are murderers? As far as I know, according to the laws of this country, someone is innocent until proven guilty. If you can prove that a vampire of American descent has committed a murder, then absolutely that vampire should be prosecuted to the fullest extent of the law. Otherwise, if you have no proof and only theoretical possibilities, then you cannot arrest them or otherwise detain them. Vampires have the same rights as other Americans, and they should be treated that way.

"At least someone is on our side."

James looked from the television to see Sarah, the tears in her eyes as she stared at the commercial on the screen, her arms crossed over her chest as though she needed to protect herself.

"Did you know?" she asked. James nodded. "James..."

She stumbled past him, pushed open the door, and ran outside. She clutched her arms closer around her chest since there was a cold breeze blowing in from the bay and her dress was flimsy. James went after her, taking her into his arms, but she pulled away.

"You're still hiding things from me," she said. "You're still tip-toeing around me like I'm a fragile egg that will shatter if I'm dropped and I'm not."

"I know that, Sarah."

"We can handle what's happening together, but you need to be straight with me."

"But you look so sad sometimes, honey. All I want is to protect you from the things that make you look sad."

"Life is sad sometimes, but we can deal with it."

"You're right. I won't keep anything from you anymore."

"You keep saying that, but then you do it anyway." She dropped her face into her hands, breathing deeply, struggling to calm herself. "Will they round up the vampires?" she asked.

"Nothing has been decided."

"Do you think we need to leave?"

James shook his head. "As far as I can tell no one's been looking for us, and if they start they'll have a hard time tracing us here. I don't see any reason to go now."

Sarah looked out into the flat black of the water. James held her close, stroking her back, pulling her into his side.

"Do you think we can outrun the madness this time?" she asked.

"I do. I know my way around the whole world. In a way, I've been on the run since I was turned. We'll do what I've always done—stay somewhere until we don't feel safe and move on."

James shook his head. This is the repercussion of the curse, he thought bitterly. And here he had promised Sarah just a moment before that he would never hide anything from her again, but even as he said the words he knew they couldn't be true. He was hiding something from her already—his fear at how this all would end.

CHAPTER TWENTY

A week later James planned a special night for Sarah. Francine told him about nearby Acacia National Park, and though the park itself closed at 4:30 in the afternoon the restaurant served dinner and he wanted to take Sarah out to relax for a while. Theresa was only too happy to spend another night with the baby.

"You two have fun," she said. "We'll be fine."

They borrowed Francine's lime-green VW Bug since she was home from her classes at Bowdoin University, and they headed around the Gulf of Maine where the land was broken in jigsaw pieces by lakes and rivers, coves and ponds, peninsulas and bays, the islands floating like sponges a mile or two away. It was an hour drive to the park, but it was a beautiful night, clear under the wide moon and flashing stars, a little warmer now at the end of April. Sarah lowered the window and breathed in deeply, savoring the salty sea air. James reached for her hand and kissed her fingers.

"I could live here forever," Sarah said. "It's like we stopped at the edge of the world, safe from everyone and everything."

"Then we should stay," James said.

The further they drove the more they were surrounded by coniferous and deciduous forests, the ocean whispering riddles in the shorelined distance. He pulled onto the Park Loop Road of Acacia National Park, past the signs for the scenic vistas and the hiking trails, the art galleries and the boats to the lighthouses and whale watching. It was dark, so most everything was closed, but even in the night they saw the meadows and the marshes, the dense evergreen forest surrounding them.

"I should take Grace here during the day," Sarah said. "She'd like to see the puffins and the sea birds. Maybe I could take her on a picnic here." James sighed. "I'm sorry," she said. "I wasn't thinking."

"Wasn't thinking about what? Of course you should take her here during the day. It's beautiful. If I'm sighing it's because I wish I could come."

"There's plenty the three of us can do together at night," Sarah said.

"I know."

They pulled into the parking log near the Jordan Pond House Restaurant. Sarah looked at the hikers and the campers walking through the parking lot, waiting near the door, chatting easily amongst friends and family as though there wasn't a care in the world.

"Do you think it's safe to go in? What if someone notices you're..."

"Nocturnal?"

Sarah laughed. "Yes, nocturnal. The nocturnal type is so public now."

James listened to the ambient conversations outside. They were mainly families with children, some couples, and a few groups of friends. They were talking about their own lives, what happened to them on the trails that day, what they saw, where they went, what pictures they took. They were engrossed in their own stories, and he didn't hear the word vampire from any of them.

"I think we're all right," he said. "I'll order a dinner for myself, you'll eat a few bites of it, then we'll get it boxed so you can have it for lunch tomorrow." Sarah looked at the people, still undecided. "We can't stay in the house all the time, Sarah. We're safe here. We look like a normal married couple out for a nice dinner."

"We are a normal married couple out for a nice dinner."

"Exactly."

Sarah exhaled. "Let's go in," she said. "I'm hungry."

James parked the car and they walked to the restaurant, located on the grassy bank of a deep lake that zigged and zagged through the scenic valley within the tree-covered mountains. Sarah walked to the wooden tables and chairs outside where customers ate lunch in the daylight hours and admired the beauty of the valley brightly lit by the gracious moon, then bent over the wild-looking blue and yellow blooms. They walked inside and found a come-as-you-are diner where visitors could stop to eat in their t-shirts, khaki shorts, and running shoes after a long day hiking or canoeing. The room was brightened by the round lantern-style lights hanging from the ceiling.

Sarah searched every face in the room as though she were wondering, "Is that man looking at James? Does that woman notice that I'm eating from his plate and not him? Do those children see his pale skin?"

James fed her a bite of her salad. "We're fine, Sarah."

She nodded, then dipped her fork into the three cheese ravioli in front of James. "I know," she said. "Your meal is really good, by the way."

"I'm glad you like it."

After dinner James found a place to park near the rocky coast where they could see the water winding past the granite cliffs and cobblestone beaches. He turned the car off, slid his arm around his wife, pulled her close, and kissed the top of her hair. Sarah relaxed into him, resting her head against his chest. They sat silently, watching the moonlight reflect off the glacier-formed peaks and valleys, the water flowing around the waving evergreen trees, the balsams, the spruce and the pine.

"Maybe it's not a bad thing this happened," Sarah said.

"What do you mean?"

"I've learned not to be so attached to things. It's like you said...our house in Salem is just a house. I love it, I'll always love it, but if I never see it again I'll be all right. You and Grace are the only things I need in this world." She looked out the window, smiling at the moon, her decision made. "Besides, we won't need to hide forever. This craziness will die down. People will get bored of it. They'll start to accept that you nocturnal types are just a part of life."

"Sarah..."

"Craziness does end. The witch trials did end."

"Yes, they did. But fear, paranoia, madness, they never go away—they just look different from one generation to the next. And some prejudices are harder to get over than others. People may have a harder time dealing with the paranormal because it seems so physically, biologically, religiously, inherently wrong. It goes against everything people have been taught to believe about the world." He looked into Sarah's eyes. "You want me to be honest with you, so I'm being honest with you. I don't think this problem is going away any time soon, and I think we need to be prepared to run at a moment's notice. I'm not saying anything is going to happen. I think we're safe here—for now. But we also need to be ready, just in case."

Sarah nodded. "I've been keeping our bags packed and ready to go." She yawned, then looked at the time on the car's dashboard. "It's midnight," she said. "We should head back."

After the accident James wondered if it was a planned attack. As if someone knew where they were. As if someone knew what he was. As if someone followed them. He didn't know how, he didn't know who, and he certainly didn't know why. In the whole world he couldn't think of one person who might want to attack him. Even if someone knew what he was, why would they want to kill him or his innocent wife?

As they drove toward Brooklin in the dark night, back around the Swiss cheese-like slices of water, James heard the car before he saw it. His extrasensory perception wouldn't allow him to miss it, the sound of a buzzing jigsaw, closer and closer, faster and faster. Suddenly, there it was, the black Hummer swerving around the trees. James guessed the driver was going at least one hundred miles an hour, and he swerved to avoid colliding with the tank-like car. Sarah had fallen asleep, but she was jolted awake as the tiny Bug jerked around branches and through bushes. When she realized they were being chased, she grabbed the handlebar above the passenger's door and held her breath.

"James?"

"Just hold on, honey. Hold on."

Suddenly, the black SUV disappeared. James was still on edge, driving faster than he should have been but he had to get his very human wife away. He checked the rearview mirror, the side mirrors, out the back window. They passed many miles since he last saw the Hummer, but he couldn't relax, not yet, not until he knew Sarah was safe.

"Probably a drunk driver," he said. Sarah nodded, but she didn't look convinced.

He didn't see it again until it was too late. Even with his extrasensory instincts it happened too quickly. The SUV shot out from the distance, hitting Francine's Bug head-on. The car was thrown from the road, rolling over and over and over, and James watched in horror as Sarah whipped around from side to side. When the car finally stopped, she was unconscious and covered in blood. James pushed the metal of the crumpled car aside like his arms were jaws of death. He ran to the passenger's side, pushed aside the airbags, unhooked Sarah's seatbelt, and pulled her from the wreckage through the shattered window. He wasn't thinking about broken bones or internal injuries. He had to get her out of the car.

"Sarah, honey? Sarah?"

She didn't respond. He pressed his ear to her blood-covered chest and listened. Normally, he could hear her metronome-like heartbeat from far away, and normally that sound brought him such comfort. Now, with his ear against her chest it was barely audible. But it was there. She was alive.

With shaking hands, he pulled the cell phone from his pocket, the one with the unlisted number, and he called 911 begging for an ambulance for his wife.

He wept with his limp Sarah in his arms, unconcerned about the blood streaking him in his misery. He patted her cheek gently at first, then more firmly, trying to sting her awake, anything to get her to open her eyes.

"Oh my God, Sarah, you have to wake up. You have you wake up. You can't leave me again. Sarah? Oh my God."

When Sarah opened her eyes, she moaned in such pain. James could hardly stand it, as if it was his own pain she voiced. He promised he would protect her, it was his job to protect her, and now this. It didn't make any sense. Suddenly, Sarah was coughing blood and clutching at her stomach. James soothed her the best he could, stroking her matted curls from her eyes, holding her sweater over the wound gushing blood from her abdomen.

"It's all right, Sarah. Help is coming. You'll be all right."

"James?"

"I'm here honey. It's okay."

He looked at his wife bleeding and barely conscious on the side of the road. The idea that she might die was too real to him, and he knew if someone didn't help her soon she would leave him again. He couldn't let that happen.

"I can fix this, Sarah," he said. "I know what to do. I've done it before." He didn't want to say the words, but looking at his wife, weaker by the moment and straining to breathe, he thought he had no choice. "I can turn you," he said.

Sarah shook her head. She was so weak she could barely say the words. "I can't...I'm so sorry."

"Sarah, please..."

"I'm so sorry, James. I love you so much."

James clutched Sarah close and wept bloody tears into her hair. "Don't be sorry," he said. "This is all because I'm cursed. I wish I were human again so I could go with you."

"Grace needs you," Sarah said. She tried to say more, but she fell unconscious in his arms.

When the ambulance arrived, too long, James moaned, it took too long, the medics raced to Sarah. Blood drooled from everywhere, her mouth, her nose, the gashes in her abdomen and arms, and the EMTs rushed to stop her bleeding. They strapped her to the gurney, pushed her into the ambulance, and when they were all inside and speeding away one of the medics noticed James, the blood staining his cheeks. The medic shined a flashlight into his face.

"No," James said, turning away, "you need to take care of my wife. Please, my wife."

"Sir, you need to let me check you. You're bleeding."

"It's my wife's blood," James said. "Please," he begged, "you have to take care of my wife."

"Your wife has massive internal bleeding, sir," the medic said. "We'll do everything we can."

James kneeled by Sarah's side, her hand in his, his head on her shoulder. "Don't leave me, Sarah," he said.

The back ambulance doors opened and a team of doctors and nurses in scrubs were waiting. As soon as the gurney hit the ground, they rushed Sarah through the emergency doors and disappeared. James tried to follow them, but a young woman wearing a surgical mask blocked his way.

"I'm sorry, sir, but you need to wait here."

"But my wife..."

"Sir, has someone examined you? You're bleeding."

"It's my wife's blood. Where is my wife?"

"We're checking her now, sir. We'll let you know as soon as we know something."

She disappeared behind the door. James heard the doctors and nurses shouting medical terms he didn't understand, she's lost a lot of blood, he heard, then something about blood transfusions and emergency surgery. The doors swung open and they wheeled Sarah past on her way to the surgical ward. James rushed alongside them.

"Sir, you need to wait here," a nurse said. And then Sarah was gone.

James would have dropped to his knees but he didn't have the strength to fall. Dear God, he begged silently, you can't take her from me. Not now. Not like this. I can't live another three hundred years without her.

He stood there, for how long he didn't know, waiting for something, someone, half-expecting Sarah to walk out on her own two feet. "Hi, honey," she'd say. "Sorry, it was all a mistake. Let's go home."

James drifted into a dream-like stream-of-consciousness as the events of the past few months drifted through him. His greatest fear had

218 | MEREDITH ALLARD

been realized in the midst of his greatest joy. He had his wife and daughter. He had the life he had always wanted and missed. And now it was all going away, and in his heart of hearts he knew all along it would happen. He was right—he was cursed. He put Sarah in danger simply by being there. She wouldn't be involved in any of this, she wouldn't be fighting for her life at that very moment if she wasn't with him. James thought he should go away, disappear, leave Sarah and Grace to themselves without the taint of the curse of the vampire to haunt their every step. But he couldn't bring himself to leave. He loved them too much.

For whatever pain his presence caused her, he knew she loved him, that unconditional love that saw him exactly as he was and loved him anyway. So he stood and he waited. And he sat and he waited. And he walked the length of the curving hospital corridor, past the emergency room, past the cafeteria, past the elevators, around the gift shop with Get Well Soon balloons and pink and yellow flowers, and waited. He sat outside in the garden with the toad fountains spitting water in the air, the rocks set out like a Japanese garden, the benches scattered under the trees, and waited. Suddenly, he saw the light of the dawn peeking tentatively from under the covers of the night. At first, James was so dazed he didn't realize he needed to get away. He forgot what he was, and in that moment he was an ordinary man whose wife had been injured in an accident. They had a daughter waiting for them. But then the sky brightened and he remembered that day, the year before, when he stood in the Salem sun and slipped into an unconsciousness he nearly never recovered from.

What to do? James panicked. He had no car since he had come with Sarah in the ambulance, and Francine's Bug was wrecked anyway. He could run away quickly, but where? They were in Bar Harbor and he didn't know the area. Besides, he needed to stay close to Sarah. He needed her to know he was there the way he needed her to know he was there when she languished in jail in 1692. Then, he sat outside the jail all hours of the day and night. Until he was turned. And then she died. Oh my God, James groaned. He realized there must be rooms in the hospital with no windows. That was the answer: he needed to get inside one of those rooms.

He walked to the woman behind the nearest desk. There were a handful of people waiting in the emergency room in pain or sick or both.

"I have a migraine and the lights are painful," James said. "The sunlight is especially hard when I have a headache like this. Is there somewhere I can lie down where there's no sunlight?"

The gray-haired woman looked at him over the top of her eyeglasses. "Let me put you in an exam room where a doctor can see you."

"The paramedics checked me at the scene. They said I was banged up but I'm fine."

"But if you have a headache, sir, you might have hit your head. That could be dangerous if you don't get it checked."

"I didn't bang my head. I get migraines when I'm stressed, and having my wife in surgery is stressful. I just need to lie down for a while."

The woman looked around as if she were looking for someone to tell her what to do, but no one was there. She gestured for James to follow her down the hall. They took the elevator to the second floor where she showed him a windowless room with two hospital beds.

"You can rest here," she said.

James shut the door as she walked away. He sighed, pressing the air from his lungs as if he were still being watched by human eyes, and he waited until the woman's footsteps grew fainter. When he felt safe, and alone, he fell asleep.

As soon as he opened his eyes he knew something was wrong. A young nurse in pink scrubs pressed herself against the wall as if the Devil himself requested her presence in Hell. A doctor with salt and pepper hair in a white lab coat sat in the chair next to James, staring at him.

"How is my wife?" James asked. "Is she all right?"

"You weren't breathing," the nurse said.

Though James cringed inside, outwardly he laughed. "That can't be true if I'm sitting here talking to you." He laughed again. When the nurse's eyes narrowed, he shrugged. "Sometimes I get sleep apnea and stop breathing for a while."

Two men in scrubs appeared in the doorway carrying a gurney between them. When they saw James sitting upright, they stepped back.

"Were you sending me to the morgue?" James asked. He tried to sound light but sounded sickly instead.

"You had no heartbeat," the woman said. She stepped to the door. "I'm calling the authorities."

"There's no reason for that," the doctor said. "Obviously, you were wrong, Nurse Tosh. As you can see, he's fine."

The nurse glared at the doctor. "I came in here to tell him his wife was out of surgery, and I called you when he didn't wake up. You're the one who said his heart wasn't beating, Doctor Masters. You're the one who said he had no pulse."

Doctor Masters's face became a caricature of silliness. "I was just joking," he said. "You came running to me saying he had died in his sleep, so I was playing along with you."

"I'm calling the authorities. He's one of *them.*"

The nurse tried to leave but the doctor closed the door in front of her. He leaned close to her and spoke firmly. "There's nothing to report. Obviously, the man is fine. He was in a deep sleep and you panicked. That's all. You need to consider if this report is worth your job."

The nurse shook her head, opened the door, and walked away. The doctor closed the door behind her and stepped close to James.

"Your wife is out of surgery," the doctor said. "She's still in serious condition, but she's stable. Come with me to my office and we can talk there."

All eyes were on James. The nurse who found him dead asleep was huddled close to two other nurses, whispering until James stepped into the hall. She stopped speaking, and the entire floor was silent. Everyone there, doctors, nurses, patients, and visitors, stared at James like he was hideously disfigured or naked or unclean somehow. They knew. He could tell by their disgusted faces. They saw his pale white skin, his shallow breaths, his dark eyes, his glasses lost somewhere along the way, and they knew. James wouldn't look at them as he followed the doctor down the hall.

"She won't say anything," the doctor said as he opened his office door. "She's a single mother and her ex-husband doesn't pay child support. She can't afford to lose this job. Besides, she has a reputation for making mountains out of molehills. No one will listen to her."

"How is my wife?" James asked.

"There were some complications during surgery. She lost a lot of blood and needed a transfusion. There's still some concern about infection."

"Can I see her?"

"Of course." The doctor's hands came together under his chin, and he watched James like a boy who stumbled upon Santa Claus on Christmas Eve. "I just have one question. Are you...?" The doctor shook his head. "I always wondered if it were possible. With all the craziness these days, I thought it had to be nonsense, but here you are, and you don't breathe, and your heart doesn't beat, and yet you're as real as I am."

James said nothing. The doctor gestured to the photos on the bookshelf behind his desk.

"This is my family," the doctor said. He handed James a picture of a pretty blond lady and two young boys. "My wife Emily and my sons Joshua and Eric."

James pulled out his wallet, surprised it was still there, and showed the doctor a picture of Grace. "This is my daughter."

The doctor pulled the picture close to his face and studied it. "She looks just like you. I didn't know...I didn't think..."

James shook his head. "She's adopted."

"But she looks just like you."

"It's a long story."

The doctor had his stethoscope around his neck, his hand on the knob on the end, stretching out towards James.

"Can I...?"

"Then can I see my wife?"

"Of course."

The doctor closed his eyes as he listened to the silence inside James's chest. "Unbelievable," he said. He sat behind his desk, his fingers forming a triangle under his chin. "What are you going to do? Congress is holding a special session to decide what to do about the Vampire Dawn. Now they're fighting between deportation and internment and..." The doctor grimaced, unable to continue.

"And..."

"It doesn't matter. The ACLU is fighting it, but a lot of angry people are worried about being attacked by bloodsuckers in the night. Look there."

He pointed through the open blinds into the corridor where a patient, hospital gown open in the back, pink fluffy slippers on her feet, wore a necklace of garlic coves around her neck. Across from the nurse's station was a silver cross banged crookedly into the wall.

James felt a grip like fingers around his throat. This wasn't a flash of red-boiling anger. This wasn't rage-filled frustration or blindly thrashing fury. This was primal, paralyzing fear.

"I need to see my wife," James said.

The doctor walked James to the Intensive Care Unit. The family before them had to be buzzed past the locked door, but Doctor Masters ran his card through the slot on the wall and the doors opened. They walked into a circular ward with the nurses's station in the center and eight rooms around, the walls of glass exposing the patients and the monitors inside. The doctor led James to a room around the nurses's station, and he saw her, Sarah, sweet Sarah, beautiful Sarah, everything he ever needed in this world Sarah, her eyes closed, breathing heavily, well bandaged, her beautiful face lacerated and bruised, a dead-pallid tone to her usual peach-like complexion. He walked to her, carefully, as though the sound of his footsteps would wake her. He bit his lip, determined not to cry.

"Sarah?" he whispered.

She didn't respond. He pulled a chair to the side of her bed and sat beside her. He tucked the blanket closer around her in case she was cold, she was always cold, Sarah, then he brushed a few matted curls from her cheek. He took her hand and watched her sleep. The doctor backed away, leaving them this time alone. James wished he couldn't hear what was happening outside. The doctor was talking to the nurse who had first found James asleep.

"I'm calling the authorities." She sounded defiant, ready to stand up to the doctor, the administration, and anyone else who would tell her she was wrong.

"I examined him in my office," the doctor said. "There's nothing wrong with him."

"Then bring him here. Let me listen to his heartbeat."

James heard the uneasy pause. "No need for that," the doctor said.

"We're not safe," another woman's voice said. "How can you let him stay here? What if he attacks someone?"

The doctor laughed. "Did she tell you about her crazy ideas? Really, Maria, I thought you had more sense than that."

"But they're real," Maria said. "It's been proven. And that man," James could feel her pointing through the wall, "is one of them."

"Does he look like he's going to hurt anyone? He has a daughter. He's worried about his wife. Leave him be."

The nurse grumbled as she walked away. James knew from the bass in her voice and the thunder in her step that she wasn't through. She would report him, and report him again, until someone took her seriously. She would tell anyone and everyone. James knew the self-righteous smile without turning around to see it, the leering glance, the turn of the head that said, "I know you're there and I refuse to see you."

The end was coming. Life as he knew it, with his wife, with his daughter, would no longer exist. He knew that as well as he knew he was sitting in a hospital room looking at his injured wife. If he hadn't been turned he never would have attracted Hempel's attention. If he had never attracted Hempel's attention, his name would have never been on that list in the cabinet in the dead man's closet. The hysteria about the Vampire Dawn sweeping the world would be an interesting aside for him, entertaining reports on the news, a reason to watch a You Tube video or two, a reason to say, "That's too bad" or "How could they do that?" and go on with his day because he would be awake with everyone else. But now Sarah was suffering because of what he was. If he could have found a wooden stake he would have run it through his own heart. At least he couldn't hurt Sarah any more.

Sarah sighed. "Sarah?" he said. But she didn't respond. He stroked her arm, stared at her face, looked for the smallest trace that she was in any pain or needed immediate medical attention.

James shook his head, blocking out the whispers coming from outside the room. When a blue-scrubbed nurse opened the door to check Sarah's monitors, they stopped speaking. They didn't need to bother, he thought. He could hear them through the wall.

"Is everything all right?" James asked.

The nurse nodded. She checked the numbers on the monitors, checked the IV bags hanging from the rack, checked the connection to Sarah's arm. She didn't seem nervous with James in the room. She didn't hesitate or back away, but he knew there were others who were afraid.

The cell phone in his pocket vibrated and he looked at the number. It was Olivia.

"James, oh thank God. Where are you?"

"I'm at the hospital. Sarah is…she's been…"

"I knew something was wrong. I felt it around midnight last night."

"Yes," James said. "That's when the accident happened."

"Oh, James." Olivia stammered her words. "How badly is she hurt?"

James explained the accident that was even then a high-speed blur in his memory. "It all happened so fast, Olivia. I should have been able to react quickly enough."

"Don't you dare blame yourself, James. You saved Sarah's life."

"I didn't help her at all. I've been promising her I would protect her, I would never let anything bad happen to her again, and she nearly died because of me."

"She most certainly would have died if you hadn't had control of the car as well as you did. You need to stop thinking that way, James, right now. You need to stay strong for Sarah."

"How is Grace?" he asked.

"She's fine. Francine said she's sad, she keeps looking for you, but she's all right. Theresa called me when you two didn't come home last night. Where were you during the day?"

James sighed. "I'll explain later," he said.

"I'm coming to Maine right away. I've closed up the shop, I'm packing my bags, and I'm coming." She paused, and James heard the sorrow cracking her motherly voice, as though her own children were suffering. "Are you all right, James?"

"I'm hanging in there."

"All right, dear. I'll be there as soon as I can."

James sat back against the chair and closed his eyes. He felt a wound of seeping sorrow, imagining his daughter going to sleep every night for the rest of her life without him. He would never tuck her in again, tell her a bedtime story, and, in later years, never help her with her homework. Never give her boy advice. Never walk her down the aisle or hold his grandchildren in his arms. He saw it all slipping away. All those lonely years he knew before he found his wife again were like a lingering dream compared to the shock of the reality he now faced.

When the pain became too much and he had to take his mind off everything or else begin to gnaw his own arm off, he turned on the television hanging high on the wall.

We've got a great show for you tonight. To begin, I have some latebreaking news to report. Congress has decided, being the learned, compassionate group they have proven themselves to be time and time again, to round up vampires for no other reason than (whispers) because they can. Here is Congressman John Heckle-Green talking to reporters on the Capitol steps explaining why, by the slimmest of margins, our august leaders decided to bury the undead alive.

(Cut to a dapper middle-aged man with salt-and-pepper hair, a well-fitted gray Armani suit, and a fixed smile. The dapper middle-aged man says, "These undead creatures take the form of wolves and bats, and they leave their coffins at night and they feed on the blood of the living.")

So they take the form of wolves and bats and feed on the blood of the living? Ooh, scary. You know where he got that from? The 1931 movie *Dracula* starring Bela Lugosi. That's right. The Congress of the United States of America has made the decision to imprison people, who happen not to breathe, based on the dialogue in an eighty-one year-old movie. And you know what? The dialogue isn't even very good. They had a habit of stating the obvious back then. Here's another example of dialogue from the movie:

(Mimicking Lugosi's vampire voice): This is very old wine. I hope you will like it.

(Mimicking a weak man's voice): Aren't you drinking?

(Lugosi's voice again): I never drink wine.

Wait, here's more: My, what a big bat!

And (in an angry Lugosi voice): You know too much to live. (Snaps his fingers) Van Helsing!

I think the learned men and women of Congress should memorize every line in the movie, and then every time they're questioned about how they can justify imprisoning those who haven't been convicted of any crime, they can repeat those quotes and look like the assholes they really are.

Now it turns out a number of vampires willingly added their names to the government's watch list in an attempt to show how they've assimilated into society and aren't to be feared. Now the government is using that list as the basis for their decision to round up the vampires. Here's Senator Ben Jove:

(Cut to another dapper middle-aged man with salt-and-pepper hair, a well-fitted gray Armani suit, and a fixed smile who looks remarkably like the first dapper middle-aged man. This one might be rounder. This dapper middle-aged man says, "At this time, there are over ten thousand names on the watch list, but we estimate that there are hundreds, if not thousands more who haven't come forward. Why haven't they come forward? What do they have to hide? We can only assume that those still slinking away in the night are not sympathetic to our concerns, which makes us afraid for the safety of the American people who are unwillingly living next door to an undead. We must act swiftly and decisively to keep the American people safe.")

Congress used the fact that there are still unknown numbers of vampires out there as the basis for their decision to round up the vampires and imprison them. Now, with the decision to round up the vampires, there's another debate raging about where to keep them. For more on this part of the story we go to Frank N. Stein. (Audience laughs. The host turns to the monitor, showing a dark haired reporter wearing the top of a Frankenstein mask.) Frank, what can you tell us about plans to imprison the vampires?

The exciting news about the upcoming internment is that, after the vampires are forcibly rounded up, expelled from their homes, their families, their lives as they've known them, and forced to live imprisoned in squalor and deprivation, at least the vampires will be surrounded by like-minded individuals such as other vampires, of course, as well as other bloodsuckers like politicians, Wall Street profiteers, and community organizers. Sources close to the White House say, contrary to popular belief, there are currently no plans to waterboard the vampires with blood since the general consensus is that the vampires would actually enjoy that, thereby cancelling the negative effect the waterboarding is meant to produce.

So where are they planning on holding the vampires?

Right now, Guantanamo Bay is the best choice for obvious reasons. Hey, who doesn't want a beachfront flat rent free? It looks like it'll be either Guantanamo Bay or somewhere near the Sierra Nevada in California's Owens Valley.

Didn't they intern Japanese-Americans in Owens Valley in the Manzanar camp during World War II?

That's correct. In seventy-one years, the United States government hasn't learned a f(beep)g thing.

And what about the fear of copy cat crimes? You know, that humans will begin pretending they're vampires and commit acts of violence?

We need to practice prevention. Watch your children. If they begin running around with a black tablecloth tied around their necks as though it were a cape, or if you catch them in front of a mirror with an emery board sharpening their eyeteeth, you must intervene immediately.

Should I be concerned if my son likes to play Dracula? Surely that's an innocent pretend game. All children like to play pretend sometimes.

Only if he has real blood dripping from the sides of his mouth and you can't tell where it came from. And the family cat is missing.

We'll be back after this.

CHAPTER TWENTY-ONE

Finally, Sarah opened her eyes. James pulled the chair as close to her as he could. He kissed her hand, watched her monitor, brushed her sweaty, matted dark curls from her face. Finally, her eyes focused and she saw him and she smiled, that sweet, beautiful smile he lived for. When he leaned over to kiss her he struggled to hold back the emotion so the thick red tears wouldn't streak his face. Sarah touched her hand to his cheek.

"How do you feel?" he asked.

"Everything hurts," she said. "Where's Grace?"

"She's fine. Theresa and Francine still have her. Olivia is coming. She'll be here soon."

Sarah closed her eyes. James said nothing, pushing every other thought from his mind except the one that told him she needed to be well again. She needed to be strong again. When she opened her eyes she looked through the glass wall and saw the nurses watching them, their faces curious, their eyes judgmental. James couldn't bear to see the anguish in Sarah's face, still swollen and bruised from the crash but every bit as beautiful as she ever was. He closed the blinds to keep the prying eyes away. When he turned back Sarah was crying.

"They know," she said. James lowered the bar on the side of her bed and he sat next to her and took her into his arms, gently, not wishing to hurt her. He pressed her head to his chest, his hand on her shoulder, holding her close, his lips in her hair.

"Yes," he said.

He wanted to protect her, to save her from the anguish, but he didn't want to lie to her. He had promised, and she needed to know. He told her what happened, how he fell asleep in the lightless room, how the nurse found him and thought he had died, how frightened she was when she saw him sit up in bed after the doctor said he had no pulse. She had called the morgue to come pick up the body of the dead man, and then the dead man opened his eyes and asked about his wife. He told Sarah about the doctor, who was doing all he could to protect them.

Sarah was startled when the door opened.

"It's just me," Doctor Masters said.

"This is Doctor Masters," James said.

"How are you doing?" the doctor asked. He listened to Sarah's heart, looked into her eyes, checked her stitches. He wrote some notes into her records. "You're doing well, Sarah. Much better than expected. You're a strong lady."

"You don't know the half of it," James said.

The doctor stopped writing when he saw Sarah sobbing.

"She knows," James said.

"Don't worry, Sarah," Doctor Masters said.

James looked at his wife with the most reassuring smile he could manage. The sleep medication the doctor slipped into her IV worked quickly and she fell asleep.

When Sarah opened her eyes James wasn't there. She looked out the window, saw the nighttime darkness, and knew something was wrong. James should be there, and the fact that he wasn't frightened her. The blinds of the glass wall that looked out into the ICU had been opened, and she saw Doctor Masters talking to two police officers. Sarah's heart raced in fear. Were they looking for James?

She saw the doctor shake his head, look at her, and she saw the urgency in his face though she couldn't make out his words through the glass. The officers walked toward her, watching her as if they expected her to run, as if she could escape in her condition. The officers were stern, humorless. They scanned the room as if they were looking for some crime to charge her with.

"Where's your husband?" the younger officer said.

"I don't know," Sarah said.

"Some of the nurses said they saw him here as soon as the sun went down. Where might he be?"

"I don't know," Sarah said. She knew they might find him, take him away, maybe even forever, but she wouldn't help them. They kept looking around, as though James might magically appear. But when Sarah said nothing more, looking at Doctor Masters for help, the doctor opened the door.

"She's still in Intensive Care," he said. "No more today."

"Let us know when she's able to talk," the older officer said. The doctor watched them walk away, then closed the door behind them.

"James is fine," he said. "He's at Theresa's house. Your friend Olivia took him there."

"He knew the police were coming?" Sarah asked.

"He overhead some nurses talking."

Sarah nodded, relieved at least to know he was safe. "Why were they here?" she asked. "Are they arresting him?"

"They said they weren't going to arrest him. They said they just wanted to ask a few questions."

"What questions?"

The doctor shook his head. "They wouldn't say."

Doctor Masters looked at the clock on the wall. He took the remote control from the nightstand and turned on the television. "I think you should see this," he said.

In other news, the armed forces, in cooperation with local law enforcement agencies, are out tonight identifying those individuals on the undead watch list. According to sources at the Pentagon, no one is being arrested or deported to another location at this time.

"We're simply verifying their places of residence," said a well-lined army general in full dress.

"Are there plans to remove them another time?" a reporter shouted.

"Are you verifying that the people are dead once you discover them?" shouted another. "Are you taking pulses and listening to heart-beats, or are you just taking people's words for it?"

"There have been reports of false accusations where some are listing the names of living people," said another.

The general grimaced, his mouth disappearing in a maze of wrinkles.

"We're in the process of verifying the living status of those we're questioning. Those with pulses and heartbeats are immediately removed from the list."

We're hearing now that the President will be coming into the White House Press Room at any moment for an unscheduled confer-ence. We have cameras standing by. I understand the President's walk-ing in now. Let's listen to the President:

My fellow Americans, we have been faced with an unusual chal-lenge, a unique circumstance in our history. With the confirmation of the existence of vampires, it's not surprising that Americans are experi-encing differing reactions. Some are for the vampires, and they're out there in their fake fangs and their Dracula capes, reminding us that un-der our Constitution all American citizens are entitled to life, liberty, and the pursuit of happiness. Others are afraid. Vampires drink blood, they say. Vampires are only out at night when it's not so easy to see who else is out there, they say. Today, after much intense debate and discus-sion with Senators Heckle-Green, Jove, and O'Bunnion, along with a joint committee representing both parties in Congress, we've decided it's best to be safe in this particular instance so we're going ahead with the removal of the undead to a desert facility. We need to know who these vampires are, what they're doing, who they're with, and, most im-portantly (laughs), where they're finding that blood to drink. Just so you know, I'm not planning on sharing any of mine, especially not with some guy who sounds like Bela Lugosi (Reporters laugh). I know there are many who disagree with this decision, but I feel it's the best for eve-ryone. We need to keep America safe.

Reporter #1: Mr. President, how long will the vampires be imprisoned for?

President: I'm not saying they're being imprisoned. We've made the decision to hold them temporarily until we can get a sense of each individual. If that individual isn't proven to be a threat to society, then he, or she, can go home.

Reporter #2: How are you planning on vetting these vampires? Whose testimony will be used to verify whether or not they're a danger?

President: We're going to have to take that on a case-by-case basis.

Reporter #3: Will the vampires have legal representation?

President: This is the United States of America. They're entitled to legal representation, and, like other American citizens, if they're unable to afford attorney fees then they'll be given a public defender.

Reporter #2: What about the charge that the vampires aren't American citizens because their country of origin can't be proven. Many don't have accurate birth certificates and weren't born in this country.

President: We're treating vampires currently living here as American citizens.

Reporter #2: Is that the only criteria you're using to determine citizenship?

President: We have it under control.

Reporter #3: I understand the ACLU has filed a class action lawsuit to prevent the internment of the vampires.

President: That's going to be for the courts to decide. However, as the President I have some say in the matter (laughs).

Reporter #1: You realize, Mr. President, that you've angered many Americans by siding with those favoring vampire internment. Many believe there must be a better way to handle the situation. By all accounts, many of the vampires who added their names to the watch list are every day Americans who happen to be dead. How can you justify pulling these families apart? Aren't you simply going along with the hysteria sweeping certain segments of the country?

President: I wouldn't say I'm going along with the hysteria. There is reason for concern about the reality of the undead in America. If they're law-abiding citizens as many seem to be, then this will be over quickly and everyone can go back to their lives.

Reporter #1: Many of those in favor of vampire internment are also in favor of extermination.

President: No one is being exterminated. We're simply trying to determine who's a law-abiding citizen and who's a threat to society. We might wave some garlic in their direction (laughs), but otherwise there are no plans to exterminate the vampires.

Reporter #4: Is there any truth to the rumor that scientists will be experimenting on the vampires in an attempt to see how they live though their bodies are dead?

President: I'm not aware of any intention to experiment on the vampires.

Reporter #1: Is that a no?

President: That's a 'I'm not aware of any intention to experiment on the vampires.'

Reporter #5: Will the writ of Habeas Corpus continue to be suspended while dealing with the Vampire Dawn? You'll retain them as long as you want whether or not they have crimes charged against them?

President: We'll hold them until we know they're not a threat, and then we'll let them go. We're going to do everything we can to make this as painless as possible for everyone involved.

Thank you very much. God bless you, and God bless the United States of America.

The doctor handed Sarah the box of tissues, standing by until the flood of despair washed her away and she was too dry to cry anymore. Suddenly, she was numb. She thought she would float away on a raft, down the road, across Maine, out into the open ocean where she and

James and Grace could drift and dream until they found a place they could live together in peace.

She began to breathe heavily, the exertion from her anguish too hard for her in her weakened condition. The doctor listened to her heart, checked the monitor, and checked the bags hanging from the IV stand.

"Your blood pressure is too high, Sarah. I'm going to give you something to help you sleep."

Before Sarah could say no the doctor added a new bag to the IV stand, and then she was sleeping. Even medicated, it was a fitful, troubled sleep. As she dreamed she knew she dreamed. She dreamed James was there, rocking their daughter, singing the seventeenth century love song "Scarborough Fair." She hummed as she remembered the words:

Are you going to Scarborough Fair? Parsley, sage, rosemary, and thyme, Remember me to one who lives there, For once she was a true love of mine...

She imagined James stroking her hair as he loved to do, his fingers in her curls, kissing the nape of her neck. She felt him on the bed beside her, his strong arms around her, protecting her. When she awoke in the morning she felt the coldness linger. The blinds of the ice-like glass walls were closed while sunlight peeked between the curtains over the windows and Sarah saw a pattern like bars on the floor. Bars from three hundred years before or bars for her husband now...it didn't matter. They were bars just the same, meant to keep her on one side and James on the other.

As she stared at the patches of sunlight she heard a faint rustling outside. She listened, then listened again, and she realized she heard voices. She lowered the bar on the side of her bed, threw her legs over, and gripped the nightstand as she pulled herself upright. Her legs ached and her back cramped and her stomach pinched, but she strained to see. When she couldn't stretch high enough, she dragged herself out of bed, limped to the window, and pulled aside the blinds.

Outside she saw a crowd, not a thousand, not even a hundred, but enough to make themselves heard. Some held signs with slogans like

"Down with Vampires!" and "No bloodsuckers in my backyard!" Most were calm, content simply holding their signs, allowing the words on the posterboards to proclaim their disdain. Others squinted, snarled, and pumped their fists in the air, wearing their frustration proudly.

"If you only knew him," Sarah thought. "If you only knew his heart you would love him as I love him." But they didn't care to know him, she knew. She dropped the blinds and turned away.

The door swung open and frightened her. Doctor Masters rushed in, checked her monitors, and unplugged the IV from the wall. "I need to get you out of here, Sarah," he said. "I thought I could keep this under control, but it got out of hand so quickly." He led her to the bed, helped her lay down, and added two bags to her IV. "I have an ambulance waiting. Hold on."

He raised the bars of the bed, unlatched the foot lock, and with the bed in his right hand and the IV in his left, he pushed Sarah through the door. She saw the surprised faces of the nurses, patients, and visitors as the doctor swung her around the corner. When the elevator door opened, he pushed her in. Sarah thought she should feel afraid at the abruptness of it all, at Doctor Master's intensity as he navigated the narrow hospital corridors, but she didn't. Maybe she was numb, she thought. Maybe what was going to happen had been preordained and there was nothing to do but wait and see. Maybe the Puritans were right. Maybe your fate was determined before you were born. What's the point of fighting what's already been decided?

The elevator opened on the ground floor, and Doctor Masters pushed her out the emergency entrance. There was an ambulance, its red lights blaring, the backdoors open, two paramedics waiting. When they saw Doctor Masters they sprang toward Sarah, grabbed her bed, lowered the legs, and pushed her into the back of the waiting vehicle. The doctor jumped in beside her. The paramedics slammed the doors and they squealed away.

"Did the crowd see us leave?" Sarah asked.

"I don't think so, but they'll figure it out. Someone will tell them."

A few miles from the hospital the siren turned off and the ambulance slowed, making regular time in regular traffic. "They don't want to attract any attention," Doctor Masters explained. "We can't have anyone following us."

He listened to Sarah's heart, checked her pulse, flashed his pen light into her eyes. Could he tell how disconnected she felt, she wondered, as if she were watching the scene from somewhere else? She felt the way she did during the past-life regression when she discovered a whole other self, Elizabeth, harbored inside her, waiting to be released to the surface of her consciousness. Sarah closed her eyes, and when she opened them she hoped she would be with James and Grace and this was all one last horrible nightmare, a residual effect from the times when Elizabeth would tap into her sleep. She dreamed they were back in the days before anyone knew vampires were real, when no one suspected her husband of being anything other than what he seemed to be—a dedicated professor, a loving husband, a devoted father. But she opened her eyes and saw the shadows on the wall of the ambulance and Doctor Master's worried gaze. She heard the scratch of the ambulance tires along the small-town roads and she knew this was all too real.

"Where are we going?" she asked.

"You're going to Theresa's," the doctor said. "I have everything set up for you. You shouldn't have left the hospital yet, but it wasn't safe there for you any more. James and I settled it last night. I'll come by twice a day, James will take care of you at night, and you have friends there to help during the day."

"Aren't you going to get in trouble at the hospital for this?"

Doctor Masters shook his head. "I don't work there any more."

The ambulance slowed then stopped, and Doctor Masters jumped out. The little tan and white carriage house seemed smaller suddenly and more isolated than before, Sarah thought as she saw it through the ambulance doors.

"Are we safe here?" she asked.

"I think. For now."

The three men pulled Sarah from the back and lowered the bed's legs. Sarah looked everywhere around her, half-expecting the crowd from the hospital to be there. She wouldn't have been surprised if Kenneth Hempel suddenly showed up, jumping out from behind the bushes, yelling, "See! I knew people would be appalled by the presence of vampires!" Though Hempel had been dead two months, nothing surprised her any more and the presence of a ghost reporter wouldn't seem so strange to her now. But there was no one there, only quiet and bird chirps around the carriage house. There were two kayakers gliding past on the water, but that was a common enough sight along the bay.

The front door burst open and Olivia ran out with Theresa by her side. Francine stood by the door with Grace in her arms.

"Look, Gracie, it's Mommy! She's home!" Francine held Grace high above her head so Sarah could see her daughter's angelic face and golden curls. Sarah smiled, her heart warmed by the sight of her baby, and she waved and looked as strong as she could. When Francine brought the baby closer, Sarah touched Grace's cheek. Grace smiled, though her joy was stunted, as if she knew something was wrong. When Sarah saw Olivia she sighed. Olivia patted her hand and smoothed her hair.

"It's all right, dear. Everything is going to be all right."

The men carried Sarah into the living room. For some reason, the inside of the little house seemed different than she remembered. Separate. As if it wasn't there, it hadn't ever been there, and she was seeing it in a dream. The red-checkered curtains fluttered in the breeze from the open windows, and the red sofa, chairs, and light wood furniture were pushed aside to make room for Sarah's hospital bed. Doctor Masters nodded to the paramedics, who nodded at him, and Sarah, before dashing back to the ambulance and racing away.

"Joe is my cousin," Doctor Masters explained. "He owed me a favor."

"Won't they be angry with him at the hospital?"

"Joe? He doesn't work at the hospital. He's a plumber."

Doctor Masters winked at Sarah, then set up her cot and IV. He pulled the coffee table closer to have a place for the medications he pulled from his backpack.

"I'm going to put these in the refrigerator," he said.

The bedroom door opened. "Sarah?" James called. "Are you okay?"

"What are you doing up?" she asked. "It's still daylight."

"I heard you come in. Is Thomas there?"

"I'm here," said Doctor Masters. "She's all right, James. Come back when it's dark."

"Will you stay with her?"

"I'm not going anywhere. It's not like I have anywhere else to go." The doctor smiled. He meant it in a joking way, but Sarah didn't find much to laugh at.

"Sarah?" James called. "Are you sure you're okay?"

"I'm all right," Sarah said. "Please, James, go to sleep. I'll see you when it's dark."

"I'm sorry, Sarah. This is all my fault."

She tried to get out of bed, go to him, but Doctor Masters wouldn't let her. "Stay in bed, Sarah," he said.

"It'll be dark before you know it," said Olivia.

"I always loved the bay windows," Theresa said, "but now I wish there weren't so many of them. I don't have enough material to cover them all."

"Tomorrow I'll run to the store to get some dark fabric to cover them," Francine said. "This way James can sleep in here during the daytime."

Sarah closed her eyes and turned away. As far as she knew, James might be gone by tomorrow night.

She must have fallen asleep. When she woke up Doctor Masters was gone and James was there, the nighttime fully descended. There was no moon, and the blackness felt heavy and overwhelming, like the black velvet Jennifer loved so much. James brushed a few stray curls from the corner of her mouth, and when she turned to him he smiled.

"How do you feel?" he asked. "Thomas showed me how to add medication to your IV. He said you could have more pain meds now if you need it."

"I don't want to feel groggy," she said.

"But he said you need to stay on top of the pain. If you let it get too bad it's harder to control."

"I'm all right."

They sat in silence, James holding her hands in his. Outside the crickets chirped, the leaves on the trees blowing fitfully in the wind. Inside the carriage house was quiet. Grace was sitting up in the playpen Theresa bought for her surrounded by stuffed toys, but she sat silently, staring at her parents with a thoughtfulness unusual for a ten-month-old. What did she know? How much did she understand about what was happening? Sarah closed her eyes and pressed her head into James's arm.

"Are we safe here, James?"

"You're perfectly safe here."

"I said we."

James paused, the pain evident in his night-dark eyes. He looked out the window at the weighted darkness. Sarah grabbed his hand and tugged until he looked at her.

"You have to tell me, James. You promised."

He looked through the window as he spoke. "The plan is to round us up and hold us until they figure out what to do with us."

"I saw the President on the news," Sarah said. "You were right. We haven't come as far as we'd like to think."

Olivia walked into the living room. She peeked over the playpen, saw that Grace was all right, and sat in the overstuffed recliner next to Sarah. "That's not legal," she said. "You're a law abiding citizen, James. They can't just take you away and lock you up."

"It's been done before," James said.

"James?" Sarah looked into his eyes. "What else do you know?"

"Nothing."

"James?"

"Nothing, Sarah. Please." He pressed the blanket closer around her and kissed her lips. "You need to rest. You still have a lot of recovering to do." He sat back in the chair, took her hands in his, stroked her fingers, her cheek, her hair. She felt tired again, the weight of the stress and her injury and the unfairness of it all made her so tired, but she didn't want to sleep. She was afraid that if she closed her eyes her husband would be gone when she opened them again.

"Go to sleep, Sarah. It's all right. Go to sleep."

She fell asleep, but it was a haphazard, worried sleep haunted by demons. She saw James slipping away, back across the years, to a time she could never recover. What if they never found each other again? No matter how many preternatural visitors, no matter how many past life regressions—what if they lost touch of each other forever? She saw herself and her daughter, their empty arms reaching toward him as he slipped out of their grasp. She gasped aloud when she opened her eyes, but she settled when she saw James sitting beside her.

"What time is it? she asked.

"Two a.m.," James said. "We still have time."

"Do we?"

He looked away.

"Tell me a story," Sarah said. She needed to keep him talking, hear his voice, know he was still there.

James sighed. He stared at her face, her hair, her hands. He stared at her as though he needed to memorize everything about her all over again so he wouldn't forget. "I never finished telling you how I met Chandresh on the Trail of Tears," he said.

"That's right."

James watched the tailless black cat scamper across the hardwood floor and smiled. He looked out the window, his eyes small in concentration, that far-off look he always had whenever he spoke of his past.

"I had been living alongside the Cherokee in the Smoky Mountains..."

"That's where you decided to stop hunting," Sarah said.

"Yes. When I realized the Cherokee were being forcibly removed from their land I followed them west."

"Why?"

"To this day I'm not entirely sure. Part of it was I wanted to help them the way I wished someone had helped us when we were caught up in the madness in Salem. And focusing on their hardships in the camps gave me something to think about besides how much I missed you."

"What were the camps like?"

James moved onto the bed next to Sarah and put his arm around her, gently. He leaned back and held her to his side, pressing her head against his chest. He rested his cheek on top of her hair while he spoke.

"Inside the camps smelled of urine and fear, the rows of people stretching far and away, like corn in the fields. Outside the camps were freshly dug graves. Most nights were silent and no one spoke. Sometimes motherless sons or fatherless daughters sobbed. Sometimes you could hear the braying of the horses or the clucks of the chickens or the barks of the dogs. Some of the richer Cherokee retained a few of their possessions and brought their looms and pack dogs along, and some sadly brought their slaves. Sometimes they whispered amongst each other, but otherwise it was quiet.

"Everyone was crowded together, huddled around their campfires, their eyes closed, their stomachs aching from the salt pork, their legs and backs sore, their hands and faces blistered from sunburns. When they could muster the energy they chanted songs and prayers. One night a man, a father who had lost his sons, began screaming, his arms reaching for the sky, or, more likely, for his dead children. His eyes grew wild and he went mad. The soldiers restrained him with rope, letting him howl in one of the wagons until they cut him loose and brought him into the woods from where he never returned. One night as we walked a woman with an infant on her back, her two older children clinging to her legs, was crying as she forced herself forward. Suddenly, she dropped dead to the ground. The soldiers pulled the three screaming children from her and tossed them into the closest wagon, leaving the woman's corpse by the side of the road." James shook his head. "Perhaps we should talk about something else."

"Tell me about the night you met Chandresh."

James sighed. "We had been traveling for about a month by then, and the walking was so hard for them. Not for me, of course. I could easily catch up to the ones who walked all the daylight hours. Their going was slow because they didn't walk over roads—they passed through the wilderness. The stronger men and women went ahead and cut the timber out of the way with axes, and it was a long, hard journey every day.

"The people were hungry, thirsty, and suffering from fever, dysentery, and exposure to the weather. They were dependent on the quartermasters for sustenance, and all they had to eat or drink was what they were given, and what they were given was given grudgingly. There was no shelter anywhere, and for the whole time on the trail I thought there were no homes left for anyone anywhere in the world.

"Every night, as I found my way forward, I passed the dead and the dying left along the trail. The shamans were doing what they could with their ancient ways, but they were in a foreign territory. They didn't know the local plants and herbs. They didn't have access to the medicine they knew could heal. A number of white doctors were there to help as they could, but there was tension between the shamans and the white doctors since they had different ways of treating the sick and each thought his way was right.

"Everyone was dying. Husbands died, leaving their widows and children to fend for themselves against an unfriendly forest and impatient soldiers. Wives died, leaving their husbands and children without hope or comfort. One night I saw soldiers dash a four-day-old baby's head against a tree because it wouldn't stop crying. I learned later that the baby's mother had just died. I tried to intervene. I grabbed the baby and brought her to the closest doctor I could find, but the child was already gone and there was nothing left to do but bury her. Everywhere along the trail were people burying their dead in shallow, unmarked graves. When it was time to go on they had to go, and often they weren't given time to bury their loved ones properly. Mothers were forced to carry their dead children all the day long until they stopped again in the night."

James stopped talking. Sarah waited, but he stayed silent.

"What is it, James?"

"What else do you want to know?"

"I still want to know how you met Chandresh."

"Sarah…"

"You asked me what I wanted to know. This is what I want to know. My heart breaks for those people, James. You have to tell me their story."

"Very well." James pressed her closer to his chest. "In the shadows of the night, after the people had finished walking for the day, I would see the Grim Reaper himself, cloaked in black and gloom, pointing at that old man with parched lips and distended stomach, grimacing at that little girl heaving for breath, laughing at that woman crying for the children she will abandon in her death, her husband already dead and gone.

"One night I heard sobbing, which was common enough then. I came around a bend in the forest to see the medicine man I was familiar with since his son was my neighbor in the Smoky Mountains. The medicine man had spoken to me once along the trail when he called me the Kalona Ayeliski."

"What is that?" Sarah asked.

"The Raven Mocker. To the Cherokee, the Raven Mocker is an evil spirit who feeds from the hearts of the dead and dying to lengthen its own life."

"He was wrong about you."

"He was, and yet he wasn't. The Cherokee believe only the medicine men could see the Kalona Ayeliski, and the Cherokee people on the trail definitely couldn't see me. The white soldiers and doctors saw me well enough and spoke to me, but the Cherokee looked right through me and never acknowledged me at all. I stood alongside them in their camps, I walked among them as they ended their long day's journey in the night, I spoke to them, I brought them food and water, I helped bury their dead, and yet they never once so much as nodded in my direction. Then the medicine man explained that they couldn't see me because they couldn't see the Raven Mocker."

"Is that why Chandresh couldn't see you when you lived next door to him?"

"Yes."

"But he certainly sees you now."

James looked away. "Yes."

"That doesn't make sense. You're not an evil spirit. You don't feed on anyone's heart. You drink blood, but you don't kill anyone for it."

"I was no longer hunting then, that's true."

"Then how could the legend apply to you?"

"I don't know, but I'm certain they couldn't see me."

"Maybe they created the legend of the Raven Mocker because they assumed that if vampires were supernatural then they must be evil."

James shrugged. "I'm not aware of vampires that eat human hearts, but they may exist. The legend may have sprung from some truth."

Sarah wanted to ask him questions to keep him talking as she had always done, but something stopped her. She was frightened suddenly, reminded of the truth of their situation, and she remembered she wouldn't have her husband by her side much longer. She pressed herself into him, as hard as she could, trying to meld into him so when they took him away she would go too. Suddenly, she was afraid of hearing the end of his story, as though when he finished he would disappear, like it had been time for him to leave when he finished reading Miriam's books.

She tried to stretch her arm across James and she was startled by the IV tubes she had forgotten about. James checked the attachment to her arm, saw everything all right, and he gripped her hands and kissed them. She had to hear his voice, that moment and every moment more, and when he finished that story she would have him tell another and another.

"You said the medicine man was Chandresh's father?"

"Yes."

"What was his name?"

"Chandresh's father was Ashwin."

"What does it mean?"

"'Strong horse.'"

"And what does Chandresh mean?"

James paused. "'Lord of the moon.' That's the name he received after."

"After what?"

James looked over Sarah's head, through the window, as though he were searching for the scenes to play themselves out so he could show her like a movie. She saw the faintest traces of a grin as he remembered.

"When Chandresh and I were living near each other in the Smoky Mountains, I would watch him return to his cabin from tending his fields, playing with his older daughter in front of their house, sitting on the porch with his wife and her mother while the girls slept. Once, at a gathering before they were swept off their land, Ashwin addressed me directly, though I didn't realize at the time that he was the only one who could see me. Then, when Ashwin saw me on the trail, he watched me closely."

"Was he afraid you were going to eat someone's heart?"

"He didn't say so, but he made it clear he was keeping his eye on me. When he realized I was there to help, to get food and water where I could, to help tend the sick and the dying, he finally began calling me James instead of Kalona Ayeliski and I knew he finally saw me for what I was. When Chandresh lay dying, that's when he called to me."

"Chandresh was dying?" Sarah's hand went to her heart. She remembered herself in the dungeon, dying tortured and alone, and she remembered herself bloody and bruised along the side of the Maine road, dying in her husband's arms, and she imagined that dying within a sea of people wasn't any better.

"Remember when I said that one day I might tell you something that would make you run away from me for good? What if what I'm about to tell you is that thing? Would you want me to stop talking?"

"There is nothing you can tell me that will make me run away from you. I love you."

James stood from the bed and paced as he did whenever he was agitated or worried. His brow furrowed, his finger pressing back the wire-frame eyeglasses he wasn't wearing, there was no reason to hide his eyes now, and when he looked at Sarah it was with such love.

"Chandresh had dysentery, and he was weak from walking and malnutrition. He didn't have the will to live any longer and he wasn't fighting. He was ready to go. His wife and daughters were already dead. Chandresh's mother-in-law had been separated from the family for days until people who knew them said they passed her unburied corpse miles back. Ashwin begged me to find her and bury her, and I did. When he realized Chandresh was dying too, I could hear his heart breaking, tightening in his chest, tying itself into a knot. He knelt over his son, tried to get him to drink the few drops of water he had, but Chandresh clamped his lips and shook his head. Ashwin removed his son's turban and brushed his hair from his eyes as sweetly as any mother tending her newborn.

"'Listen,' he whispered to his son. 'You cannot leave me. You are all I have in this world. We will survive this together, you and I. We will go west, and we will grow strong. Stay.'

"I had to bite my lip to keep from crying. I knew Ashwin knew what I was, and yet I couldn't stand for him to see my bloody tears. It reminded me too much of my parting from my own father, and I knew the father's pain, and the son's for leaving him. Suddenly, Chandresh choked and gasped for air. He was taking his last breaths in this world.

Ashwin spun toward me. "'Help him!' he cried. I saw the others stare at Ashwin. As far as they could see the medicine man was begging for help from the air, or maybe from the Great Spirit who was nowhere to be seen along that forsaken trail. But I knew he was talking to me.

"'There's nothing more I can do,' I said.

"'Help him!' Ashwin cried again. The sight of this man, so strong while he helped others along the trail as best he could, who had lost everyone he loved day by day, one by one, begging me to help him tore at me in ways that are still too painful. Again, he reminded me of my own past, this time when I sat outside the jail begging anyone I saw to help you. It was too much and I turned away.

"Ashwin grabbed my arm. 'There is one thing you can do,' he said.

James's eyes darted from side to side as though he were seeing it all over again. "Then it dawned on me. A father desperate to save his son would be open to any solution to keep him, even a supernatural one.

"'Absolutely not,' I said. 'I wish this life on no one.'

"Ashwin shook me, pressing my arms to move like he was the puppeteer and I was his marionette. 'Save him!' he cried.

"'You called me the Kalona Ayeliski,' I said. 'You watched me around the people like I was some crazed monster ready to rip their hearts out of their chests and make a meal of them. Do you realize what you're asking? Is this the life you want for your son?'

"Ashwin dropped to his knees, his hands in the air, his eyes closed, his head bobbing. He chanted in his native language, softly at first, then louder and louder, a rhythmic, mesmerizing chant. I don't know what words he sang, but they touched me. I understood this man. I knew his pain. I had felt it myself, and that is when I realized that everyone's pain is the same. He was a Cherokee medicine man. I was...well, I was me. And yet in that moment we were the same."

"'If I do this it's without your son's permission,' I said. 'He isn't choosing this life—we're choosing it for him. Are you willing to suffer the consequences if he doesn't like our decision?"

"'He is a medicine man's son. He understands the spirit world. He will not be afraid. He understands there are good spirits and bad spirits. He will only be the Kalona Ayeliski if he chooses to be. You could have become the Kalona Ayeliski, yet you are not.'

"Chandresh gasped for breath. He was nearly gone.

"'Now, James,' Ashwin cried. 'Now!'

"I bit Chandresh's neck and sucked his blood until he was dry. Then I bit my own wrist and pressed it to his lips. At first, he didn't respond and I was afraid it was too late. But finally, he did begin to drink, and then he fell into the coma where the body regenerates into...into...'"

"A nocturnal?"

James smiled. "Yes, a nocturnal."

Sarah sat up. She clutched her stomach, it was still painful to move, but she pushed James's hand away and did it on her own. She looked into her husband's eyes and patted the bed beside her. He sat, stiff, holding himself at a distance from her, just as he had the first time he came into her rented brick house and he was afraid to get too close lest she discover his secret. Now she knew his secret and she didn't care. She held her hands to his cheeks and turned his face so she could look into his eyes.

"You turned Chandresh," she said. "Is that it? Is that what you've been so afraid to tell me?"

"Yes."

"But Chandresh's father begged you to turn him, and you understood his pain because of what happened with your own father. What's so terrible about what you did? Why were you afraid to tell me?"

James stroked Sarah's curls away from her face. "I was afraid that if you knew I turned Chandresh, perhaps you'd be afraid of what else I'm capable of." He looked out the window toward the bay as though he were searching for something far away. "I'm no better than Geoffrey."

"No better than Geoffrey?" Sarah laughed. "Here you are with all your advanced degrees, Doctor Wentworth, and you still miss what's right in front of you. You helped Chandresh."

"Does he think I helped him now?"

"What's happening now is not your fault, James."

"Perhaps. But whether or not I helped Chandresh, he certainly helped me. For as long as I had been living without you, I felt cold inside. Chandresh showed me I could still feel emotion, I could still care for someone. He needed my help, and that gave me some purpose. Even with you gone, I realized I could still be of some use in this world."

"You have the most caring heart I know. I will always love you."

"I know, honey. I'll never leave you..."

He stopped. Sarah knew why, and she couldn't give her usual reply—it wasn't true any more. He clutched her to him, and she clutched him just as hard, and they wept together, trying to wash it all away, out into the bay, to the other side of the world, somewhere far where they would never have to deal with the madness again.

CHAPTER TWENTY-TWO

For the next two nights James wouldn't leave Sarah's side. Doctor Masters came by twice a day as he said he would. He examined Sarah, adjusted her medication, said how quickly she was recovering. James passed the time sitting next to her, holding her hand, monitoring her medication, changing the dressing over her wounds. He lay on the bed next to his wife, his arms around her, feeling her breathe, memorizing the curve of her hips and the stretch of her neck. He held her head to his chest. He felt her warm softness and basked in the scent of strawberries and cream. The only reason he didn't cry out in pain was because somewhere he knew that, though the separation would be hard, they would survive. He would survive. His wife and daughter would survive and they would be reunited. He didn't want to leave his wife, he would never willingly leave her, or Grace, but if he had to go away for a while to settle his end of the madness then he would go and he would be all right, and then he would come home to his family. He had decided.

Perhaps they won't take me, he thought. Perhaps I've escaped their notice. But he knew. There was such an uproar at the hospital when he went to visit Sarah. Someone called the police on him. They'll find me soon enough, he thought. You can't hide anymore.

Agitated, angry, and unsure how to deal with it all, James paced the length of the living room, there and back, there and back, with such force that the wood floor showed the weight of his step. Olivia, Theresa, and Francine sat around the dining room table, whispering amongst themselves, casting anxious glances towards him, but he ignored them. Talking aloud to anyone but Sarah would feel like a chore right now.

He saw Sarah stir, and he wanted to wake her and talk to her, make sure her pain was under control, but she was still so swollen and bruised, so he let her sleep. He glanced through their open bedroom door and saw the large duffle bag Sarah had packed for them weeks ago, long before they ever had to flee. *We should do it again,* he thought. *We could run anywhere in the world. We have money, and I have access to cash so we wouldn't need credit cards. Madness couldn't have broken out every place across the planet, could it? There must be somewhere we could hide and wait it out. Some day soon there will be something else in the news that will capture the public's attention. It might take a year or two. Perhaps five or ten. But nothing stays the same, and this too shall pass.* They could outrun it, the three of them, moving on and moving on. He had always done that, though never with the urgency he would need to do so now with his wife and daughter along for the ride. They could do it. He knew they could. They needed to leave right now, this moment, to steal whatever part of a head start they could. Where to start? His thoughts turned immediately to his first home, London, just a few hours away by plane.

James rushed into the bedroom, threw the duffle bag onto the bed, and checked to see that it was mostly packed as Sarah said she left it. Then he went through the closet, pulling the few items of clothing Sarah had hung up on the hangers and tossed them into the open bag. They needed to go. There was no time to waste. He would let Sarah sleep a little while longer, get their plane tickets over the Internet, find the next flight out of Bangor International Airport, and they'd be on their way. He zipped the bag closed and carried it into the living room where Olivia and Theresa stood huddled by the front door as though they wanted to block him.

"Are you leaving?" Theresa asked.

"We have to go," James said.

Olivia took James's hand. "Sarah can't go, James. She's still recovering."

James shook his head. He couldn't admit, even to himself, that Olivia was right. "She'll be fine. I'll take care of her."

Then James heard it, the smug, self-satisfied footsteps shuffling toward the house. The knock startled Olivia and Theresa, but James knew. Theresa peeked through the peephole, worried about who it might be.

"You can let him in," James said. Theresa opened the door, and Geoffrey walked inside. "This is Geoffrey, everyone."

"You were at James's wedding," Olivia said. "I believe we met there."

Geoffrey nodded. "That is correct. Very nice to see you again." He looked past James to Sarah. "How is the little human person? She doesn't look so very bad. And the littlest human person?"

"Sarah is getting better. Grace is fine." James noticed Geoffrey's haggard look, how tired and gaunt he seemed. James thought Geoffrey looked on the outside the way he felt on the inside. "How did you know we were here, Geoffrey? Who else knows we're here?"

"Good God, James, everyone in Maine knows you're here. You didn't need to cause such a ruckus at the hospital."

"I was..."

"I know, James, I know." Geoffrey's nodded, his voice soft, even comforting. "But Maine isn't a big place, and everyone around here knows everyone else and some kayakers saw the ambulance bringing Sarah here. It didn't take long to put the pieces together." Geoffrey sighed. He walked to Sarah, still sleeping, and looked at the IV bags connected to her veins. "She's very strong," he said.

"I know," answered James. "How do you know all this?"

Geoffrey shrugged. "I have ways of finding out, that's all. Aren't you going to ask why I'm here? You always ask me why I'm here."

James sighed. "Why are you here, Geoffrey?"

"I've come as your own personal town crier." Geoffrey stood tall, pushing his shoulders back and stretching his head toward the ceiling, lengthening his already long frame. He pretended to unroll a scroll and held his hands out as though he stretched the imaginary paper so he could read whatever was written on it. He cleared his throat. "Hear ye, hear ye. They're sending soldiers out in force. The Vampire Dawn has officially ended and the round ups have begun. All vampires must be ready to report at their appointed time."

"No!" James said. "I'm not reporting to anyone. I'm leaving with my wife and daughter and we're going somewhere far away where we'll be safe. We're leaving now."

Geoffrey grabbed James's arm. "And go where? With her?" He pointed his elbow at Sarah, who was oblivious to them. "Do you see what your little human person looks like? She's so pale right now she could be one of us. You can't run anywhere with her. She's too damaged."

"He's right," Theresa said. "Her wounds are still healing, James. She can hardly sit up yet. She can't sit in a car, let alone for hours in a train or an airplane, and what about the time you have to wait in the airport? I'm so sorry, but she just can't leave on a journey like that right now."

James sat on the sofa, his hands on his knees, his head down. He was gasping for air, odd since he hadn't needed oxygen since 1692. He felt his preternatural body knotting up muscle by muscle from the inside out, and he couldn't stand the crimping pain. He felt the way he did the night he sat awake while his human body died because now it was happening all over again. He was wasting away inside and he shuddered from the knowledge that he might never see his wife again. He felt Olivia's hand on his but he wouldn't look at her. He knew he'd see the truth he couldn't bare to acknowledge in her motherly steel-gray eyes. She tugged on him, and finally he turned to her.

"Sarah can't go," she said, "but you can. If you need to run, James, then run. Sarah will understand."

"No," James said. He pulled away from Olivia and walked the room again, back to smoothing the tire-like grooves he was working into the wood floor with his frenetic pacing. "I can't live without her. I've tried, and I can't. We have to go together—all of us. I know it will be hard, but as long as we're together everything will be all right. I'll take care of her."

Geoffrey knelt besides James, took his vampling's hands in his, and brushed a few stray gold strands from his brow, a fatherly gesture that suddenly seemed natural between them. His voice was soft, concerned, such a contrast to his usual irreverence. "You can't take Sarah," he said. "Your little human person is so delicate, and she's hurt right now." He looked at Theresa. "All you human people are so delicate, I hardly know how most of you make it through the day without injuring yourselves somehow. How you live into your eighties with your soft skin and fragile bones is quite remarkable really." He tugged on James's hand and looked at him without a flicker of sarcasm anywhere in his features. "I can see it in your eyes you know what I say is true. Your little human person needs to stay here now, and you need to go where they tell you to go. It's the best thing for you, and it's the best thing for her too."

James dropped his head, shuddering in spasms, and Geoffrey, still kneeling, looked up into his vampling's sad face. "You have to decide whether or not you're going to run, James, but if you run it will have to be alone, and it will be hard. It's not so easy to hide anymore. Are you going to drive? They'll find the license plate of your car. There are security cameras everywhere. Are you going to fly? You need a passport to leave the country."

"I know how to get new passports with different names," James said.

"There's no time!" Geoffrey shook James's shoulder, trying to rattle some sense into him. "Didn't you hear me? They're coming to take you away. And me too. Every one of us. And if we don't go willingly they're going to hunt us down." Geoffrey sighed with frustration. "I knew you'd do something rash like try to run. That's why I'm here now—to stop you. We both need to go, James. We'll be all right, and your nice little human people here will be all right as well. But there's no running. If the government wants you gone they'll make you go away. You know that all too well, don't you? They'll find you, and it frightens me to think what they'll do to you once you're found. Now as your..." Geoffrey closed his eyes, and he was silent a long moment. "As your friend, I'm begging you. Don't run. Don't risk all the happiness you have to come back to. Do you know how fortunate you are to have these nice human people who love you? Do you know how proud I am of you?" Again, Geoffrey stopped himself, and again he took James's hands in his. "You have too much to risk, James, by being foolish now. I'll be there to help you. I won't leave you alone again. And these lovely human ladies will be here to help Sarah and Grace."

"Of course that's true, James," Theresa said. "They can live here with me."

"Or with me if they want to move back to Salem," Olivia said. "We'll take care of them."

James pulled his hands free. He stood and towered over Geoffrey, who was still on his knees, his eyes still begging James to understand. James pointed at Geoffrey like he was calling the attention of the heavens onto that horrid vampire man.

"You're telling me to go along with it?" James laughed a wicked laugh. "The way you wanted me to go along with it when you said you could help me when I was sitting outside the jail where they held my wife? The way you wanted me to go along with it when you bit me and turned me into this? You're the reason I'm in this hell in the first place." James turned the entire force of his fury onto Geoffrey. "Damn you, Geoffrey! This is all your fault! If you just left me alone, if I wasn't this unhuman, cursed atrocity! You cursed me, Geoffrey, and now my wife and daughter have to suffer for it and I will never forgive you. You're not going to leave me alone again? What's so special about this time? Why are you going to help me now when you abandoned me when I needed you most?"

Geoffrey sighed. He walked to the window, unlatched the lock, and slid it open. He looked toward the blackness of the bay, invisible in the night. He breathed in deeply though he didn't need to.

"I deserve all your wrath, James, I know I do. You don't know how I've suffered knowing what I know. I reproach myself nightly because of it. You and I are connected, James, and though I made mistakes in the past, I'm here now. I won't abandon you again."

James was stunned into silence. Geoffrey—loving and considerate? The world must be coming to an end. He would have laughed if he wasn't so sad. Finally, he asked, "Is there no other way?"

Geoffrey shook his head. "I'm so very sorry, James."

Olivia covered her eyes with her hands, and her shoulders shuddered with her sobs. She sobbed the way James wished he could have but he was numb suddenly, unable to feel anything. Someone might have staked him right then and he wouldn't have known the difference and kept going as though nothing had happened until he disintegrated into a splat of blood on the floor. Finally, when her tremors slowed enough so she could gather her voice and speak, she said, "I think Geoffrey is right, James. It breaks my heart to say it, but I don't see a way around it. You need to go."

"But what's going to happen to you after you're rounded up?" Theresa asked.

Geoffrey shook his head. "I don't know," he said.

When Sarah awoke Geoffrey was gone and James sat with Olivia and Theresa around the dining room table. Olivia was weeping, keeping a white linen handkerchief to her cheek while she wrote whatever James told her into a spiral notebook. Theresa dropped her head onto her arms on the table. Sarah pushed herself onto her elbows, straining to hear what they were saying but they whispered closely to each other and their words were muffled. She watched her husband, his stillness, his blank stare at the red-checkered tablecloth under his clenched fists, his inability to look at either Olivia or Theresa, the way his mouth hardly moved while he spoke.

"What's wrong?" she asked.

"Nothing," James said. He left the table, sat on the bed beside her, and brushed a few stray curls from her eyes. "Everything is going to be all right, Sarah, I promise."

When they heard the angry banging on the door they froze. Theresa peeked around the red gingham curtains and gasped when she saw the two grim-faced army officers outside her house. Her hand shook as she opened the door.

"We're looking for James Wentworth," said the dark-haired officer.

James stood from the bed, still gripping Sarah's hand. "I'm here," he said.

The soldier held an envelope in James's direction, which James took. Theresa gave the soldiers a glaring stare which made little impression on them. James turned the envelope over in his hands, stared at his neatly typed name, then ripped the top, pulled out the letter, and scanned the contents inside. Sarah saw his jaw tighten and his eyes narrow, and she could see in his straining muscles how he struggled to keep his expression still. But she didn't need him to speak in words to understand that something was wrong. She knew him so well. She struggled into a sitting position to try to see what the letter said, but she felt dizzy suddenly, caught up in the tornado, the house and everyone in it spiraling through the wind-swept sky, higher and higher, then lower and lower until they crash landed somewhere through the rainbow and over the woods, from to the full life of color to the limited shadows of black and white on the other side.

"James Wentworth, as a resident of the state of Massachusetts you're ordered to report to the Boston South Station at 10 p.m. on Friday, May the fourth. You can pack one bag to take with you. Anyone not following the directive will be subject to immediate arrest."

"But I'm already being arrested," James said. "Isn't that what this is?"

"You're not being arrested, sir," the second officer said. "You'll be detained awhile."

"And the difference is?"

"Make sure you're on time. That's all."

The soldiers turned away, and Sarah heard the marching cadence to their heavy steps as they disappeared through the front yard. They had handed James his notice, given him his directions, and now they were gone, their work done. James stood by the door, his head to the side, listening. Even Sarah from where she sat on the bed could hear loud crunching of the jeep's accelerator as they drove away. James turned to the anxious faces watching him.

"Well, there it is," he said.

Suddenly, without reading the letter, Sarah understood. Her breath came in short, strained bursts and she struggled to breathe.

"Are they taking you away?" she asked.

James took her into his arms. "Yes," he said, "but don't worry. Everything is going to be all right. I promise you, Sarah. We'll be all right."

"Friday the fourth," Sarah said. She had been sleeping so much she realized she had no idea what day it was. "What is today?" she asked.

"It's Wednesday the second," Olivia said.

Sarah looked at James. "Two days? You're leaving in two days?"

Her hands went to her cheeks, first squeezing, then slapping, trying to awaken herself from this nightmare. James took her hands from her face and held them to his chest.

"Sarah, please..."

Please what, she wondered? Please go? Please stay? She wanted to scream, cry, run, anything other than stare helplessly in the direction the army officers had gone. Suddenly, she felt herself chained to the walls, the pock-faced monster—that ghoul who had haunted her night after night, year after year as he stood tall in the shadows—triumphant after all. I have caught you again, my pretty, she heard him say, and I will catch you again and again until you understand you will never truly get away. I will hold you in my night-dark dungeon forever.

Bang! Bang! Bang!

Sarah started. What was that? Knocking on the door? A gun going off? She couldn't tell. Her shaking shoulders betrayed her terror at the living nightmare she saw acted out everywhere around her. But she couldn't move her hands to hide her eyes from the horror, weighted down by the chains as she was.

"What is it?" she cried. "James, what is it?"

James looked at the door. He listened, intent, his head tilted, his extra senses alert, but he shook his head. "I don't hear anything, Sarah," he said. He looked at Olivia and Theresa, and they both shrugged.

"I didn't hear anything, either," said Olivia.

Theresa peeked around the curtains. "There's no one there, Sarah," she said. "The soldiers are gone."

Knock! Knock! Knock!

"No, he's there." Sarah cringed in terror, trying to hide behind James, trying to disappear. If you can't see me, I'm not here, she thought, like a two-year-old playing peek-a-boo.

"He's here!"

"Who's here?" Theresa asked. She opened the front door, afraid she missed the intruder through the window, but all was still outside, the bay flat, the trees bent in the breeze, bowing in reverence at the sad scene before them. "Sarah, I promise you, there's no one here."

"Oh my God," James said. He knelt beside his wife and kissed the top of her hair, her forehead, her cheeks, her hands. "Sarah, he's not here. That was a very, very long time ago, honey, and he's not here now. He won't be here for you ever again. They were here for me, Sarah, for me. You're safe. No one is going to take you away."

Bang! Bang! Bang!

Knock! Knock! Knock!

Sarah shook her head and waved her hands faster with each sound, trying to brush the pock-faced man away. "He's here, James. He followed me here. He's coming with his chains. He's going to drag me away. We're going to die again. Grace! We're going to die again."

"Oh, Sarah..."

"Ssh. Listen." Sarah strained her head toward the window, and she cringed when she heard the wagon stop, the horses bay, the thud as the constable jumped to the ground, the rattle of the chains. "He's here. He's coming. Hide me, James. You have to hide me!"

And then it all began again. Bang! Bang! Bang! Knock! Knock! Knock! The door opens and he's there, the pock-faced constable, talking nonsense about witches and confessions and warrants of arrest. But I'm innocent, Sarah screamed in the silence of her mind. How can you take me away? Her hands went to her stomach where she knew her baby waited, the baby she knew was a girl, the baby she named Grace, and she wept because they would die all over again.

She is taunted, yelled at, manhandled, chained. Driven to the dungeon, yelled at, manhandled some more. She is bodily searched, for witches markings and whatever else they want to see. Her head is shaved. She is chained to the wall. When their coercions and threats do not sway her, she is no witch and will not confess, she is forced between the walls, caught in the limbo agony of screaming muscles and traumatized bones. It will never end, she thought. We are caught in limbo forever.

She sees him coming, his weighty, snake-like chains slithering alongside his feet, inch-by-inch toward her, each step a nail in her coffin. He grabs her arm, drags her to the wagon, chains her on, and drives her away. She looks back, sees her husband on his knees on the ground, her dear and loving husband, his hands outstretched toward her as though if he could reach her he could pull her back and keep her with him where she belonged. Where else in the world could she belong but with James? But he couldn't reach her, and then he was gone...

James heard the moaning from deep in Sarah's gut, a guttural moan that began in anguish and ended in horror. Olivia and Theresa rushed to Sarah's side, brushing her hair from her face, stroking her back, saying sweet motherly nothings to soothe her. When she settled some James cradled her head against his chest.

"Sarah, please. It's going to be all right. We're all going to be all right." He brushed her matted curls from her eyes and wiped her tears away with the tips of his fingers. "I know you're thinking this is like 1692, but it's not the same. Then, they accused you of something you weren't, but I am what they say I am. Which is why I'm going to be all right. I'm immortal and I'm strong. Don't ever forget that, Sarah. I'm immortal and I'm strong."

"No, no, no," Sarah said, her tears flowing freely down her face and onto James's chest, soaking his shirt through. "No, no, no."

"Sarah..."

"No, no, no...."

James tried to calm her, to convince her that everything would be all right, but she was too far gone to hear him. As he sat on the bed, still trying to soothe her, he pulled his cell phone from his pocket and called Doctor Masters. The doctor was on his way.

James watched nervously as Doctor Masters added some medication to Sarah's IV and she was sleeping in a matter of moments. James slumped over, the anguish everywhere within him. He turned to Theresa, and Olivia took his hand.

"You need to take care of Sarah while I'm gone," he said. "While I'm gone..." The words echoed in his head and he felt hollow suddenly. His voice sounded strange to his ears and he wondered what language he was speaking.

"You are my family," Olivia said. "I will take care of them. I will take care of them until you come home because you will come home." Olivia was so overcome with emotion she turned away. She walked into Theresa's open arms, and Theresa hugged her.

After the doctor left and Olivia and Theresa retired for the night, James sat on the bed next to Sarah. He sat there for hours, unstirring, holding her hand, watching her in her drug-induced sleep. He didn't need to memorize her face. He did that years before. Years before. He knew her wide, full smile. The luscious rosebud lips he needed to kiss whenever he looked at her. He knew the silky softness of her dark curls, the wondering curiosity behind her dark eyes. He knew the warm softness of her touch. He had had her in his mind every night for three hundred and nineteen years, and he thought he would have more time before he had to rely again on his memory of her.

When dawn would soon shine through, James went into the bedroom and emptied his frantic packing from earlier. He filled the duffle bag with a few items for himself, a change of clothes, two photographs—one of Sarah and one of Sarah, Grace, and him, the triumvirate of Wentworths laughing, holding hands. Joyful. It was a shock to realize that photo had been taken only three months before. Grace had grown so much. He packed some composition notebooks he had bought from the general store and a handful of ballpoint pens, and he dropped in his cell phone with the unlisted number though he suspected he wouldn't be able to keep it. He had seen these round-ups before. He reached into his pocket and pulled out the small antique-looking key, turning it over in his hands, remembering the touch of it, as though he were reacquainting himself with an old friend. He stared at the key, through it to the memories on the other side, and he dropped it into the bag and zippered the bag closed.

As he walked around the quiet little carriage house, looking at the whitewashed kitchen, the living room with the red gingham curtains and the red overstuffed sofa and chairs, he thought of his wooden gabled house sitting lonely in Salem. He pictured the great room with his seventeenth century wooden desk—to which the antique key belonged—the flat screen television mounted onto the wall, the bookcases overflowing with books, and the bedroom where Sarah and he slept. He was surprised at his numbness. He thought he should be reduced to tears or fuming with red-blood anger. He thought he should be raging, or at least feeling sad. He looked again at Sarah, and though she was unconscious from the drugs the doctor had given her he could see the strain in her tight eyes and pulled lips. She was sleeping, but she wasn't resting. He kissed her forehead and stroked her arm, then walked away, afraid of waking her. He had to stay strong. He would be the strength for all of them. He had decided.

His resolve nearly broke when he heard his daughter's voice.

"Dadda," she said.

James looked in Grace's crib and smiled. She was nearly eleven months old, and she had been babbling for a while now. But this was the first time he heard something that sounded like an actual word. His name. He wanted to cry, but he refused. She wouldn't see him bleed from his eyes, not now.

He took a moment to compose his voice. "Hi, Grace," he said. He lifted her from her crib and he sat with her on the rocking chair in the bedroom. He rocked them slowly, gently, needing to soothe himself as much as his daughter.

"It's going to be all right," he said, his voice a whisper. "I have to go away for a little while. It's just a little while, but I'm going to miss you very much. I love you, Grace. I'm so glad you found your way home. Now I'm going to be fine, and your mother and you are going to be fine. We're all going to stay strong, and then we'll see each other again very soon and everything will be fine. Do you understand what I'm saying?"

"Dadda," Grace said.

"I love you, Grace."

James heard footsteps down the hall. He smelled the familiar sandalwood scent and turned to see Olivia standing in the open doorway. In the deepened lines in her motherly face he saw his own fears reflected back to him. Looking at Olivia, he felt numb, nothing, like when your body is injured and at first there's great pain to alert you that something is wrong, but then the body becomes kinder and shuts down. That was where James was. He was experiencing the greatest pain he could imagine, and now he was shutting down.

"Don't worry about a thing," Olivia said. "I'll take care of them. But you need to stay strong too, James." Olivia stuttered as she spoke, and though she struggled to hold her face tight she couldn't stop the emotion from cracking through. "You need to come back because we all need you. Your wife and your daughter need you."

"Don't worry, Olivia. I'm coming home. I've decided."

Olivia kissed the top of Grace's head and smiled.

"I believe you," she said.

CHAPTER TWENTY-THREE

When Sarah awoke the next day everything was hazy. She opened her swollen eyes to a darkened room and blurred vision, gradations of gray blanketing everywhere she looked. She expected to see the dark brown wood of her gabled house, her husband asleep beside her in their bed, her daughter asleep in the room next door. She threw her legs over the side of the bed to go to Grace and moaned aloud at the sharp pain in her stomach, like she was stabbed by newly sharpened knives. Suddenly, the gray blanket cleared away, leaving a clear view of the hospital bed, the IV tubes connected to her arm, the white walls and red furniture of Theresa's house. She saw a shadow and started, but recognized James in the lightless room, asleep in the overstuffed recliner by her side. She looked at the windows at the heavy black curtains blocking out any semblance of sunlight and sighed. The sharp, butchering pain returned, only this wasn't in her stomach where her stitches healed. This was in her heart, which wouldn't heal nearly as well.

"How are you feeling? You look better."

Olivia stood by the side of the bed, a tray with medication in her hands. She had that detective seeking clues look as she studied Sarah's careworn face. But Sarah was too consumed by watching James, still lost in his catatonic sleep, and she looked at the window again, wondering how bright the sun was and how much longer until it was dark.

"Doctor Masters said you can have some broth," Olivia said.

Sarah nodded. She couldn't take her eyes from James. She had a vague recollection of the night before and she knew he was leaving. She remembered seeing the pock-faced constable, the chains, the walls, but the rest of it was a blank.

Olivia put the tray on the end table near the bed, then sat next to Sarah and took her hands. "I've been wanting to do a reading on you for some time now, Sarah," she said.

"Jennifer said you've been wanting to do one since we went to the exhibition at the college."

"That's right. May I do one now?"

"What if you learn something I don't want to know?"

"Wouldn't you rather know what you're dealing with?"

Sarah nodded. "All right," she said.

"Good girl." Olivia gripped Sarah's hands tighter, closed her eyes and began rocking back and forth, the same bobbing Sarah remembered from her psychic reading when she first arrived in Salem. Olivia said nothing, squeezing her eyes tighter, shaking her head from side to side like she was saying no to a voice inside her head. She turned her face down toward her shoulder as though she needed to concentrate. Sarah held her breath, waiting for the static she felt in the air during her past-life regression, like shocks of light touching her everywhere, waiting for the strange electric connection she felt to everyone and everything whenever she was confronted by the supernatural. She turned her ear toward Olivia so she could catch her Wiccan friend's wise predictions for her future, James's future, their future together. Finally, Olivia opened her eyes and shook her head, her mouth opened like she wanted to speak but didn't know what to say.

"What do you see?" Sarah asked.

"Nothing," Olivia said. "I can't fall into a trance. I can't get a read on you right now."

"What does it mean?"

"It doesn't necessarily mean anything. It's nothing to worry about, dear. It happens sometimes."

"Olivia, if you know something you need to tell me. Good or bad, I need to know."

Olivia kissed her cheek. "There's nothing to tell."

Sarah grasped Olivia's hand and held it to her heart. "There's nothing to tell about my future?"

"It doesn't mean you don't have a future. It just means I can't connect to it right now."

"Is it true what you said when we brought Grace home? That there's no such thing as coincidence? It's not a coincidence that James and I are being torn apart again for reasons beyond our control? Is this our destiny?"

Olivia put her arms around Sarah. "Do you remember what Martha said to you at the past-life regression last year? About your soul, and James's?"

"She said our souls were intertwined. She said we'd be together whenever, wherever because it's our destiny."

"She was right, Sarah. No matter what comes between you, you will always find your way back to each other. *That* I'm sure of."

Sarah sighed. She closed her eyes and leaned her head back on the feather pillows Theresa bought to make her more comfortable in the narrow stretch of the hospital cot. She exhaled deeply, trying to release the nail-biting worry she felt everywhere inside her, in her stitches, in her injuries, in her heart. She tried to let herself drift away, float upwards to the clouds, float away from that hospital bed, away from her wounds, away from the accident that debilitated her for who knows how much longer. She didn't have time to be weak now. Suddenly an influx of questions flooded her tired mind and she tapped her temples trying to make the unwanted thoughts go away.

Olivia took Sarah's hands in hers. "What is it, Sarah?"

Everything else filtered away and there was one nagging question left. And Olivia was the one who could answer it.

"Why did I come back? Why am I here?"

"You came back because you had to. Neither you nor James could have found peace if you hadn't."

"I came back to be separated from him again? It doesn't make sense."

"We don't always understand what's happening when it's happening," Olivia said. "Patience, dear. All in good time."

Sarah struggled to sit up. She still had such scratching pains in her stomach from the littlest movement, and she still felt dizzy whenever she turned her head too quickly. Olivia fluffed the pillows, propped them against the back of the bed, then helped Sarah straighten into a half-sitting, half-laying position.

Sarah grimaced as a wave of sharp-knife pain slashed across her abdomen, and Olivia wiped her brow with a cool, damp cloth.

"I'm all right," Sarah said. Olivia sat beside her and took her hand. "When we were in Salem, Jennifer told me how Chandresh didn't believe his wife would come back, and she believed that too. She said Chandresh loved his wife, but he said that was his past and his present was with Jennifer in Salem. How can they be so sure Chandresh's wife won't come back when I came back to James?"

"Chandresh said good-bye to his wife. He made peace with her death. She was taken from him cruelly, as you were taken from James in 1692, and Chandresh suffered himself while they were on the trail to Oklahoma. It doesn't mean he loved his wife less than James loves you. It means he was able to accept their fate and he moved on. James never said good-bye to you, Sarah. He couldn't. His life in this world didn't matter to him if he didn't feel connected to you somehow. Everything he did, everything he thought, was about finding some bond to you. In a way, you could say he called you back to him. He never let you go, and now here you are. You see? It's all part of the master plan."

"Can't you try again to get a reading on me?" Sarah asked. "Jennifer said you're a powerful witch and witches all over the world come to you for advice. Use your powers, Olivia. Tell me what's going to happen." She managed a weak smile. "That's how desperate I am—I'm begging you for a reading now when you scared me out of my wits last time."

"You weren't familiar with the supernatural world yet," Olivia said. "You're more open to what I have to say now. Besides, I wouldn't say I'm so powerful. I do my best, that's all."

"When I was at the Witches Lair you had no problem falling into a trance."

"There are many reasons for disturbances in the energy. It might be because you're injured, or because of the difficult circumstances and your mind is too anxious and your body is too tight to let your energy flow, or it might be because things aren't clear yet. Not everything is decided for us, Sarah. Often it's our own choices that guide our future." Olivia looked around and shrugged. "I wish Theresa were here now, or Martha. They're so much better at explaining this than I am."

"I understand what you're saying."

"Good. If there's one thing I want you to remember it's that there's something larger, something benevolent in your life guiding you, there for you, giving you the strength you need whenever you need it if only you'll allow yourself to depend on it. It's there now."

"I don't feel anything benevolent now," Sarah said. "All I feel is anger and pain and fear."

Olivia nodded. "Trust in it, Sarah. It will carry you through the worst of the worst and help you understand when you're standing on the other side."

"I need it now," Sarah said.

"Yes," Olivia said, "you do."

"You need what now, Sarah?" James sat upright as he reached for Sarah's hand, his eyes fixed on Olivia. "What does she need, Olivia?"

"It's nothing," Olivia said. "I tried a reading on her, but I wasn't able to focus on anything. Her energy wasn't clear."

"What does that mean?"

"It doesn't mean anything. Don't worry." She pointed at the tray on the side table. "Eat your broth, Sarah," she said as she disappeared into the kitchen.

James sat in the bed next to his wife. He put his arm around her shoulders and held her close. He kissed the top of her hair and breathed in deeply.

"Do I still smell like strawberries and cream?" she asked.

"Always."

"What does Grace smell like?"

"Cinnamon."

Sarah nodded. "I like cinnamon."

"Me too. Strawberries and cream and cinnamon go well together."

She pressed herself into his side, trying again to meld into him and again finding they were all too separate.

"I want to go with you," she said.

"They'll see soon enough how human you are."

"I should have let you turn me."

"No, Sarah. You were right to say no. You need to stay exactly as you are. You're perfect exactly as you are. Besides, you need to stay with Grace."

"I know," she said.

James kissed her tears away, and Sarah savored each moment his flesh touched hers. He sat in the overstuffed chair so he could look into her face, they had just a few more hours to see each other, able to reach out and touch each other before they parted until who-knows-when. James kissed her forehead, then stroked her face from her curls to her chin.

"I never finished telling you about the Trail of Tears," he said.

"After you turned Chandresh?"

"Yes."

"Was he angry you turned him?"

"At first. But his father was there to help him, and I was there to help him, and he came around in time."

"You did for him what Geoffrey didn't do for you."

"I couldn't live with myself if I left him to figure this life out for himself. I needed to make sure he was all right. I needed to teach him how to deal with this curse."

"How many times do I have to tell you—you're not cursed."

"The curse is more obvious now than ever, Sarah. We're all suffering for it. I hope Chandresh doesn't hate me for what I did to him. It's because of me he has to leave Jennifer."

"You saved his life because his father begged you to, and in a way, Timothy is your vampling too. No man with your heart can be cursed. I told you before you're like the Tin Man. We've pulled the curtain back from the scary-looking wizard and found an ordinary man, and the ordinary man is telling you that you already have the heart you've been wishing for. That heart has been filled with undying love for me for over three hundred years, and Grace, and Chandresh, and Timothy. For Miriam's whole family down the generations. Don't you ever say you're cursed again. I don't care what the anti-vampire protestors say. I don't care what the media says. You're my dear and loving husband, Jamie. You always will be."

James was silent, and he looked far away, over Sarah's head, somewhere she couldn't join him, like she couldn't join him on this journey he would soon be traveling. Finally, he sighed, then continued talking as though he hadn't stopped. "Now the others couldn't see Chandresh like they couldn't see me, though Ashwin saw us both. When Chandresh was strong enough, we did what we could to help the others as they continued to Oklahoma."

"How long did it last?" Sarah asked.

"About three months," James said. "It's where the legend of the Cherokee Rose began. During the Trail of Tears, the mothers of the Cherokee were crying so much because they couldn't help their children survive. They say the elders prayed for a sign that would lift the mothers's spirits to give them strength. The next day beautiful roses grew where the mothers's tears fell, white for their tears, with a gold center for the gold taken from the Cherokee land, seven leaves on each stem for the seven Cherokee clans. The trail was arduous, even painful at times, but they did finally arrive in Oklahoma."

"Many died along the way, and the soldiers were brutal to them."

"That is true, but don't lose sight of those who survived. Remember, you said it yourself—they're still here. It was hard going for them for a long time. They left everything behind—their politics, their social systems, their culture. They left their homes, their ancestors, everything about their way of life, but as soon as the survivors arrived in Oklahoma they began to rebuild. They rebuilt it all, Sarah. They created schools for boys, and for girls. They reestablished their culture. They had a newspaper in both Cherokee and English. They started businesses, created a new Constitution, and they thrived. The years after the removal were called the Cherokee Golden Age."

"But then they had problems again."

"They did, but they overcame those too. They overcame problems caused by the Civil War, problems caused by Oklahoma statehood. They've overcome every obstacle put in their way. People have used harsh measures to deal with the 'Indian problem,' and yet they're still here."

"They're using harsh measures to deal with the Vampire Dawn."

"They are." James grasped Sarah's hands and clasped them to his chest. "But we'll survive. We'll survive, we'll heal, and we'll rebuild. We're immortal and we're strong, Sarah. Don't ever forget that."

"I'm not immortal," she said.

"You're here now, so in your way you are."

Sarah nodded. "And then when this madness is over we'll be together again."

"Yes. We'll be together again."

Sarah struggled to brighten her mood—she knew he needed to see it, she knew him so well. After her hard-won smile, she threw her arms around his neck and buried her face in his chest.

CHAPTER TWENTY-FOUR

The lines of the weary, broken-hearted undead stretched down all the miles of the road as far as James could see. A storm lingered overhead in the moonless night, bringing heavy gray clouds and the fresh-air scent of early May rain. Beneath the storm they came in a cluttered throng, rows and rows of them, white-skinned, black-eyed, marching to the tempo of a common-time drumbeat only they could hear. Many stood straight-backed, eyes ahead, stoic, as though this were nothing, they had suffered worse before, they had suffered over more years than the oldest humans could imagine. Others wept openly, the blood staining them in their sadness, their white faces streaked pink. They were the elders, the wisest and the most respected, with gray in their hair and wrinkles in their faces. They were husbands and wives, fathers and mothers, sons and daughters, uncles and aunts, nephews and nieces, cousins, friends, neighbors, and anyone else you ever knew from the day you were born. Some held hands with others of their kind or with the humans they loved. The young women caught the lewd glances of the khaki-suited soldiers who didn't hide their delight at the sight of the pretty raven-eyed girls. They walked across the narrow streets of Boston, just as others of their kind were doing in every major city in the country, passing cars whose drivers slowed to gawk and wonder, passing pedestrians who stood in rows on the sidewalks to see the undead go by. Some called for family members they couldn't find in the crowds. Some watched their feet as though their numb legs had become detached from their torsos and they wondered how they moved. The storm in the sky left its gloominess over everything and everyone. Those heading into the train station looked around in bewilderment, as though they hardly knew why they were there. But everywhere was a heaving of sorrow so deep it cut through all the many generations these beings had seen.

273

The media was there, hundreds of them from all over the world, their film crews capturing the moment, their on-the-beat reporters talking into their microphones as they tried to make sense of the scene for those watching at home. A boisterous crowd blocked the way into the train station, and there were twice as many spectators there to watch the proceedings as there were those being rounded up. Cell phones and digital cameras flashed and filmed. Some in the crowd shouted curses while others shouted encouragement. Many held placards, some for, some against the vampires. The army soldiers were there, guns out, on guard, their muscles tense, their shoulders high, waiting for someone to start with them, ready to use the force they were trained for. They created barriers on either side of the entrance as a walkway for the vampires to pass through.

As the vampires and their families made their way into the train station, the armed guards pushed back the spectators who pressed forward. The people held their placards over their heads, pumped fists into the air, flashed peace signs or waves with less than five fingers. When the vampires arrived in greater numbers, the crowd broke out into a frenzy of shouts and gestures and signs and cameras.

James held onto Sarah's arm in one hand and his duffle bag in the other, seeing everything—the advertisements for local Boston sights, the fast food stands, the newspaper racks, the ticket booths, the shouting confusion as the undead searched for where to go—through an avalanche of bleary-eyed bewilderment. He hadn't expected the chaos. He thought the vampires would disappear as unheeded and unnoticed as the Cherokee had left the southeast in 1838. There was no fanfare then, little media coverage except propaganda to cheer the evacuations, certainly not crowds hovering to see them off. One day they lived in the southeast and the next they were gone. Sarah held her head down, staring at the ground beneath her feet, refusing to acknowledge the madness surrounding her. James pulled her into the train station since he was afraid of being separated from her in the crowd and not finding her again before he had to leave. Inside, they were given directions over the loudspeaker. They were assigned trains according to their county of residence. James found the number for Essex County and brought Sarah to stand beside him. In his confusion, he looked around for Grace until he remembered Olivia stayed behind with her. He said good-bye to her at home. He looked around for Chandresh, who was boarding the same train since he had moved to Salem to be closer to Jennifer, and Jennifer was there too, but they had been separated in the crowd. Timothy was boarding the same train, as was Jocelyn, but he didn't see them either. He realized with a nervous tick that there was something he meant to tell Sarah before he left, something important, and he shuddered when he couldn't remember what it was. He remembered telling himself, "Don't forget to tell Sarah..." Don't forget to tell Sarah what?

James bit his lip. He would stay strong for Sarah. He had decided. When a single tear fell, he wiped it away quickly, hoping she hadn't noticed.

But she saw. She looked into his blood-streaked eyes and took his dead-cold face between her hands and squeezed with all her strength. Suddenly, the early May thunderstorm broke though, and though they sat inside they could see the ferocity of the storm pelt the glass walls, the bursts of lightening flashing while the harsh water pellets hit the trains outside. Sarah shivered though it wasn't a cold rain, the gray-cloud sky matching her grief at their impending separation. James kissed her forehead and let his lips linger.

"This will all be over soon," he said, for himself as much as Sarah.

He found two seats on a bench near the glass doors that led to the platform outside. He slid his arm around Sarah's shoulders, trying to comfort her. He knew her so well. He knew what she was thinking before the realization crossed her own mind, but that was their way. He guessed she could see the crack in his heart through her weary eyes. She was still recovering, still in pain, but she came with him to say good-bye, and he loved her for her strength. For the first time since they were reunited over a year before, he didn't know what to say to make any of this better. He couldn't make this better. He was going away when he promised he would never leave her ever.

James watched Sarah as she eyed the throng pushing forward and back, here and there, side to side, pressing against them in one moment and emptying through the glass doors in the next. Despite the cries, the yells, the whispers, the questions, James pulled Sarah close and they managed to create a moment for themselves within the confusion, like they were enclosed in a soundproof bubble.

Sarah kissed James's hand and rested her head against his shoulder. "I remember the first time I saw you," she said. "I mean the very first time. I was talking to my sister at supper, and I looked up and there you were, the most beautiful-looking man I had ever seen."

"Do you recall it from your own memories? I told you that story in the library last year before you went through the past-life regression."

"No, I remember it. I remember sitting next to Mary Grace, telling her that she was too young to help with the reaping and the plowing, and if she lost a finger or an arm in the sickle I wasn't enough of a seamstress to sew it back for her..." Sarah's hand went over her mouth, her eyes wide with the memory. "My sister's name was Mary Grace. That's where I got the name Grace."

"That's right. Mary died of typhoid when she was eleven years old. You were sure the baby you carried was a girl so you named her after your sister."

"I was right."

"Yes, you were." James watched the people pass by, heard the shouts as they called to each other, heard the footsteps, some quick, some slow, some shuffles, some stomps. For a moment, he thought he heard Kenneth Hempel's heavy, plodding footsteps. This whole scene was part of Hempel's master plan. Damn you, Hempel, James thought. This is all because of you.

"Next month is our first anniversary," Sarah said. "Our first anniversary this time around." The sadness was back and her voice cracked and her chest heaved. Her hand went to her stomach where she was still stitched from her surgery. When James moved to help her, she shook her head. "I'm all right," she said.

James nodded. "I know it's our anniversary. I never forgot you for a moment over three centuries. Do you think I could forget something from a year ago?"

"Do you think you'll be home by then?"

"I don't think so, honey."

Sarah dropped her face into her hands, and James pulled her closer to him, closer, closer, as though if he pulled her tight enough they would meld and they could stay together somehow because either others would mistake him for human or her for one of his kind. Then, after giving into her grief, she sat up, her face set, her shoulders firm. She looked James in the eye and nodded.

"We're very lucky," she said. "Most people don't get a second chance at love the way we did."

"Our second chance isn't over," James said. "This is just a bump in the road." James leaned his face close to Sarah, and he whispered in her ear with all the love he could channel into his words:

> "I prize thy love more than whole mines of gold,
> Or all the riches that the East doth hold.
> My love is such that rivers cannot quench,
> Nor ought but love from thee give recompense.
> Thy love is such I can no way repay..."

He waited. Sarah lifted her head and said:

> "The heavens reward thee manifold, I pray.
> Then while we live, in love let's so persever,
> That when we live no more we may live ever."

James sighed. "Do you understand why I'm doing this, Sarah? I need to know that you understand why I'm leaving."

"They'll hunt you down if you don't go."

"And the sooner I go, the sooner this nonsense will be over and I can come home."

"I know."

Sarah watched the white-skinned men and women boarding trains, saw their weeping families, and she looked as blank as James felt, as though everything passed by in a haze. As a new train was called and a fresh crowd brushed past on their way to the platform, Sarah grabbed James's hand, and he clutched hers, tightly, pulling her toward him to protect her from trampling feet or grabbing hands.

"By leaving I'm protecting you, Sarah. Now the government has what they want, me, and you won't be dragged who-knows-where for who-knows-how-long, always running, always paranoid. You can rest and recover and grow strong again without having to look over your shoulder every five minutes to see who's there. By giving myself up, I'm setting you free. I will always sacrifice myself for you and Grace. I will give myself a thousand times over for the two of you."

"I know," Sarah said. "I love you."

"I love you more."

And he still, even as they sat in the chairs of the terminal waiting for his train to be called, even as they clutched each other as if they were the only things keeping the other from falling through the crust of the earth to the nothing on the other side, insisted that everything was going to be all right.

"This too shall end," he whispered. He shook his head, remembering again there was something he wanted to tell her, something else, something...but no matter how hard he tried he couldn't recall what it was. Knowing there was something he couldn't remember gnawed at him, chipping away at his brain in painful bites, and he was afraid he would be too far away before he recalled what he wanted to say and then he wouldn't be able to tell her.

His train was called. He heard his number over the intercom and saw it flash on the screen overhead. He took Sarah's hand and guided her through the press of bodies, paranormal and normal, the terminal buzzing with confusion and sadness and anger and every other emotion besides. As they walked past the glass doors outside to the platform where the trains waited in two long lines on either side, he gripped Sarah's hand tightly, afraid to lose her in the dizzying maze of careworn faces. He couldn't bring himself to look at the slick gray train that would take him away to some great unknown, a prison perhaps worse than the one he saw in his mind, the one as squalid as the one Sarah knew from over three hundred years before. He stopped near the first door, unable to look into Sarah's face, unable to see her despair. When he double-checked the number on the screen, he saw a flash of recognition, a face he knew, but it was so fast it hardly registered in his brain. Who is that, he wondered? Then the face was gone but he heard the voice, the detached, hearty, assuring voice he heard when he questioned whether or not they should bring a child into their home. And then they found Grace. James, despite the tumult of the chaos around him, despite his weeping wife in his arms, was grateful to hear the warmth then.

"You will be all right," he heard. "And Sarah and Grace will be too."

There was the flash of the face again, too fast even for his preternatural senses to grasp, and then the face and the voice were gone. But James felt strong again. When the call for his train echoed on the platform, James tried to step away from Sarah but she wouldn't let him go.

"No," she said. "Not yet."

James watched the army guards direct others onto the trains, vampires being led away, a sacrifice for the slaughter. Then a stocky guard in an overlarge uniform spotted him and James knew he had to go.

"Let's go," the guard said. "All vampires for the next train should be boarded now."

"No, James. No!" Sarah grabbed his arm, refusing to let him go.

"It's all right," James said, stroking her long dark curls, brushing her tears away with his fingertips. "I'm immortal and I'm strong. I'll be home soon."

The soldier drew closer, impatient now. "Let's go!" he yelled. He grabbed the back of a nearby vampire's shirt and tried to drag the white-skinned man toward the train. The guard's face grew red and wet when he realized he couldn't make the vampire move, and he turned his attention onto other undeads a few feet away. "Now!" the guard yelled at them. Then he turned to James and pointed. "Let's go!"

James was tempted to ignore him, or at least to show the world the inferior strength of humans compared to his kind, but Sarah was nearly liquid in his arms and he had to make this as easy on her as he could.

"I'm coming," James said. "I'm saying good-bye to my wife."

"She'll be all right, James. I'm here to help."

Jennifer appeared like an auburn-haired angel out of the crowd and slid her arm around Sarah. Howard and Timothy and Steve and Jocelyn were there too, Howard huddled close to his son, who was also being hounded about the train.

"Where's Chandresh?" James asked.

Jennifer shook her head, her eyes red and swollen. "He's already on board. He's not very good at good-byes." Jennifer pushed her long hair from her eyes, no longer pretending to hide her tears. "Don't worry, James. We'll be fine. Right, Sarah?"

Sarah stood between them, James holding onto one of her arms, Jennifer holding onto the other, and he marveled at how limp she stood, ready to be broken like a wish bone, left to see who was left with the larger piece of whatever shards were left of her. Jennifer tried to smile, tried to make light of the darkness surrounding them, but her usual playfulness deserted her long before she arrived at the train station.

"Can't you snap your fingers and make this go away?" James asked.

"I wish I could, James."

James put his arm around Sarah's waist, then grabbed Jennifer's arm so tightly she flinched under his strength. "You promised me three wishes," he said. "That Halloween at the Witches Lair, you promised me three wishes. You said I used my first wish for the spell to bring me back after I saw Hempel in the sunshine. This is my second wish, Jennifer. Take care of Sarah and Grace. Whatever you need to do, however you need to do it, you make sure they're all right. You help them stay strong, even if you have to use your magic."

Jennifer smiled through her sadness. "Are you giving me permission to cast a spell?"

"I am."

"And what about a spell for you? Do you give me permission for that too?"

James watched the swarm of soldiers barking orders, and he saw the vampires parting from their loved ones. He thought of Chandresh when the blue-suited officers ransacked his house and his muscular, manly friend could only look on, unable to do anything to protect his wife and children. He looked at Jocelyn and Steve as they whispered their own tearful good-byes. James nodded. "I'll take whatever I can get right now," he said.

"I'll call Martha and the rest of my coven," Jennifer said. "We'll have a special ceremony. I have an acorn and white, yellow, and orange candles for Sarah's spell for inner strength, and I have colored threads, scissors, and a screw-top jar for your spell for protection." She hugged Sarah close. "And my mother, the great and powerful Olivia, will cast the spells for you. This way they're guaranteed to work."

"Don't forget us," Howard said.

"We won't forget any of you," Jennifer said.

Howard clutched his son to his chest with one arm and reached for James with the other. "You'll watch Timothy, James?" Howard said. "You'll make sure he's safe."

"You know I will," James said.

Howard nodded, but James saw his friend's furrowed eyes under his heavy, close-knit brows and he knew Howard wasn't convinced. Howard was thinking what James already knew, that there were forces even

James, with all his preternatural strength and extraordinary senses, couldn't control.

"You should get on the train," Howard said to his son. "It's all right. Everything will be fine."

Timothy threw his arms around his father's neck. "I love you, Dad."

"I love you, Timothy. I always thought I would never have a family because I was so different, but then I found you and suddenly my life made sense. I'm proud to be your father."

They hugged tightly, but Howard stepped away. "I'm going to do everything I can to get you out, Tim. And I'm coming to see you. On the night of the full moon next month I'll be there. Wherever you are I'll find you. Do you understand what I mean?"

"Howl and I'll know you're there," Timothy said. "Just be careful. We don't want them to come after you next."

"Don't worry, Son. I'll be fine. And you will too."

Timothy looked at James with a sarcastic grin. "Guess what?" he said. "I got a call from that publisher this morning. He wants to have a look at my vampire book after all."

"What did you say?" James asked.

"I told him I was a little busy right now. Maybe some other time."

"I bet you could start a bidding war over your memoirs when you get out," Jennifer said. "Then everyone will want to publish your book. A guaranteed *New York Times* bestseller."

Timothy smiled. "Maybe," he said. "Vampires are even hotter than they already were. Some movie called 'The Vampire Killers' is number one at the box office right now. It's like vampires and cowboys and Indians. It's the stupidest premise for a movie I've ever seen, but people are eating it up. I heard they're already planning a sequel."

James looked at Sarah but said nothing. Jocelyn took Timothy's hand.

"We should go, Timothy," she said. "Everyone else is on board and they're waiting for us." Jocelyn kissed Steve one last time, managed a weak smile for her husband, then helped the vampire boy onto the train, holding his hand, gently leading him forward as though she was afraid of how the shock of it all might affect him, forgetting, even turned as she was, that he was a young man trapped in a fourteen-year-old's body. They hopped onto the train, found Chandresh waiting for them by the door, and they stuck together in a cluster, afraid to let any of the others out of their sight. James saw Geoffrey through the window of the next car, his long face pressed against the glass, his nose flat, his mouth blowing steam circles like a boy at the window of a candy shop. They caught eyes, and Geoffrey nodded. James didn't know whether to laugh or cry.

The guards barked again, and James stepped toward the train but Sarah clung to him, her fingers fastened into his shirt, oblivious to anything but him. The train's engine stuttered, and the guard next to James waved at other guards, who saw him, the last vampire on the platform. They shouted at more guards, and five armed guards ran toward him.

"I have to go, honey," James whispered in Sarah's ear. "I'll be home soon."

"I love you, James. I've always loved you. Even when I didn't know your name I loved you."

"Sarah, I have loved you every night for three hundred and twenty years."

He kissed her, passionately, because this kiss had to last awhile. He kissed her the way he kissed her after more than three hundred years of missing her. His lips burned, as his unbeating heart did, for the love of her.

As the guards reached him he flashed onto the train and out of their grasp. He saw his wife weeping, limp with grief, and he saw Jennifer, Steve, and Howard rush to her side to embrace her, to keep her strong, because together they would see this through. James, praying for one of the few times since he was turned, asked God to send strength Sarah's way. Please, God, he begged. She needs to stay strong. I need to stay strong. We need to see this through so we can be together again. I can't wait another three hundred years before I see her again.

The train chugged away, faster and faster away from the woman he loved, her beautiful face pulled in a spasm of torture as though she were trapped between the walls again, feeling the cracks in her bones and the ache in her muscles and he wanted to scream. Most of all, he felt an overwhelming urge to vomit back every ounce of the blood that consumed his life and allowed him to live that unnatural way. It was just as he had told his father all those years before—it was always about the blood.

As the train picked up speed, James decided he needed to see his wife one last time. He jumped over the railing onto the ground below, flashing back to the platform with his supernatural speed, the human heads popping from side to side as they watched him race the wind to take his wife into his arms one last time. Sarah saw him as he drew closer to her, and she ran to him and threw her arms around his neck. James swept her up, clutching her tightly to him, and he kissed her passionately, basking in her warm softness, savoring strawberries and cream, letting his lips linger on hers. When he heard the rushing footsteps and angry yells from the stampede of guards charging toward him, he stepped away.

"I love you, Sarah," he said. "I love you more than anything in this world." Finally, he remembered what he wanted to tell her. He reached into his pocket, took out the antique-looking key, placed it into her palm, and closed her fingers around it. "When you get home, look in my old desk near the window. This key will unlock the bottom right drawer, and there are papers in there—notes and letters—I want you to read. You were right, Sarah. They're letters for my girlfriend." He smiled. "I want you to see how much time I spend thinking about you when you're gone. You are always on my mind. You are my Sarah. *My* Sarah. And remember Miriam's prophecy. I will return. I will."

"I love you, James."

"I love you more."

He turned, saw the guards closing in on him, and he flashed away. With a deft cat-like leap he grabbed the railing of the train that was already miles away from the station. He knew he was too far, a speck in the distance to Sarah, but he could still see her lean into Jennifer for support, see her hide her face away from the place where he disappeared. He heard the smacking footsteps of the guard behind him.

"Let's go. You won't be pulling that again."

The guard led James back to the compartment where the other vampires sat. "Stay here," the guard said. James saw Jocelyn, Timothy, Chandresh, and Geoffrey and sighed. This should be interesting, he thought, grateful that for now, at least, they would be together. As much as he ached at the loss of Sarah, he knew he had to stay watchful, aware. He needed to stay strong. Just as he promised his wife. He needed to triumph over this damned curse that sent him away from her. He needed to get out of this so he could go back to his life with the woman he loved and their little girl. He had to. It was their destiny.

EPILOGUE

Sarah stared at her wooden gabled house as though she had never seen it before, as though she had only known it in her dreams. It was nearly silent outside that spring afternoon, the dusk settling as pink and gold on the break in the horizon, the crooked oak tree bent even closer to the ground, as though it had grown older in the family's absence. The fresh blooms flittered in the bay breeze, and everywhere Sarah looked was oddly deserted of people, as though everyone stayed away in deference to the old house's new mournfulness. Usual traffic flows, the earliest tourists of the season, even walking locals were nowhere to be seen. For decades, neighbors saw the wooden gabled house, noticed the phantasmal man in the shadows, and they were convinced the old house was haunted—by memories. Now, with Sarah and Grace back without James, that intuition was more right than ever—the memories would be hard again. The house had a reprieve from the specter-like recollections for a while, nearly a year, but now there was more sadness, more worries, more madness to overcome. For a moment, Sarah thought she saw the long wooden slats of the exterior walls shudder and bend under the weight of the heavy beams of the gables, and she wouldn't have been surprised if the house bowed in prayer then disintegrated into dust before her eyes. But even as she felt the agitation, the old place called her name—Sarah or Elizabeth, it was all the same to her now. Just as it had when she saw it when she first arrived in Salem, the house spoke to her, she knew it, and it knew her, and James or no James, it was her home. She and that house still shared their secret, and she needed it. She thought of the poem she shared with her dear and loving husband, and it brought her some comfort.

"I prize thy love more than whole mines of gold..."

287

Sarah sighed. She pulled herself slowly from Olivia's silver Prius, it still hurt to move, and Olivia helped her unstrap Grace from her seat in the back. Sarah held her daughter to her chest as she walked to her green front door with determination. This would be hard, she knew, but she and Grace would get through it because they had to. James was strong and immortal. He would be all right. It was just as he said. This was a roadblock, a bump in the road, but she would be strong enough for all of them.

"Or all the riches that the East doth hold..."

Inside the great room Olivia took Grace from Sarah's arms.

"You're still recovering, Sarah. Let me have her. She's getting bigger every day."

Sarah nodded though her arms ached with the emptiness.

Olivia stopped, clutched Grace to her chest, and watched Sarah, her detective seeking clues look on high alert. "You don't need to stay here by yourself, dear. You can stay with me as long as you need."

"I want to be home," Sarah said. "I need to be home."

"What about Child Services?"

"Mrs. Jackson said as long as I can prove I'm human they won't take Grace."

Olivia smiled with the motherly compassion Sarah loved her for, then carried Grace into her bedroom to lay her down for a nap.

Sarah was mesmerized by the old house, looking around as though everything inside were new to her, as though she had awakened from an odd dream and she knew this house from somewhere only she wasn't sure where or how or why. She looked at the remodeled kitchen, the hearth empty without the black cauldron, the books on the shelves, the diamond-paned casement windows. She looked up at the loft-style attic and the seventeenth century wooden desk.

Then she remembered. She reached into her pocket, pulled out the antique-style key, and wandered to James's desk. His laptop computer was closed, his lecture notes filed, everything in its place as he always left it. She imagined him sitting at his desk, writing something, reading something, thinking something, and she walked to his chair and imagined that she pressed her hands into his strong shoulders and he smiled at her and brushed her hair from her face. She wanted to talk to him. She wanted him to hold her and she wanted to feel his strong arms clutching her close and she wanted to hear his strong, sweet voice tell her everything was going to be all right. But he wasn't there.

For now, she reminded herself. For now.

How quickly things changed. At first, after their wedding, it seemed as if no time had passed since their first marriage in 1691, but now everything was different. Whenever she wondered about what James must be facing on his journey to the camp or the prison or whatever it was, she had to force those thoughts from her mind because she couldn't go there. She filled herself with happy memories instead.

"My love is such that rivers cannot quench..."

She sat before the old desk and pushed the key into the lock on the bottom right drawer, the same drawer from where he had pulled the newspaper clipping of President Jackson. She saw a manila folder with the words 'For Sarah' in her husband's calligraphy-like handwriting, and she pulled it from the drawer and saw a stack of timeworn papers inside. With trembling fingers, she pulled out the pages, staring at them, reading and rereading them as though to verify they were really there and not a figment of her imagination, something she wanted to see. She read them again, one by one, and saw the proof of James's everlasting devotion. They were letters to his girlfriend. They were letters to her:

...But now I am here and you are still gone. I cannot live without you, and yet I cannot die. What do I do? Oh my God, Elizabeth. What do I do?

...Dear God, Elizabeth. Where should I go?

...I am writing to you because you are still all I have to live for.

...I am certain that here, nestled high in this nook in the mountains, that I can kiss the close-looking stars, kiss you, if I stretch hard enough.

...I want to help them, Lizzie. The fear you can hold in your hands like sharp-edged razors—can you feel it? The wails of the mothers as they're dragged from their children—can you hear it?

...They look the way I felt when I watched the constable drag you away. This is torture, Lizzie. No other word will do.

... I will find water for as many of them as I can, Lizzie. You will be proud of me.

As she read his words of love, words he wrote to her even when he thought she was gone from him forever, words he needed to share with her even when he thought she would never read them, she realized that neither space nor time could keep them apart. Their love was, just as her father-in-law predicted over three hundred years before, eternal. And James knew what she would need when he was gone and, planning for an event such as this, they had lived through something similar after all, he left it behind for her so she would know how he thought of her wherever she was, wherever he was. He knew her so well.

Suddenly, she felt his strength envelop her, as though he slid his strong arms around her from wherever he was, and she knew that, whatever may come, she would be strong. That wisp-like iridescent thread she felt lassoing around them and pulling them together the first time she saw him outside this very house, that invisible connection that held them tight to each other over three hundred years, was still there, spread wider now to cover the miles between them, but it was still there, keeping them close. And just as he wanted her to be proud of how he handled himself while helping the people on the Trail of Tears, now she wanted him to be proud of how she navigated their own difficult path. She would not give up on him, not now, not after everything they had been through to find their way back to each other. They would be all right again. They had to be.

It was their destiny.

ACKNOWLEDGMENTS

I had the opportunity to visit the town of Salem, Massachusetts in the summer of 2011, and I loved it so much I wanted to move there. My worst fear was I'd get there to discover I had the town's landmarks all mixed up. Fortunately, everything was where I thought it would be. For anyone with an interest in the Salem Witch Trials or in the beginning traces of American history, a trip to Salem, and Boston, is mandatory.

And, of course, thank you to the editors at Copperfield Press.

When I put *Her Dear & Loving Husband* out into the world, I had no idea what to expect. I hoped I had written a story people would like if they had a chance to read it. I have been overwhelmed with gratitude for the warm reception readers have given James and Sarah. A most hearty thank you to everyone who has taken the time to share their kind words about the book. You are all greatly appreciated. Most authors would argue that their readers are the best, but I know my readers really are the best.

The Cherokee were not the only native tribe forced to walk west. The Choctaw, Chickasaw, Seminole, and Moscogee-Creek also endured that perilous journey. I hope readers are intrigued enough by the Trail of Tears to seek out nonfiction accounts of that sad episode. *The Cherokee Nation and the Trail of Tears* by Theda Perdue and Michael D. Green is a good place to start.

ABOUT THE AUTHOR

Meredith Allard is the author of the *Loving Husband Trilogy*, *Victory Garden*, *Woman of Stones*, and *My Brother's Battle*. She received her B.A. and M.A. degrees in English from California State University, Northridge. Her short fiction and articles have appeared in journals such as *The Paumanok Review*, *The Maxwell Digest*, *Wild Mind*, *Muse Apprentice Guild*, *Writer's Weekly*, *Moondance*, and *CarbLite*. She has taught writing to students aged ten to sixty, and she has taught creative writing and writing historical fiction seminars at Learning Tree University, UNLV, and the Las Vegas Writers Conference. She lives in Las Vegas, Nevada. Visit Meredith online at www.meredithallard.com.

Her Loving Husband's Curse is Book Two of the *Loving Husband Trilogy*. Book One, *Her Dear & Loving Husband*, and Book Three, *Her Loving Husband's Return*, are also available from Copperfield Press.